"I'll See You Inside,"
Jud Offered.

"No." Meli faced him. "I meant what I said, Jud. I don't want to see you again. This is good-bye."

For a moment he watched her silently, then he started after her and caught her at the door. Leaning against the doorframe, he imprisoned her with his arms. "And if I refuse to accept that?"

"You have no choice."

"That's for me to decide, isn't it?"

"No, Jud. This is *my* decision." She spoke with her back to him, not wanting to look at him. "Get out."

JOANNA SCOTT
has been a Californian for many years, and has no plans ever to leave her adopted state. Writing is a satisfying career for this former teacher, who now has plenty of time to spend with her family and to travel as far and as often as she likes.

Dear Reader:

There is an electricity between two people in love that makes everything they do magic, larger than life. This is what we bring you in SILHOUETTE INTIMATE MOMENTS.

SILHOUETTE INTIMATE MOMENTS are longer, more sensuous romance novels filled with adventure, suspense, glamor or melodrama. These books have an element no one else has tapped: excitement.

We are proud to present the very best romance has to offer from the very best romance writers. In the coming months look for some of your favorite authors such as Elizabeth Lowell, Nora Roberts, Erin St. Claire and Brooke Hastings.

SILHOUETTE INTIMATE MOMENTS are for the woman who wants more than she has ever had before. These books are for you.

Karen Solem
Editor-in-Chief
Silhouette Books

In All Honesty

Joanna Scott

Silhouette Intimate Moments
Published by Silhouette Books New York
America's Publisher of Contemporary Romance

SILHOUETTE BOOKS
300 E. 42nd St., New York, N.Y. 10017

ISBN: 0-373-07086-1

First Silhouette Books printing March, 1985

10 9 8 7 6 5 4 3 2 1

Books by Joanna Scott

Silhouette Romance

Dusky Rose #50
The Marriage Bargain #68
Manhattan Masquerade #117
Lover Come Back #169
Moonlit Magic #187

Silhouette Special Edition

A Flight of Swallows #26
A Perfect Passion SE SAMPLER
Exclusively Yours #136
Corporate Policy #186

Silhouette Intimate Moments

In All Honesty #86

Chapter 1

A HAZY GRAY DAWN SPLAYED ACROSS THE SKY, BANISHING the flickering stars. Soon the veil of night would lift, singed beneath the glow of a fiery Hawaiian sun. In the garden, parrots chattered through the silence, their wings fluttering above flowers that waited for the morning's warmth. Dewdrops glistened on plumeria petals—pink, yellow, white.

On her terrace just above the garden, Meli Fancher also waited for the night to end, waited and wondered about Jud. Was he safe? Had he escaped? Her gaze swept over the trees and shrubbery, beyond the black lava cliffs and out to sea, where two sailboats and a yacht bobbed on a calm turquoise ocean. The trawler was gone now, but it had been there last night and Jud had been on it. Nothing could make her doubt that.

Her thoughts drifted back to the events of the night that was now fading into daylight, and the scenes from the past unfolded in her memory as vividly as if they were happening right now. But they weren't. This morning she was sitting calmly on her terrace. When she had first noticed the fishing trawler last night, she had been alone on the rocky shore searching the crevices for marine specimens swept in by the tide. If she stopped to think about it, that was when her uneasiness had first started. It hadn't been anything definite, just a haunting intuition that something had been wrong. She closed her eyes and remembered.

The big gray boat hadn't belonged out there, not in the darkness of night. All the other fishing trawlers had returned to the pier late that afternoon in time for the four-o'clock marlin weighing. The day's winner would be posted above the stands and the crews would rest while the boats remained dockside. None of them would venture out again until morning, yet last evening one trawler had remained at sea, hovering in an ocean as silently black as the lava rock from which Meli watched it.

Well, it wasn't any of her business, she had decided as she had lowered herself into a tidepool and aimed her flashlight at a pink anemone clinging to a rocky crevice. Carefully, she reached for it, then placed it with some accompanying sea water in the plastic bag she had taken from the canvas tote on the ledge above her. The anemone had been an unusual example of tropical marine plant life, which she would study at leisure when her Hawaiian vacation was over and she returned to her lab in Maryland.

A sudden gust of wind had sprayed across the waves and tousled the curling tendrils of her long auburn hair. She had tried to tie it back with a white silk scarf, but, as usual, it seemed to have a mind of its own. Sometimes she wondered why she even bothered; she would never achieve that pristine cover-girl look that came so naturally to her sister, Sue, but then Sue was the image of dainty femininity while she, Meli, had always been a tomboy— her father's shadow and her mother's disappointment.

It had been that way ever since childhood. Pink organdy and blond curls for Sue, patched jeans and brown braids for Meli. Through the years Meli had persuaded herself that she preferred it that way; organdy was hardly suitable for tree-climbing, horseback riding and the camping trips she had taken with her dad. These activities didn't involve her mother or Sue, and her father had always loved her just as she was.

Now Sue and she were adults, and neither had really changed; Sue was the pampered wife of a Washington judge while Meli divided her time between teaching marine biology and playing nursemaid to a menagerie of stray, mistreated animals, a lifestyle which earned Sue's constant disapproval. Meli's mother, as usual, couldn't have cared less. She had written her younger daughter off years ago. Edwina had never believed in pursuing lost causes, but Sue hadn't given up. Not yet.

"You're twenty-nine, nearly thirty," she would tell Meli, "and it's time you started thinking about your future . . . marriage . . . children. A single life can be very lonely, and you're not getting any younger."

Not getting any younger, Meli thought wryly. A statement she had always shrugged off. Unlike her mother and Sue, she had never been obsessed with youth and beauty, but Dr. Carrow's latest diagnosis had changed all that.

"Endometriosis isn't always a serious problem, Meli. Your Pap test doesn't show any sign of a malignancy. I didn't think it would. But your menstrual flow has become dangerously heavy during the past year, and the hormones I've been administering haven't helped any. If you were married and planning on children, I'd advise you to start your family immediately, but since that's not the case, surgery seems to be the best solution. It's a simple operation, and if you're not planning on children . . .''

And that's when the ache in her heart had started.

"Think it over," Dr. Carrow had said, "and let me know what you decide."

So she had come to Hawaii to think it over, but the ache in her heart had crossed the ocean with her. Although she had had her share of male friends, she hadn't been seriously attracted to any of them, and her career had always occupied so much of her life that she had never really thought about marriage and a family, had always assumed that there would be time for that later somewhere in the nebulous future. But now time had become her enemy and she was faced with a decision that might make having a family an impossibility forever.

Moonlight had streaked between two smoky clouds as, blinking back dry tears of indecision, she had glanced out to sea toward the trawler. Her personal problems had been forgotten when a door had opened to reveal a momentary flash of light, and Meli had caught her first glimpse of Jud as he had trotted through it.

He had sprinted across the deck and had paused at the prow. In that brief instant he had seemed to be focusing, looking at her. She had stared back, unable to drag her eyes away, and even from this distance her first impression had been one of power and masculine sexuality. He was naked to the waist, and his bronze skin had glistened in the moonlight as he had raised his hands over his head.

Forgetting about the tidepools, Meli had reached for her binoculars and had brought him into focus. He was tall, about six foot two, she guessed, with broad shoulders that tapered into lean hips and long, muscular legs. His hair was tousled and black, his features were Caucasian, but his skin was tanned, almost teak. Was he part Polynesian? she had wondered.

Then, as she stood watching, he had dived into the sea. Refocusing her binoculars, Meli had tried to follow him. Impossible. She had scanned the mirrored surface, but he had vanished. Insane, she had thought, dangerously insane. No one swam here, especially at night. The Kona coast of Hawaii was too rocky, no white sandy beaches, just jagged cliffs of black lava rock, and although the water wasn't shark-infested, there were certainly some around.

So what had happened? Had he fallen off the boat? No, she didn't think so. She had clearly seen him raise his arms above his head and dive into the water. Still, he might be in trouble. She had turned hesitantly back toward the white brick hotel curving above the rocky cliff and had wondered if she should go for help.

No, she had decided. Wasn't that another fault Sue was fond of pointing out? Meli's habit of offering help before it was requested, of taking chances and fighting for lost causes?

"You're a bleeding heart, Meli. It's like the whole universe is on your shoulders. Mark my words, one of these days you're going to get yourself in trouble. Being a good Samaritan is one thing, but you can't cure the ills of the world. Keep your green eyes closed and your nose out of other people's business; some of them might resent your interference."

Maybe Sue was right. Maybe she had to learn to mind her own business. If the man was just enjoying a moonlight swim, she would be creating a scene over nothing. Why look for trouble? She'd give it a little more time.

But waiting made her too nervous to work. She hated just standing by, doing nothing. Not knowing what to do, she knotted her specimen sack and slung it around her wrist, then wiped her palms on her white bikini. August nights were warm in Hawaii, warm enough to swim, but—

Ah, there he was. Meli smiled in relief when she saw the swimmer's dark head breaking through the surface. He was closer now, and his hair gleamed as he cut through the water heading for shore. He's not having any problems, she thought. He's a strong swimmer. She was glad she hadn't interfered.

The man swam rapidly, turning his head, raising one strong arm and then the other. He was heading her way. Had he seen her? She remembered seeing him stare at her just before he dived off the boat. Was he actually swimming here to meet her? Ridiculous, she told herself. Her imagination was playing havoc with her rationality. This was reality, not some romantic movie.

Lights flashed aboard the trawler and swept over the water. They're looking for him, she realized. But why? He wasn't in trouble, hadn't fallen overboard.

Three men raced across the deck and lowered a dinghy. The swimmer had nearly reached the rocky shore, but his pace had slowed. He was only a few feet away now and aiming directly for her.

He's winded, Meli thought. The swim must have been farther than he had supposed. The firm strength of his arms had diminished and his strokes were weaker now. He was exhausted. Interfering or not, she was going to help him. Dropping her specimen bag, she hopped to a lower ledge.

Gunshots rang out from the trawler, tearing up the water only inches from the swimmer. He disappeared beneath the surface, and Meli ducked behind a craggy pillar. Fear clutched at her heart. What was going on? Why were they shooting at him?

She clung to the rock, her heart racing and her breath

echoing through the silent night. Thoughts came quickly, incoherent, colliding with each other. *They're trying to kill him. Protect yourself. Has he been hit? You can't cure the ills of the world.*

A wave broke against the shore, spewing foam around her feet. She shivered. The shooting had stopped as suddenly as it had started, and now the sea felt cold, cold and eerily calm. What had happened to the swimmer? She had to know. Peeking cautiously from her shelter, she saw him crawling onto the rocks. Low, barely off the ground, he clutched his left shoulder and scanned the area.

Hurt, Meli thought, he was hurt. He must have been hit. "Over here," she called, disregarding the sharp lava scraping her knees as she scrambled toward him and held out her hand.

"Drop, you fool," he growled, rolling onto his back and pulling her down on top of him. "Do you want to get us both killed?"

Why on earth was he yelling at her? Didn't he realize she was only trying to help? "I . . ." She tried to speak, but his flesh muffled her voice as her lips opened against the salty tang of his skin. Her breath caught in her throat when, turning away, she inhaled his scent—sea and spice and musky masculinity. Her fingers splayed against his chest—thick dark hair and flexing muscles that made smaller muscles hidden deep within her own body respond, curling to his touch. "Look," she said, her voice low and breathy. "Look, I—"

"Shh . . ." Pressing her head to his chest, he lifted himself and stared beyond her out to sea. "They've spotted me. I've got to get out of here."

"Who are you? Why are they chasing you?" This couldn't be real, none of it; the bullets had to be blanks. They filmed movies in Hawaii, didn't they? TV shows? Only where were the cameras? Where were the lights?

The swimmer's wiry black beard brushed against Meli's cheek when he scrambled to his feet and drew her up beside him. Rough, she thought, rough, yet somehow intimate, intimate and comforting. She liked being close to him, but not at the risk of being killed. Why didn't he explain things, tell her it was some kind of game? *Please make it be some kind of game*.

"This hardly seems like the right time for a formal introduction, but you don't have to be afraid of me. I'm not going to hurt you. My name's Jud Thompson. I'm with the F.B.I. and I've got some information those boys on the boat don't want me to deliver. Now you're caught up in it. Come on." Holding her hand tightly, he sprinted over the cliff and ran toward the hotel. "I'm sorry you got mixed up in this, but I guess you were in the wrong place at the wrong time."

The story of my life, Meli thought, grasping his shoulder as her rubber thong caught in a crevice. "Wait. I can't."

Sounds blew in from the ocean—rippling waves, a chugging motor, loud, angry voices—then the voices softened and came closer.

If this was a game, it wasn't one she wanted to play. "Go without me," she said, "it will be faster." He had to get away, but she wasn't in any danger. She didn't have any secret information. They weren't chasing her. She would probably be safer away from him anyway.

Stifling a snarled expletive, Jud bent and lifted her in his arms. "You fool," he said. "Do you think they'll let you go? Don't you understand that this isn't a game?" His dark eyes flashed as he glared at her and shattered her last illusions. "These boys are playing for keeps." He ducked his head and his back formed a protective shield behind her as he raced into the hotel gardens. "I can't leave you here. If they find you and think you might have seen me, don't you know what they'll do to you?''

What they'd do to her? Why? She wasn't involved, or was she? Why hadn't she stayed in her room tonight? She would have been safe there. Suddenly Dr. Carrow's diagnosis didn't seem so important. If Jud was right about the men being after her, her life expectancy might well have shrunken to a matter of minutes, hardly the time to think about having children.

The sweet scent of plumeria and jasmine wafted through the air. Romantic Hawaii, Meli mused wryly, so peaceful and relaxing, the ideal place to think things out according to her travel agent; but the advertising brochures had never mentioned bullets.

''Are you staying here?'' Jud asked, stepping behind an oleander bush, setting her on her feet and pointing to the hotel.

''Yes,'' Meli whispered. ''I'm on the ground floor, right through there.'' She indicated the patio door. Now, if only he would let her go— She crossed her arms over her breasts and looked up at him. His eyes were deep obsidian pools caressing her face with tender concern and, for one brief instant, she forgot about gunshots and danger. What would it be like to kiss him? she wondered.

''You'll be okay now.'' He loosened her scarf and brushed her hair back from her face. A silver ring glistened on the third finger of his left hand, two entwined snakes with blackened coils and turquoise eyes. ''I know it's been frightening.'' His gruff voice smoothed to whispery velvet. ''But it's over now. Just get inside and forget this ever happened.'' He folded her scarf into his pocket, grasped her shoulders gently, then turned her toward the hotel.

Standing there, barefoot and bare-chested, clad only in

wet, clinging jeans, his damp wavy hair falling over his forehead, he looked virile yet sensitive, an odd combination that Meli found totally intriguing. Suddenly she realized that he was sending her away to protect her. But what about him? If his story was true, and he was with the F.B.I., then he was the one in danger, so how could she think only of herself and leave him to his pursuers? "What's going to happen to you?"

"I'll be all right. I'm used to this." He looked over his shoulder.

Meli rejected his response. No one could get used to running for his life and dodging bullets.

The dinghy had reached the cliff. "Now, just disappear, will you." Jud's hands trembled as he rubbed his bare arms for warmth and searched the grounds. "And remember, none of this ever happened. It doesn't concern you. Forget you ever saw me." He pressed his lips together as his gaze shifted to the upper floors of the hotel. "Get back to your room. You'll be safe there."

Meli watched him scan the building. A handsome, dynamic man, the kind who didn't like to be dependent on anyone else. *Forget about him?* In that brief instant she knew it wasn't possible. She wouldn't . . . ever. "I can't. I can't just leave you."

"Don't worry about me. I'm not your problem. Just take care of yourself. *Numero uno*. Remember that. Now you're wasting precious time. Get moving."

Remembering how he had refused to leave her behind and had scooped her in his arms when she couldn't keep up with him, Meli shook her head. She was in no way going to leave him. If she devoted her life to saving sick animals, how could she turn her back on a human being who needed her help? She couldn't. "My room's over there," she said, grasping his hand and motioning toward a first-floor balcony. "You can't stay here. They'll find you."

Jud shrugged indifferently. "I'll be okay."

For a moment Meli stared at him, studying his features. He was so strong, yet there was something very vulnerable about him and she didn't want him hurt, not anymore than he had been already. "No," she insisted, pulling herself up to her full height of five feet four. "Now, will you stop being so damned macho and come with me?" Next to his, her stature didn't seem that impressive, yet she wasn't in the least bit intimidated. Jud Thompson didn't frighten her at all.

"No." He shook his head and the droplets of water glistening on his tousled black hair fell to his forehead. "I won't involve you anymore. It's too dangerous."

"I'm already involved. What if those men have seen me? Didn't you say they might come after me? Please, I'm too frightened to be alone," she admitted, truthfully believing that she needed Jud's protection as much as he needed hers, and that she couldn't feel safe while he was in danger. Together, they had to stay together. She couldn't explain why. Her decision was more instinctive than rational.

He lifted her chin with his thumb and studied her face. His fingers were callused, and their roughness scraped against her skin, harsh, yet somehow compassionate. "You're a tenacious little thing, aren't you?" Pressing his lips together tightly, he looked back over the rocks and frowned. "I don't like dragging you in any deeper, but at the moment it doesn't seem that I have much choice. They'll be here any minute now. I'm grateful for your offer. Let's go."

Holding his hand tightly, Meli sprinted across the lawn toward the glass garden doors. Gravel grated against her bare feet and slipped between her toes; then the hallway carpeting felt warm and soothing as she led him to her room. Once inside, she automatically reached for the light switch.

Jud covered her hand with his, flattening it against the wall. "Don't," he whispered, locking the door and slipping the chain into place. "The light will only draw their attention. We'd better keep it dark for a while." His glance drifted to the balcony door, the drapes billowing in the breeze. "Is that open?"

"I'll close it," Meli said, starting for the door.

"No," he grasped her wrist. "Just leave it. Don't do anything to make them notice this room. We'll have to be quiet, that's all."

She pulled her hand free and stared at it. A warm sticky liquid clung to the flesh that Jud had touched. "You're bleeding," she said, crossing to the telephone. "We'd better get a doctor." She knew about nursing sick animals, but a man with a bullet wound was way out of her league.

"No doctor," Jud insisted, sprinting after her and dropping the receiver back in its cradle before the operator had a chance to answer.

"But you've been shot." She pointed to his blood-covered arm. "You need to see a doctor."

"We can't risk using the phone. Someone may be monitoring the calls." he rubbed his palm over his bleeding upper arm and winced.

For one fleeting moment Meli longed to caress his face, to erase the pain and ease the lingering tension that had to have been etched there long before tonight. Jud Thompson was a man who had suffered, and his anguish had become a part of him.

"It's just a flesh wound," he said, his gruff voice gentling once again. "Don't be frightened. It's not that serious. I can handle it myself. I've done it before. Do you have a towel?''

"In the bathroom.'' She pointed behind him. "But even if it's only superficial, the wound should be cleaned.''

"Do you have some antiseptic?''

Meli thought for a moment. "Alcohol.'' She used it to clean her specimens.

"Get it.''

Hastily, Meli gathered up a washcloth, two towels and her plastic bottle of alcohol. When she returned to the bedroom, Jud was standing by the window holding back a corner of the drape and looking out over the lawn.

She padded across the floor and stopped behind him. "I've got—''

Jud spun around quickly. His knees bent and his hands shot up in a slicing motion.

He's going to hit me, Meli thought, dropping the towels and alcohol as she backed away in fright. Sue's warning echoed in her mind. *You take too many chances. One of these days you're going to get yourself in trouble.* She had been stupid to bring Jud to her room. What did she really know about him? What proof did she have that he was actually who he said he was?

Taking a deep breath, Jud backed into the drape. His fingers flexed, then relaxed. "Sorry. Force of habit. Don't ever sneak up on me again.'' His large, comforting hands grasped her shoulders with a gentle strength. "Hey, I didn't mean to frighten you.'' Drawing her closer, he stroked slowly down her arms, his hard, fibrous fingertips sending a rasping message racing through her skin. "You're trembling. My God, you're trembling. Don't be afraid of me, honey. I'm not going to hurt you.''

He was tender now, soothing, a complete contrast to the threatening man who had hovered over her only moments before, and Meli didn't know what to make of him. Should she fear him or trust him? Swallowing the panic rising in her throat, she forced herself to speak. "You didn't have to snap my head off. I was only bringing the alcohol and towels." Her voice was raggedly uneven, on the verge of breaking.

"Hey, don't cry. It's been so long . . . I've forgotten how a woman . . ." He knelt beside her and brushed a bent knuckle across her glistening lashes. "Please don't cry." He caught both her hands in his. "I meant what I said. I'm not going to hurt you." His fingers tightened over hers, and as he closed his eyes she could feel the tension coiling through his body. "I'm grateful for your help, more grateful than I can ever say." He pressed her head against his chest and stroked lightly over her hair, calming, soothing. "You're so gentle, so very sweet and gentle. I'd never do anything to hurt you."

Closing her eyes, Meli rubbed her cheek against his chest. She felt so comfortable with him, so very much at home. Yet what an enigma he was, an odd blend of aggression and tenderness. Her hand shifted to his shoulder, returning his caress. She felt the sticky ooze and remembered his wound. "We'd better get that arm taken care of," she said, pulling away from him. "But I'm going to have to put on a light. I can't see what I'm doing."

"The bathroom," he said, helping her up.

They sat on the edge of the tub while Meli sponged his arm with warm water. He was right; the bullet had just grazed his flesh, but blood oozed from the circular gash and there was still the danger of infection. She rinsed out the washcloth, rubbed on some soap, then washed the wound again. The creases on Jud's face tautened, but he said nothing. That blasted masculine suffering-in-silence bit, Meli thought. Why is he so afraid to show what he's feeling? She felt as if she were sponging off a stone statue, only stone didn't bleed.

"It's all right to complain," she said, sitting back as her gaze flickered over his chest. Tiny ovals, hard, white and shiny, glistened beneath the crisp dark hairs. Scars, she thought. Of course, hadn't he told her he'd been hurt before? When? she wondered. How? She wanted to know more about him, all about him.

"I have nothing to complain about," he said. "You're not hurting me." He circled her wrists lightly, then turned her hands over and studied her palms. "Your hands are small and very gentle."

Meli stared at his chest. She longed to run her fingers through the crisp dark hair, to touch the scarred flesh beneath it and somehow erase all memory of the pain that had created them.

As if Jud could read her thoughts, he touched her hands to his chest and held them there. "Small and gentle," he whispered in a gruff, gravelly voice. "You're so small and gentle."

Erotic wings fluttered deep within Meli, and when she looked into Jud's eyes she saw the reflected images of her own imprisoned passion yearning for release. He was going to kiss her. She wanted him to kiss her.

Blood seeped down his arm and onto her fingers. He stared at it for a moment, then tensed and released her. "My blood is getting all over you," he muttered, toweling her fingers clean before wiping his arm. "I bloody everyone I touch."

The pain on his face seemed to reflect the agony of his thoughts, not his wounds, and Meli's heart ached for him. Even without knowing the causes of his misery she wanted to help and comfort him. "Don't say that." Reaching up, she ran her index finger across his cheek, his bearded jaw. "Please don't say that."

His brow furrowed and once again his eyes captured hers. ''I told you that I haven't been around a woman in a long time.'' His voice was low and husky, but the desire darkening his eyes strained against something else.

Meli studied his features and tried to read his mood. Reluctance? Fear? Was he trying to warn her about something? She couldn't be sure.

He brought her hands to his mouth and kissed her fingertips before releasing them. Erotic little prickles quivered up her arm, and her breath caught in her throat.

''You shouldn't be touching me like that,'' he whispered gruffly. ''It's too . . .'' Closing his eyes, he combed his fingers through his unruly hair, brushing it back from his forehead. ''So long, it's been so long. It's not right . . . I can't do this.''

Rejection, Meli thought. The story of my life. And the fact that it was compassionate didn't make it any less painful. Here she was, falling all over him, and he was telling her that she was being too forward, that although he was grateful, he didn't want her, couldn't force himself to want her. Of course. She should have known. Why would a man as attractive as Jud be interested in her? Now, if she had been as beautiful as Sue . . . ''We'd better take care of that wound,'' she said, turning away to hide her embarrassment. ''I'll put on some alcohol, then bind it.'' She picked up the bottle. ''I'm sorry, but the alcohol's going to sting.'' She despised the thought of hurting him; instinct told her that he had been through enough.

His long shoulder muscles flexed. ''I'll take care of it,'' he said as he grasped the bottle and dripped some alcohol on his wound. ''You've done enough already.'' Perspiration beaded on his forehead, and his teeth cut into his lower lip as he bit back the pain. ''That should stop any infection." He leaned back against the white tile wall, closed his eyes and sighed. "Sometimes silence is more than a matter of pride; it can mean your life."

Of course, Meli thought, annoyed with herself for thinking his reticence was a matter of masculine pride. Hadn't he told her that he lived with danger? That risk and peril were a routine part of his life? Hadn't she seen the scarred proof of his statement? She longed to enclose him in her arms, to somehow soothe and protect him, but he had told her that he didn't want that from her. Silently she reached for a towel to bind his wound.

"Hey, don't look so grim," he said. "I'll survive. I'm too mean to die. Come on, honey, talk to me. Tell me about yourself."

"There's not much to tell, at least nothing very exciting. I'm Melinda Fancher, Meli for short. I teach marine biology in Maryland." She tightened the towel around his wound and tried to ignore the perspiration-dampened hair beneath his arm, the musky, masculine scent of him, primitively male, definitely sexy. "This should stop the bleeding," she said, keeping her voice calm and unemotional. Hadn't he told her not to touch him? She wasn't about to embarrass either of them any more than she already had.

"The university?" he asked, watching her closely as she knotted the towel.

"No, a small private school just outside Baltimore." Looking directly at him, she raised an eyebrow quizzically. "Are you familiar with the area?" Why did she feel that his eyes could touch as well as see, that they could sense and explore her innermost thoughts and emotions?

Jud took a fresh washcloth and gently sponged her scraped knees. "You got raked over the coals."

"At least they weren't hot."

"Hot lava. Not a pretty thought," he said, frowning. "My home base is Washington. I had my training at the academy, then did some desk time in D.C."

"Desk time?" His hand was a downy feather fluttering across her skin, and she wondered how such a strong man could be so gentle.

"You know, punching a time clock, wearing a suit, sitting behind a desk. Deadly," he said, tossing the washcloth over the towel rack.

"Sounds a lot less deadly than what you're doing now."

"It's boring. Too much time to think." He stretched his good arm above his head and yawned. "Definitely not for me. The last thing in the world I want to do is think."

What an odd remark, unless his thoughts were too terrifying to contemplate and excitement was his only means of escape. Meli could understand wanting to avoid a problem. Unfortunately her current one was a part of her, not the sort she could run away from. "You're exhausted," she said. "Even if it was only a flesh wound, you've lost quite a bit of blood. And those wet jeans can't be too comfortable. You'd better take them off." She handed him a towel. "Wrap yourself in this and then lie down."

Jud hooked the towel with his good arm. "The last few days I haven't had much sleep. Maybe I should catch some shuteye. It's probably too soon to leave anyway. They could still be out there." He got to his feet, and clutching the wall, walked unsteadily out of the room. Then he stood behind the chair as he slipped out of his jeans and tucked the towel around his waist. He took two more steps, threw back the dark brown spread and fell across the bed. "I can't sleep too long, but I'm so tired. Wake me in fifteen . . ."

Watching from the bathroom door, Meli listened as his

breathing slowed to an even rhythm. He had fallen asleep immediately, but remembering how he had turned on her earlier that evening, she was certain that he never slept too deeply, and that he would awaken instantly the minute she approached the bed.

Quietly she stepped out of her wet bathing suit, slipped into the short, flowered robe hanging on the back of the bathroom door and padded to the bedroom chair near the window. Jud's jeans hung over the back of the chair, and she ran her hands over them as if touching his clothing would give her a clue to his character. But she felt only damp denim and a musty sea odor wafted up at her.

She turned toward the bed and studied Jud as he slept. A ray of moonlight slivered between the drapes and fell across his face. For the moment he looked peaceful and, except for the beard, young. What would he look like without the beard? she wondered. Would his cheeks be teak brown like the rest of his skin, his jaw as stubbornly set as she imagined? And his lips, could their silent arrogance be softened by a kiss? She longed to find out, yet knew she never would. He had told her that she didn't interest him as a woman, but he couldn't stop her from looking at him, especially when he was asleep and totally unaware of what she was doing.

Jud turned onto his back, his face contorting in a painful grimace. ''No,'' he screamed, rocking the bed and grasping the pillow as if he were going to strangle it. ''Don't do it. Leave her alone. Don't do it. Not her.'' He turned again, pounding the pillow against the mattress.

For a brief instant Meli froze, frightened by Jud's shadowy terror, then she jumped to her feet and rushed to the bed. Was he still worried about the men chasing her? She had to wake him, tell him that it was only a dream, that she was all right, that they were both quite safe. Surprisingly her movements didn't wake him. He was still caught up in his dream, fighting the demons of his nightmare, but his shouts had slackened into mumbles. Sweat beaded on his forehead, streamed over his temples and glistened in the dark waves of his hair; his trembling body shook the mattress.

"Jud," she whispered, touching his shoulder gently. "Jud, wake up. Everything is fine. Please, Jud."

His palms shot out as he rolled onto his back and stared at her. Silent tears pooled in the terror-filled depths of his eyes. Fear, anger, pain—what horrible visions were locked in his mind?

"You were screaming in your sleep."

Two tears streaked down his cheek.

Meli wiped them with her fingertips, then lightly caressed his knitted brow.

"A bad dream," he said.

"It's all right," Meli said, grasping his wrists and nestling his hands beneath her chin. She longed to ease his aches, to comfort him. "It's all over."

"All over? How I wish it could be all over." Taking a deep breath, he gently freed his hands, drew her into his arms and tumbled her onto the mattress. One hand moved lightly up her leg, parting the short, flowered robe, caressing the bare, rounded flesh beneath it and lifting her to him. Shrugging the robe aside, he feathered his other hand over her abdomen and cupped her tautening breasts. "So sweet, so gentle and so very sweet."

His mouth shaped itself to the rosy pink tips and the throbbing force of his passion winged lower, fluttering lightly between her thighs. She had been drawn to him from the first moment she saw him, and now he was tugging on the silken cord, coaxing her to respond.

She could sense his trembling as he clutched her to him, and pressing her hand against his chest, she felt the rhythmic throbbing of his heart. The towel had fallen away; he was strong and hard, yet warm and tender. Her body melted, fitting itself to the inflexible contours of his; she had wanted him long before she met him, had known him forever in her dreams. Her arms circled his back, her fingers savoring the firm, sinewy flesh, pulling him closer.

Gasping, he buried his face between her breasts. "Oh, Carrie," he said. "Sweet Carrie. Let me hold you. Let me hold and love you." His hands stroked hungrily over her breasts, down her abdomen, between her thighs.

"I'm not Carrie," Meli said, a freezing chill icing down her spine as she pushed him away from her. Who was Carrie? She glanced down at the snakelike ring, narrow enough to be a wedding band. His wife? If not, then definitely a woman he cared for enough to call in a moment of need. Carrie, not Meli. Meli's fragile dream shattered into the shards of a heartbreaking nightmare.

She could feel his body tense as he set her away from him and looked at her intently, as if she were someone he didn't recognize, as if he were seeing her for the first time. Pain flashed across his features and merged with confusion before they cleared in recognition. "The lady biologist," he whispered. "What happened? What did I do? For God's sake, what did I do?"

Before Meli could answer, three raps sounded at the door.

Chapter 2

AT THAT MOMENT MELI AND JUD WERE SO CAUGHT UP IN their own private world that the knocks on the door seemed to be coming from outer space. Startled, they stared at each other and waited. Neither of them welcomed the intrusion.

"Shh," Jud cautioned. "Don't answer. Maybe they'll go away."

The raps sounded again, louder this time, more insistent. "Miss Fancher?" The thick fireproof door muffled the man's voice but couldn't mute the demanding tone. "We know you're in there, Miss Fancher."

Jud pressed a finger across her lips. "Ask who it is, but don't tell them anything," he whispered. "Pretend you're sleeping."

Meli nodded. Her heart was beating in such a fearfully rapid staccato that she pressed her hands against her chest to still it. "Who is it?" she mumbled in a groggy voice, praying they'd go away.

"Sam Adams, the hotel detective." The man's voice was calm but firm. "Sorry to disturb you, but we have to come in. We're searching all the rooms."

Meli sighed as she turned to Jud. "It's okay," she whispered. "It's the house detective." What a break. Relief washed over her. Sam Adams could provide the help Jud needed. He had probably been alerted by the F.B.I. and had come looking for Jud to rescue him and guarantee his safety.

"I hardly think so." Jud's hands tightened on her arms, and he pulled her closer until their faces were a scant hairbreadth apart. "He's one of the men who's after me," he said, glancing furtively around the room. "I've got to get away."

"The house detective?" Meli's palms framed Jud's cheeks, forcing his face back to hers. If Jud was who he said he was, why would the house detective be after him? "You're not making sense." Then again maybe he was; maybe she had been too gullible, too eager to help.

"I can't explain now, but you've got to trust me. You'll be safe in your room. They wouldn't dare touch you while you're in the hotel."

"Yes, but what about you?"

"I'll be okay. Just don't believe anything they tell you and don't tell them I've been here." His lips pressed lightly against hers, then bit down in a brief, demanding kiss so fleeting that it seemed to end before it began; yet its intensity etched an imprint and a need for more. "Please . . . believe me. Help me." His fingers tensed for a moment, then he released her, snatched his jeans from the chair, crossed to the sliding glass door and disappeared behind the drape. Almost inaudibly the screen squeaked along its track.

The sound grated on Meli's already-taut nerves and she wanted to scream, but she didn't. What had Jud told her about silence sometimes saving a life? If she trusted, believed and wanted to help him, then this, doubtless, was one of those occasions when self-control meant everything.

"Miss Fancher," Adams bellowed. "We're coming in."

Meli heard him fumbling with the lock, trying to force in a key. He couldn't; Jud had pressed the privacy button. Jud's plea echoed through her thoughts. *Trust me and don't tell them I've been here.* She remembered how he had carried her across the rocks when he could have moved faster by leaving her behind. She had to believe in him. "Wait a minute. I'm not dressed. I was sleeping." She had to stall them and give Jud time to hide. "Give me a chance to put on a robe." She glanced at the slider. The drapes were billowing gently. No sign of Jud. He must be out on the terrace. "I'm coming," she said, pulling on some pajama bottoms, then tightening the belt on her robe as she walked to the door and unlocked it. Maybe she could deal with them in the hall and stop them from coming in.

Three men stood outside. The one in the middle, shorter than the other two, wore white cotton trousers and a blue and red flowered shirt. His ruddy complexion extended to his bald head, which was fringed by a halo of wiry gray hair. She had seen him around the hotel, in the lobby, at the reception desk, the coffee shop. He flashed a leather wallet and badge at Meli.

"Sam Adams, hotel detective." He stepped forward, motioning for the others to follow.

"Just a minute," Meli said, blocking his entrance. "Let me see that." She grabbed his wallet, then slammed the door. The photo beside the badge matched the man who had shown it to her. Still, the longer she kept them outside, the safer Jud was.

"Hey, what do you think you're doing?" Adams pounded on the door and jiggled the knob. "Open this door."

"I'm checking on you," Meli said, reaching for the phone. "How do I know you're telling the truth, that you are who you say you are?"

When the hotel operator verified Adams's description and also that he was searching hotel rooms, Meli had no choice but to admit her uninvited visitors; anything else would only make them more suspicious, which was the last thing she wanted to do.

"Would you mind telling me what's going on?" she asked, returning Adams's wallet.

"We're federal agents, miss," the olive-skinned man with a half-moon scar in the middle of his chin said. "A man in our custody escaped tonight, just a short while ago." He looked at the carpet, then knelt to touch the darker spots. "It's wet," he said, eyeing her accusingly. His partner's left eye twitched in agreement.

Federal agents? Escaped prisoner? For a moment Meli was stunned into silence; she hadn't considered that possibility. What if Jud were lying to her? What if he were an escaped prisoner? At this point she didn't know who was telling the truth. Instinct told her to believe Jud, but how reliable was her instinct? "Do you have any identification?" Why hadn't she asked Jud for his? What was it about him that had made her so certain she could trust him?

"We're not carrying any," the man with the scar said. "We're undercover and our I.D.s could prove fatal if they fell into the wrong hands, but Sam can vouch for us."

"They're legit," Adams said, nodding judiciously.

"Now, what about this?" The scarred man tapped the damp carpeting and sniffed, reminding Meli of a ferret snuffling out his prey.

Jud had said that Adams was one of the men after him.
Trust me, he had pleaded. And she did. She had no proof;
her decision was more emotional than rational, but she
couldn't let them catch him. "There's nothing unusual
about that," she said, shrugging off the damp circle. "I'm
a marine biologist. I was out collecting specimens. Then it
got windy and I came in." She scanned the room,
searching for her canvas tote. "That's funny, I thought
I—"

"Looking for this?" Adams asked, taking her specimen
bag from the silent agent standing behind him. "We found
it on the rocks. Jud Thompson—he's the man we're
after—was out there tonight. We thought you might have
seen him."

"I wish I could help," Meli said, reaching for the bag,
"but I didn't see anyone. I'm out there practically every
night and I never see anyone. You know how it is, during
the day everyone's outside soaking up the sun, but when it
gets dark—"

"Yeah, we know," Adams interrupted. "But about
Thompson?"

"I never saw him." She peered anxiously inside the
canvas bag, checking the contents. "Thanks. I found
some specimens I wouldn't have wanted to lose." Eager
to get their minds off the damp carpeting and Jud, she took
out the anemone and studied it admiringly. "This is
tropical, indigenous to the Pacific, nothing like it on the
Atlantic coast." Now, if only they were as interested in
marine biology as she was—

They weren't interested at all. They were concentrating
on their search, and for all they cared she might have been
talking to herself. The agent with the twitching eye had
wandered into the bathroom, and now he came out holding
the blood-stained washcloth with which she had cleansed
Jud's wound. "What about this?" he asked, his icy blue

eyes narrowing suspiciously as he rubbed his hand over his temple to still the twitch.

The washcloth. How was she ever going to explain that? Don't panic, she told herself, you can handle it, you can handle anything you have to. Think about what's at stake. Put them on the defensive. Remember, this is your room. Play innocent. How would you act if you were innocent? Indignant, that's it, indignant. "How dare you!" she demanded, reaching for the cloth.

The agent pulled it back. "Not so fast." A cynical smirk curled the corner of his pale, thin lips. "First tell me what it's doing here . . . all bloody like this."

"That washcloth wasn't here . . ." Her knees, she thought. No, there was too much blood for a scrape. She reflected for a moment, then reached a decision. "It was in my bathroom. It's personal, female, and I don't think I should have to explain it to you." The flush pinkening her cheeks was real. Instinctively she knew that these were the sort of men who humiliated women, used them, abused them, and she hated reminding them of her femininity. Still, she couldn't fall apart; Jud was depending on her and, embarrassed or not, she couldn't let him down. "You had no right—"

"I'm sorry. We . . ." The agent's pasty complexion turned crimson as he twitched and stammered his apology, but his partner and Sam Adams were crossing to the slider. They weren't contrite enough to call off their search.

The terrace. Where Jud was hiding. She had to divert them. "Imagine," she said, stalking toward the terrace and positioning herself between the men and the door, "searching my bathroom. The nerve of you, the supercolossal nerve. Did you really think that I had this Jud character hiding in there?" She stood in front of the drapes, holding up the washcloth, blocking their way.

"Bleeding? Really. I think this has gone far enough. You'd better leave."

"Sorry," Adams said, sidestepping her, then opening the drape and peering through the screen. "But this is for your own protection. With a guy like Thompson you just can't be too cautious."

Meli hardly heard what Adams said; the fearful clamor of her thoughts blocked him out. *They can't go out there. I won't let them. I won't let them find Jud.* She was certain they'd kill him if they did. "He's not out there. I would know if he were. He's not anywhere in my room and I resent the intrusion." She stepped in front of the drape and clutched her stomach. "Now, will you please leave. I really don't feel well."

"He's a dangerous man," Adams said, ignoring her pleas, sliding the screen open and scanning the terrace.

Dangerous? No, Meli's heart shouted. You're the one who's dangerous, not Jud. Jud had held her so gently, been so comforting, and there had been nothing in the least bit dangerous about his tears. They had been real, painfully real, while beneath a thin veneer of civility these men were brutes, cruel, vicious brutes.

"Look at this," Adams said, "over here."

His agent pals pushed past Meli.

They had found him. Oh, no. She should have realized that there wasn't anywhere he could hide on the terrace. There was just a potted palm and some wrought iron furniture out there. Swearing under her breath, she raced outside. How could she have been so stupid? But how could she have stopped them? She had tried, hadn't she?

Adams and the agents were peering over the railing. "Look at those shrubs," Adams said. "All trampled as if someone had jumped on them." Arms akimbo, he stared at Meli. Jud was the unspoken accusation.

"I don't know anything about any shrubs," Meli said,

her heart sighing in relief when she realized that Jud had escaped. "I suggest you speak to the gardener." She hadn't considered that Jud might jump. Although her room was on the first floor, the hotel was angled into the cliff and there was at least a twelve-foot drop from the terrace to the garden. Still, she should have known that Jud would take the chance. What was a twelve-foot drop to a man who spent his life dodging bullets?

"Well, I guess he could have hidden on the terrace without your knowing it," Adams had said doubtfully. "But he's not there now." He had followed her back into the room and closed the screen. "He's around here somewhere, so remember, if you should see him, call us right away." He had handed her a card. "My number's on there. He's dangerous. People don't matter to him, and if you get in his way . . ." His fingers had made a slashing motion across his throat. Then, turning, he had walked toward the door and stopped, his hand circling the knob . . . . "Don't let him fool you. He's a con man, talks a sweet game, but he can be vicious, a potential killer." Adams had hesitated for a moment as if to emphasize his statement. "Good night, Miss Fancher. Sorry to have bothered you. Lock your door and remember what I've said about Thompson; he's vicious." Adams and his two cohorts stepped out into the hall and disappeared.

Meli locked the door, raced out to the terrace and looked out over the railing. She started when she heard some bushes rustle, but it was only a mongoose. Jud had vanished as suddenly as he had come.

Now, hours later, as she sat on the terrace watching the early morning sun shoot its honey-streaked rays across the still-pale sky, her thoughts returned to the present and she wondered what had happened to Jud. It was pointless to wait here any longer. Obviously he wasn't returning. Still, she couldn't stop worrying about him, wondering if he was all right. She had to know, but she wasn't going to find out by haunting her room. She would have to do some investigating of her own.

She showered quickly, then dressed in white shorts and a flowered pink midriff that tied just above her waist. Hawaii's sunny climate made anything heavier impractical. The hotel rooms were comfortably air-conditioned, but the stifling tropical heat made itself felt outdoors immediately.

Although it was barely past dawn, chambermaids were cleaning the rooms of guests who had already checked out, and Meli sidestepped two carts stocked with fresh linens and cleaning supplies that stood in the hallway. The doors of the rooms she passed were ajar, and as she passed by she heard the whir of a vacuum cleaner. A man wearing khaki shorts and an open-necked white T-shirt left a room across the way, followed her toward the elevator, then turned and took the stairway.

Not everyone in Hawaii was on vacation, Meli thought, not the hotel staff or Jud, or Sam Adams and his sleazy cohorts. Sam Adams was the logical one to ask about Jud, she decided as she circled the garden atrium and walked toward the elevator. After all, wouldn't any normal woman want to know if the dangerous criminal he had been looking for last night had been caught? In fact it might seem suspicious if she weren't curious about the outcome.

From past experience she knew that at this time of morning Adams was usually in the upper lobby lolling around the reception desk, sipping coffee and chatting with the registration clerks. Today the outdoor lobby was noisier and more crowded than usual because, as the activity board behind the desk indicated, two tour groups were checking out. Their harried guides were stamping luggage tags, shouting directions and trying to ensure that the suitcases of a busload of senior citizens from Cincinnati didn't get mixed up with the baggage of a family tour returning to Tokyo. Just beyond them, studying the recreation schedule, she recognized the man from the downstairs hallway. Well, why not? He was staying at the hotel, wasn't he?

"Excuse me," Meli said, skirting a potted palm and leaning around the corner of the reception desk. "Is Sam Adams around?"

"Sam's off duty," the receptionist replied, brushing her short brown hair off her forehead as she looked up from her computer. "Are you having a problem? One of the bellmen is covering for him. He might be able to help. Shall I call him?"

Not unless the bellman was one of his henchmen, and Meli seriously doubted that. Neither of Sam's cronies had looked as if they had ever done an honest day's work. "No, I have to see Sam. Any idea where I can find him?"

"Probably down at the pier. He's one of the judges in the fishing tournament."

Meli thanked the receptionist, then jogged down the steps to the parking area where her rented bicycle was chained to the rack. The man she'd seen in the downstairs hallway was studying some travel brochures as he walked toward his car. Meli smiled to herself and thought that if he weren't so engrossed in his reading, she would have motioned to him and made some joke about their minds operating on the same wave length. He might even be having breakfast in town and would probably be willing to give her a lift. No, she needed the exercise, and the bike ride would help give her time to think.

She kept to the edge of the road, staying behind a group of teenagers heading for one of the few white sand beaches on Kona and cycling past the tiny wooden church perched at the side of the minuscule beach. Her friend from the parking lot had passed her, and she had waved to him, but he hadn't noticed. He was probably too busy trying to avoid the joggers and pedestrians. The two-lane road was too narrow to accommodate the heavy tourist traffic.

After chaining her bike to a rack at the end of the pier, she bought some pineapple–macadamia nut bread and coffee, then strolled along the water's edge. The flags of many nations fluttered alongside the pier near the grand-stands and judges' box where the marlin were weighed each afternoon at four.

A young family studied the flags, the parents identify-ing each nation to the small boy standing between them. The boy said something that made his father smile. When he bent to whisper into his wife's ear, she turned sideways and Meli saw the protruding bulge of an advanced pregnancy. A sharp tightening sensation that was becom-ing all too familiar clutched at her heart. She had been seeing a lot of pregnant women lately, or perhaps she was just more aware of them. It didn't matter. Now wasn't the time to dwell on her personal problems. She had come here to find Sam Adams.

The hotel registration clerk had told her that he was one of the judges in the billfisher contest, but as far as Meli could tell he wasn't among the three men and two women conferring in the judge's box. She finished the last of her coffee, tossed the cup into the trash bin and walked toward the judges' box. Maybe someone there would know where Adams was.

A tall, dark-haired man wearing brown-lensed sun-glasses was chatting with the chunky Polynesian woman seated at the scoring desk. When he saw Meli he quickly concluded the conversation, turned his back to them and began checking the daily weight charts posted in front of the grandstands. It was almost as if he were trying to avoid her. Ridiculous, Meli told herself. Why would he be trying to avoid her? They didn't know each other; she had never seen him before, unless . . .

For a brief instant Meli felt a pang of recognition. There was something about the way he moved. Jud, she thought, then dismissed the possibility. The tan complexion was the same, she mused, studying his arms and the back of his neck, but his short, razor-cut hair was neatly tapered, his face clean-shaven. She'd noted that before he turned away. If only she could see his eyes . . . Stop being silly, she told herself. He wasn't Jud, but apparently she was so preoccupied with Jud that she was imagining him in every man she saw. Had he escaped? Was he safe? She had to know, and Sam Adams could probably tell her.

"May I help you?" the woman asked, looking up at Meli.

"I hope so," Meli replied. "I'm looking for Sam Adams and I was told I might find him here."

"Sam Adams?" Lowering her eyes, the woman cleared her throat and shuffled through some papers on the desk. "Sam Adams," she repeated, tapping her fingers on the desk and glancing over her shoulder at the dark-haired man whose attention was riveted on the scoring chart.

Was there an almost imperceptible shake of his head? Meli wondered, or had she just imagined it?

"No," the woman said, smiling at Meli congenially. "As a matter of fact, I haven't seen Sam since yesterday." She held up a small pad and pencil. "If you want to leave your name, I'll tell him you were asking for him."

Meli shook her head. No point in letting Adams know how concerned she was about Jud. An inordinate amount of interest would only arouse his suspicions. She had to make her inquiries seem casual. "No thanks, it's not that important. I'll probably run into him later today."

When Meli began walking away she felt a warm prickling at the back of her neck, the uncomfortable sensation that she was being watched. Turning her head slightly, she glanced behind her out of the corner of her eye. The dark-haired man had returned to the front of the booth, and although his sunglasses made detection difficult, she was almost certain he was watching her. Was he a friend of Adams's? she wondered. Probably. Well, she'd better not make it look as if contacting the hotel detective had been her sole reason for coming here. Casual, she told herself, keep it casual.

Nervous beneath the man's scrutiny, she walked to the end of the pier, where a glass-bottomed boat was docked. The man who had left the hotel with her was buying a ticket. Apparently he had found the brochure describing this boat ride particularly appealing. She could understand why; Kona's offshore waters were so clear that the glass-bottomed boat was like a window into the sea, its underwater lights illuminating the ocean bottom, revealing fish, coral and plants. The harbor ride was an exciting experience even for a pro like herself who had been on it several times. She knew the captain, and Chuck, one of the divers on the boat, had been her student last summer when she had taught a class at the University of Hawaii in Honolulu. Now he dived beneath the glass-bottomed boat, pointing out coral reefs and feeding fish to amuse the tourists. Although jobs were scarce in Hawaii, Chuck, like most of his friends, wouldn't consider any work that kept him indoors and away from the sea.

Meli stepped on board and asked Chuck if he had ever explored the white coral reef she had discovered just beyond a rocky spit behind the hotel's outdoor swimming pool, but his answers barely registered and she watched indifferently as the man from her hotel pocketed his ticket and walked to the edge of the pier. Her attention was tuned to the mysterious man in the judges' booth. By now she was certain of his surveillance, but whenever she looked in his direction he turned away.

This is absolutely ridiculous, she decided. She had never been a shrinking violet and she wasn't about to let some snoopy stranger study her like some glass-encased specimen. She would confront him and put him on the defensive. If she was wrong, she would apologize, but she was certain that she was right. She said good-bye to Chuck with the intention of challenging her covert scrutineer, but when she headed back to the booth, he was gone.

It's probably nothing, she told herself; this Jud incident was making her paranoid. Maybe the man was just girl-watching and she should be flattered rather than annoyed. She wasn't totally unattractive—and in this brief outfit, just shorts and a scanty top . . . The explanation was logical, but it was the kind of logic she used to silence an insistent intuition, an intuition that invariably proved correct.

Trying to put her suspicions at rest, she pedaled through town and stopped off at some shops to buy a few souvenirs: pearl earrings for Sue, a swirling pink and green shirt for Dave, Sue's husband, and a scuba outfit for Bobby, their son. Then, loading her purchases into her basket, she began bicycling back to the hotel. Perhaps Adams had returned. She hoped so because she wanted to find out about Jud and she didn't know whom else to ask.

Adams hadn't returned, but it didn't take more than two minutes to discover where he was—in jail. The bellmen, activities director and desk clerks were all buzzing with the news.

"It's unbelievable," one desk clerk said, waving the newspaper and setting it down in front of Meli. "You're the one who asked about him this morning, aren't you?"

"Yes," Meli said. "What happened?"

"Read the article. It's unbelievable."

Meli scanned the column. Sam Adams and two other men had been arrested by the authorities. The photos above the article were of Adams and the two men who had accompanied him to her room last night. So Jud had been telling her the truth, she thought, more grateful than ever that she had believed him.

"Isn't that something?" the desk clerk asked, shaking her head in disbelief. "Who would have thought it about Sam? I mean he was always such a stickler for honesty and obeying the law. Do you remember that time when some money was missing from the cashbox and he accused—"

"May I borrow this?" Meli asked. She wanted to read the article in the privacy of her room, scrutinize it for information about Jud.

But there wasn't any. After returning to her room she had carefully reread the article three more times, but Jud wasn't mentioned. There would probably be some information on the evening news, but that was hours away and she was too anxious to wait. She had to know if he was safe, and she had to know it now.

Maybe the desk clerk had some additional news. Meli folded the newspaper and opened her door just in time to see the man who should have been on the glass-bottom boat disappear into the room across the way. Something was wrong. There was a limit to coincidental meetings. Was he connected with last night? One of Sam Adams's friends? Apprehension, fright—Meli wasn't certain which emotions she was experiencing, but confidence and bravery weren't even on the list. She stepped back into her room, closed the door and locked it.

Now what? She might be getting paranoid, but she was suddenly as uneasy about her own welfare as she had been about Jud's, and she was too frightened to leave her room.

What to do? Pacing the floor nervously, she reread the article. *Anyone with information concerning these men is urged to contact the FBI.* A phone number followed.

Well, Meli thought, dialing the number, she had information and she wanted some as well. If the man in the room across the hall was connected with Adams—and what about the man in the judges' booth? Too many people were watching her all of a sudden, and she needed help, protection maybe.

The man answering the phone announced that he was agent Simonson and Meli heard the intermittent beep that indicated their conversation was being recorded.

"I read the article in the newspaper," Meli said after identifying herself, "and I was wondering if there was any information about Jud Thompson."

Meli could hear Simonson catch his breath and the line quieted for a moment as if he were covering the mouthpiece. Then the phone clicked. Had someone else picked up an extension? she wondered.

"What was that name again?" Simonson asked.

"Jud Thompson. I know Sam Adams was looking for him last night. Is he all right?"

"I'm afraid I don't know any Jud Thompson."

Didn't know any Jud Thompson? Meli felt as if she were losing her sanity. Was it all a dream? A Kafkaesque nightmare? "Look, I don't know what's going on, but Jud Thompson came to my room last night. I helped him escape and now I think I'm being followed."

"Hold on a minute." The mouthpiece was covered again and Meli heard the sound of muffled voices. "Look, Miss Fancher, we're quite sure you're not in any danger, but we're in a sticky situation and we'd rather you didn't discuss Jud Thompson with anyone until we've had a chance to talk with you. Is there some convenient, inconspicuous place where we can meet later today?"

Meli's sigh of relief echoed through the telephone. If Simonson didn't want her discussing Jud, then Jud existed, and she wasn't losing her grip on reality. Thank God for small favors.

"Can we meet somewhere, Miss Fancher?"

"Yes, of course." Not her room, she decided, but somewhere close by, with other people around. There was safety in numbers, wasn't there? And at this point her safety was a prime consideration because she didn't know whom to trust. After several more moments of thought, she suggested meeting in the hotel cocktail lounge at six o'clock that evening.

Chapter 3

THE HAUNTING TONES OF A UKULELE PLAYING 'SWEET Hawaii' greeted Jud as he stepped through the bamboo arch of the thatched-roof Paniolo Lounge. It took a moment for his eyes to adjust to the shadowy light, a brief hiatus during which he didn't move. Force of habit—don't walk in blind; always check the layout.

At least that rule was still operational, but by coming here to meet Meli Fancher he was definitely bending one of his others, a vow he had made never to become involved with a woman like her. Not that he didn't enjoy female companionship, the take-it-or-leave-it kind, one-night stands, no strings attached. But Meli Fancher was different; one night with a woman like her seguéd into a lifetime commitment, something he wasn't capable of giving. So what was he doing here? Why hadn't he been able to stay away?

Sure, he was grateful for her help, but gratitude wasn't his reason for being here. No point in deceiving himself with that canard when the pure, unvarnished truth was that he had simply wanted to see her again, that he had tried to stay away and hadn't been able to.

As soon as he had escaped last night he had reported back to headquarters and had had arrest warrants issued for Adams and his two henchmen. The problem was that other members of the espionage ring were still at large—most important, the top man—and the Bureau didn't know who Adams and his friends had contacted before their arrest.

At the moment Jud's main concern was that Meli's explanations hadn't completely convinced her late-night visitors of her innocence and that one of them might have had second thoughts and mentioned her name to someone higher up, someone still on the loose. She wasn't involved in the case, had no classified information, but they didn't know that, and they might come after her, which was why he had had her put under surveillance. He hadn't told her; the less she knew, the better. What was the point in making her nervous?

He had intended to leave it at that, strictly professional, in the hands of another agent, and then he had seen her down at the pier. She hadn't recognized him; he had turned away as soon as he had noticed her approaching the booth. Besides, he had gotten a haircut and a shave since the last time she had seen him. Then, safely hidden behind a pair of dark glasses, he had been able to listen to her voice—intelligent, inquisitive, unafraid—he had watched her walk—long, tanned legs, undulating curves, honeyed skin that he knew was as softly feminine as her voice. An unforgettable woman. He wanted to, had to, see her again. She seemed so independent and self-assured. A brief affair might not be an impossibility after all.

So when she had called the office this afternoon he had broken his rule. Instead of sending another agent to meet her, he had come himself. And now that he was seeing her again, he knew that he had never really intended anything different. From the first moment she had called to him across that rocky cliff, he had thought of her as his salvation, had wanted to hold her in his arms, to feel the sweetness of her flesh against his.

Now he surveyed the half-empty lounge and found her seated at a small table near the back of the room, signing for her drink, leaning forward and pushing the check toward the flickering candle. She didn't see him, but he could see her. He could see her long auburn hair and honey-toned complexion glowing in the candlelight. Pink-gold, he thought, velvety, strokable, pink-gold.

He wanted to watch her unobserved for a few minutes, so he stepped to the side of the door and found a dark corner untouched by the day or the candlelight. Then, crossing his arms over his chest, he leaned back against the wall and studied her. She looked different now, softer somehow, more feminine. Her hair, that was it. Loose, it swept over her ears and down the back of her neck, a coppery wreath of wildly swirling curls that he longed to touch. Why did she ever keep it tied up? His appreciative gaze slid lower. She wore a striped sundress, green and turquoise, some kind of backless halter arrangement that plunged between her breasts and wrapped around her neck. He smiled to himself; she looked nothing like any college professor he had ever known.

Closing his eyes, he remembered how he had caressed and kissed those breasts. He had been half asleep yet awake enough to know that he had wanted her, just as he had wanted her this morning, just as he wanted her now. Yet even in this moment of wanting he knew he couldn't have her, knew he had no right to want her, not unless she was willing to accept the little he had to offer. And he was certain that Meli Fancher wasn't that sort of woman. Even in his cynical mind she evoked images of white picket fences and children. She wasn't for him.

The music stopped and a scattering of clapping filled the silence. Taking a deep breath, Jud opened his eyes and began walking toward Meli. He had been a fool to come here. He should have sent another agent, someone who would have smoothed things over and told her he was all right and that she wasn't in any danger. He should have but he hadn't. He was insane to start down a path that could only end in nothingness, but from the moment he left her last night, he had known that he would be seeing her again. Now he was inexplicably nervous at the prospect, and his heart pounded against his ribs as he stepped closer.

She looked up as he approached the table, and he could see the confusion in her eyes, the same confusion he had seen that morning when he had watched her on the pier. She recognized him as the man she had seen in the judges' booth earlier that day, but he was certain she still hadn't made the connection, didn't realize he was Jud Thompson.

"Miss Fancher," he said, stopping by her table and offering her his hand.

Her hand shot out in automatic response as she pushed back her chair and began rising. Then she sank down in her seat and stared at him in disbelief. "Jud," she murmured, a relieved smile wreathing her face. "Jud Thompson." Thank God he was all right.

"None other." He returned her smile as he sat down beside her.

"You were at the pier this morning." A perplexed frown canceled her smile. "I thought it might have been you, but you looked so different, and you never said anything to me . . . not one word," she accused him angrily. She had been so concerned about him; he must have overheard her inquiry and realized that he was the reason she was looking for Sam Adams, yet he had concealed himself without saying anything. She felt like a fool; Jud had made her feel like a fool. "How could you do such a thing?"

"Look, I can explain . . ." Jud fumbled for the right words, but couldn't find them. He had thought she would be glad to see him and hadn't expected this angry reaction.

"Do you have any idea of how worried about you I was? Why do you think I was looking for Sam Adams? I was up all night, thinking God knows what . . ." Now that she knew he was out of danger, all her pent-up feelings exploded and Jud was her target. "How could you just skulk in the background without saying one word? Didn't you even care about the way I felt? Common courtesy would have dictated—"

Common courtesy had nothing to do with F.B.I. regulations. Jud had been busy checking out Adams's contacts, and Meli hadn't been cleared until late that afternoon, just before she had called. "I'm sorry about that, but if you'll just listen—"

"Listen?" Meli ignored his plea and rose to her feet. "This morning I would have listened; I was so damned worried I would have listened to anything, but now . . ." Still fighting to control her temper, she picked up her purse and slipped the strap over her shoulder. "I'm glad you're okay." She was angry enough to strangle him, but she controlled herself, stepped behind him and began walking toward the exit. Listen, indeed! she snorted to herself. The way she felt right now she wouldn't listen to Jud Thompson if he were yelling "Fire" in a burning building. The colossal nerve of the man.

"Wait a minute." Jud grabbed her wrist and pulled her back. Things weren't going at all the way he had planned them. Where was the gentle, caring woman he had met

last night? Talk about temper—he was dealing with a
virago.

"Let me go." Two minutes ago she had been ecstatic
that he wasn't hurt. Now she wanted to pulverize him,
which is exactly what she would do if he didn't release
her. She had to get out of here—fast.

"No. You can't just leave." He had to make her sit
down again so they could talk. That was why he had come
here to speak with her and get to know her better. Besides,
he had promised Rick Simonson that he would keep an eye
on her. For her own safety she was still under protective
surveillance, and he had told the agent watching her to
take the night off.

"Oh, can't I?" Meli said, her eyes glittering from the
anger boiling within her. Who did he think he was,
controlling her life as if she were a puppet on a string?
Disappear and Meli worries, come back and Meli smiles.
All is forgotten, all is forgiven. A mindless, insensate
woman. Well, she'd show him exactly what she thought of
his attitude. "Just you watch." Reaching down, she
picked up her glass of mineral water and tossed it in his
face. She was still seething when Jud released her, and she
strode rapidly away.

For one dumbstruck moment Jud did exactly as she had
commanded. Too stunned to do anything else, he just
watched her leave. He didn't know which had been more
shocking, the wet chill of the drink or the fact that Meli
had actually thrown it at him. And to think, he had called
her sweet and gentle. But she had been last night. Well, if
she thought he was going to let her get away . . . He
snatched a napkin from the table, patted his face dry and
started after her.

She had run faster than he had expected, but he caught
up with her on the garden path between the lounge and the
main building. He jogged in front of her, blocking her

way. She tried to sidestep him, but he wouldn't let her, and when she tried to push past him, he captured her wrists and drew her to him.

"Let me go, damn you, let me go." Her hands flayed ineffectively, and she didn't know whom she was angrier with, Jud or herself. She hated losing her temper, but there were times when she just couldn't control it, and this had been one of them. Now that she had had a chance to calm herself, she was mortified to think that she had actually thrown her drink in Jud's face, and she wanted to be alone with her embarrassment.

"Not just yet. You owe me an apology," Jud said, his voice husky from sprinting after her. Fire and ice, he thought. She was like fire and ice. No way was he letting her go.

"I owe *you* an apology? That's rich. You were standing there on the pier watching me, probably chuckling at the cute trick you were pulling, while I had visions of you lying somewhere . . ." She winced as his fingers tightened around her wrists when she tried to pound her fists against his chest. She was doing it again, letting her temper run away with her. She bit her lip and forced herself to stop.

"You were worried about me?" He stepped closer, covering her hands with his and pressing them to his chest, where they remained motionless.

"That's right, I was worried about you, fool that I am." She could feel his heart racing beneath her hands, and she remembered last night when he had held her in his arms. Then, she had wanted him to make love to her, but now . . .

"But now that I'm all right you're angry?" Jud's mouth parted in a boyish grin that weakened her knees. "Why? That doesn't make sense."

"You've treated me like an idiot. I feel—" She didn't

need him to tell her that she wasn't making sense. The calm, predictable pattern of her life had stopped making sense the minute she had seen him dive off the trawler.

"Hurt?" Jud finished for her. "I've hurt you and now you want to hurt me back. All right." He released her wrists, put his hands behind his back and presented her with his chin. "Go ahead. Hit me. I deserve it. Keep punching away until you get it out of your system." He brought one hand forward and tapped his chin with his index finger. "Come on now. Right here."

Meli's hand clenched into fists, and for one brief moment she actually raised them toward him. Then, realizing how comical he looked, she lowered her hands and started laughing. She didn't want to hit him, it was just that when she had seen him in the lounge and had realized the unnecessary anguish he'd put her through, she hadn't been able to control her rage.

It wasn't Jud's fault. He had no way of knowing about the inner tensions that drove her. How she hated being patronized and shunted aside like an unwanted child. And so she had reacted like a child. What could be more childish than tossing water in someone's face? "I can't," she said. "I just can't." She wasn't proud of her temper, but there were times . . . Oh, how could she explain her need for acceptance? Jud would never understand.

"All right then." He cupped her chin lightly, lifting it toward him. "I'm sorry I made you worry. It was thoughtless and cruel. Now, will you settle for an apology and dinner?" His thumb feathered her cheek, stroking lightly down to the corner of her lip.

Meli felt a tugging deep within her, as if his hands had taken control of her body. She wanted to accept his invitation, yet she knew she couldn't. The closer she got to him, the more she'd be exposing herself to pain. She was almost certain that he was involved with another woman, which made him off limits to her. She wasn't like her mother, not in any way. "I accept your apology," she said, "but the dinner isn't necessary."

"I know it isn't necessary. It's just something I want to do." His hand dropped to her shoulder, his fingers massaging the pulsing cord in her neck. "I understand how you feel about me, but even a condemned man gets one last dinner."

Meli saw a haunting need deep in his eyes, and she couldn't say no, not bleeding-heart Meli, who spent half her life drowning in a sea of compassion. So we'll have dinner, she thought. What can happen in a crowded restaurant?

"Do you like Japanese food?" Jud asked, equating her silence with acquiescence. "I know a great place where the locals go."

When she told him that Japanese food would be fine, he clasped her hand in his and began walking to the parking lot.

During the short drive to the hilltop restaurant, Meli kept telling herself that this was the wisest thing to do. Seeing Jud in danger had made her think of him as some sort of exotic hero, an off-the-screen James Bond. But this secret agent had feet of clay, so she would have dinner with him and wait for him to tarnish his golden image by lying about Carrie. Once she saw him for what he was, her compassion would evaporate and she would get him out of her system. She had always despised a liar, and that went double for any man who cheated romantically.

They left their shoes in the restaurant entryway while a bowing hostess clad in a silk kimono slid back shojis and led them to a private booth overlooking the water. As they walked through the restaurant Meli noticed the female diners lift their eyes to follow Jud. They appraised, approved, then looked at her with envy. But Jud didn't belong to her, so she pretended to be unaware of their attention and concentrated on the hillside view. Far below the rocky cliff sailboats bobbed in the moonlight. She remembered the trawler and shivered.

There were no chairs in the booth, just floor cushions. Jud held Meli's hand while she knelt by the teppan table and tucked her feet beneath her. Then he seated himself and crossed his legs in front of him.

The waitress handed them hot towels, and Jud began speaking to her in Japanese, interrupting the conversation to ask Meli if she enjoyed sake or would prefer another beverage. When Meli replied that sake would be fine, the waitress bowed and left the room.

"Your command of the language is very impressive," Meli said, searching his face. No, the tan complexion definitely wasn't Oriental, yet he spoke Japanese as if it were his mother tongue.

"Not so impressive when you consider that I lived in Tokyo until I was four years old. You know what they say about a young child's mind being like a sponge. I picked up the language and it stayed with me. I was an Air Force brat. My father was a test pilot. For the next two years I lived in New Mexico near my grandparents, then my father got transferred to Berlin."

"Ah, so you got to see the world." Meli had always envied the cosmopolitan sophistication of classmates who accompanied their parents to exotic foreign assignments. Jud carried himself with that same air of ease and confidence. "Lucky you."

"Yes, lucky me." Resentment clouded his features and mocked his words. "I hated every minute of it."

"How could you hate it? Seeing all those wonderful places? Why it's an invaluable experience for a child, for anyone."

"Great if you're a jet-setter," Jud said, "but all a kid really needs are two loving parents, a stable home, trees to climb . . ." His voice broke on a note of wistful depravation.

Two loving parents. Meli could understand that need. Reaching across the table, she patted his hand sympathetically, but Jud drew away when the hostess returned with the sake and poured the warm liquid into the small china cups. What had Jud's childhood been like? Meli wondered. Although her world had fallen apart when she was twelve, she still remembered the camping trips she had taken with her father. Had Jud ever shared a similar experience? His cynicism made her doubt that he had ever enjoyed a happy home. At least she had—for a while.

"Do you have any particular preferences in food?" Jud asked, "or would you like to rely on the expertise of a near native?"

"I'll trust you."

"A mistake," Jud said, his voice slightly rougher, "a very big mistake."

"Oh, should I order for myself then?"

"I wasn't talking about the food," Jud said, watching her carefully. "You can trust me with that."

"That's all we're talking about, isn't it?" She hated this double entendre, had never been at ease with the flirtatious patter that came so easily to her mother and Sue. "I can rely on my own judgment for everything else."

"Can you?" Jud's gaze was a cogent blend of protective tenderness and restrained desire.

"You'd better believe it." Her independence was a matter of need rather than of choice. She had never had anyone else she could count on, not since her father had died.

"And if I don't?" Her blush surprised him. Last night

she had reacted so well under pressure, yet now this light banter seemed to be unnerving her. He studied the rosy hue of her cheeks and found her more intriguing than ever.

"That's not my problem." But as Meli bent her head and sipped her sake she wondered if it was. She watched Jud as he turned to give the waitress their order and decided that her scheme to get him out of her system wasn't proceeding well at all. Not to worry, she told herself. Just this one dinner and you'll never see him again. What can happen over dinner?

"Have I shocked you?" Jud asked after the waitress had gone.

"Not at all," Meli said. "It's just the sort of thing men do, isn't it?" If they were talented, she mused, they wrote sonnets; otherwise they quipped over sake. As a general rule, she was more comfortable with the written word.

"Maybe I'm not your average man."

"Definitely not." Meli grinned mischievously. Didn't he have any idea of how attractive he was? Hadn't he noticed the women's eyes tracking him through the restaurant? "I can't remember the last time I met a man running from a barrage of bullets."

"Ah, that." Jud sat back as the waitress placed bowls of clear broth and cucumber salad before them. "Well, I hope we can close that case soon. At least my undercover part in it is finished. I blew my disguise last night on the trawler. That's why they were trying to kill me." He lifted the bowl between his palms and began sipping his soup. "Not a very pleasant way to pass the time, but that's what I get paid to do."

His words sent chilling prickles racing along Meli's arm. She sipped her soup, letting the hot broth trickle down her throat. She had been with him last night and she knew what he said was true. They both could have been killed. "Why were they after you? The newspaper mentioned something about espionage."

"Quite a scheme," Jud said. "It might have worked, too, if one of our contacts on the island hadn't overheard something he shouldn't have. An engineer in Seattle pilfered the plans for a new jet under government contract, then he spoke to Adams, who arranged for him to enter the billfisher contest and meet a foreign agent who was also registered in the contest. The deal was practically set when I came along pretending to be a Middle-Eastern agent with a better offer."

"You caught them all?"

"Not the one we were after, not the kingpin nor his foreign contact. When I kept insisting that I would deal only with the head man, they got suspicious and did some checking of their own. That's when I made a speedy exit and dived off the boat." He smiled wryly. "You know the rest."

"I don't know if my imagination is playing tricks on me, but I think someone may be following me. There's a man in my hotel—"

"Don't worry about him. You're perfectly safe. You have my word for it."

Meli was about to ask him how he could be so certain, when the shojis slid open and admitted the waitress. She bowed, lit the burner at their table and began preparing yosenabe, a Japanese fish stew not unlike bouillabaisse. Her movements were such a study in grace that a mundane chore like slicing vegetables became a sacred ceremony.

Meli watched and listened as the waitress smiled and explained each step of her culinary arrangement, but another, more disturbing thought, occupied her mind— what if the man they hadn't caught knew about Jud? Then wasn't he still in danger? And who was the man following her? They hadn't even discussed him. The question hurtled through her mind and jarred her physically. When the waitress finally bowed and left, Meli was too upset to eat; she just wound a long noodle around her chopsticks and stared at it.

"Something wrong?"

"That man, the kingpin, does he know about you?"

"We're hoping so."

"You're hoping so?" Meli repeated in disbelief. Wouldn't that place Jud in danger?

"It might be our only chance to make him reveal himself . . . if he thinks I know his identity and comes after me." Shrugging, he caught a piece of fish between his chopsticks. "That's enough shop talk for now."

"That's awful," Meli said, putting down her chopsticks and pushing the bowl away. Any remnants of appetite had vanished with Jud's admission that he was playing decoy. And she had assumed that he was safe, that Sam Adams's arrest had ended Jud's involvement. "How can you just set yourself up and wait—"

"Drop it, will you?" The tense man who had threatened her with a karate chop had returned. Tossing down his chopsticks, Jud closed his eyes, folded his arms behind his neck and leaned back. "I don't want to talk about it." His brow furrowed and his lips pressed together as if some desperate battle were raging within him. Abruptly, he stood, walked to the window and stared silently out. "I knew this couldn't work out." He had been a fool to get involved with her, he thought.

"Jud?" Meli stepped up behind him and put her hands on his shoulders. "Jud? What happened? What did I say?"

"Look. I know you deserve some explanation about last night, and I tried to give you one, but there are some things I can't talk about. Don't ask me to justify my job."

"Justify your job? I only asked—"

"I know what you asked, and I don't want to talk about it."

If he didn't want to discuss his job, then why had he invited her to dinner? After all, that's what last night was all about, wasn't it? His job? "All right. Forget I ever mentioned it." Unbidden, another image formed in her mind: her mother and Sue bent over a fashion magazine. Little Meli edging between them and her mother shooing her away. 'This doesn't concern you, Meli. It's for an older girl like Susan.' In Meli's mind older had translated to prettier. She closed her eyes and blinked away the memory. That was then and now was now. But she still hurt and she still hated being shunted aside. She bent down to pick up her purse, then stopped for a minute, biting her lip as she tried to regain her composure. "Set yourself up as a sitting duck. Get yourself killed. Why should I care?"

"Oh, Meli." Jud knelt beside her and pulled her into his arms. Without meaning to hurt her, he knew he had and he wanted to make it up to her. "You care because you're sweet and gentle." He kissed the top of her hair, smoothing it away from her face. "Extraordinarily brave." His lips feathered her temple, her cheek, the corner of her mouth. "And I'm all kinds of a fool for blowing up like that. It's just that there are things I have to do, things I can't talk about, things you can't understand. Can you forgive me? Please?"

"It doesn't matter."

"Yes, it does. I didn't mean to hurt your feelings." He drew back, studying her features as his index finger traced lightly over the curve of her jaw. She was trying to hide her hurt, but she wasn't succeeding. She was too sensitive, and he was behaving like a brute. "It's just that sometimes I get . . . I know my work is dangerous, and if

I stop to think about it . . . I don't want to, not when I'm with you. This has to be something separate or it won't work. Do you understand?''

"I'm trying to, but . . ." Pushing him away, Meli rose to her feet and began smoothing her dress over her hips. She liked Jud, liked him a lot, but she hated being shut out. Did he think she was too naive to understand the problems of his job? *This doesn't concern you, Meli.* "I wasn't making idle conversation. I'm genuinely interested in what you do."

"Drop it, Meli, please?"

"Fine, I'll drop it," she said, making no attempt to conceal her annoyance. "What would you like to talk about? The weather? Is that topic simplistic enough for a lamebrain like me?" If Jud didn't want to discuss his job, then what could they talk about? Carrie was the only other aspect of his life that aroused Meli's curiosity, and she doubted that he would find that any less controversial.

"Don't be like that."

"Don't be like what? If you want to know the truth, Jud, I don't enjoy being tongue-tied." She glanced down at the food and realized that she couldn't swallow even one chopstickful. "And I don't enjoy being treated like a fool. Look, I'm not really very hungry." She motioned to his plate. "But there's no reason for you to miss your dinner, so why don't you just sit down and finish your meal. I'll catch a cab back to my hotel."

"Why the hasty exit? Because I won't discuss my work? Don't you think you're carrying this a bit too far?"

"Good night, Jud." As far as she was concerned, Jud Thompson was a man of too many secrets, secrets he didn't want to share. Well, right now she had enough problems of her own without taking on Jud Thompson's.

"No cab," he said, tossing some bills on the table. "I brought you here and I'll take you back."

They spoke very little during the ride back, inane remarks punctuated by long, suffocating silences. As soon as Jud pulled up in front of the hotel, Meli muttered a polite combination of thank you and good-bye, then hopped out of the car without waiting for his answer. The evening had been a complete fiasco, and she was certain that she had seen the last of Jud Thompson. It was all for the best, she told herself. In fact, the situation would have been infinitely worse if they hadn't argued. Her life was confusing enough as it was, and the last thing in the world she needed right now was an affair with a man she couldn't talk to.

She supposed she should have spent a sleepless night, tossing and turning and thinking about Jud, but since that was how she had spent the previous night she was too mentally exhausted to think and too physically drained to do anything except sleep.

Chapter 4

MELI DIDN'T WANT TO WAKE UP. SHE WAS DREAMING—
Jud and her on a tropical island, cut off from the world,
nothing but blue water, green palms, lots of orchids,
purple and white—and children, small, dark-eyed children. Lately children played an important part in all her
dreams.

Jud was holding her in his arms, gently, talking to her,
confiding in her. "Only you, Meli, only you." She felt
special, and the pleasure was so palpable, so intense, that
she wanted to prolong it. She snuggled deeper into the
pillow, but the dream was fading, chased into oblivion by
an insistent rapping.

She tried to ignore the noise, but it continued, a pattern
now, five short, two long. Someone was at her door, and
he wasn't going away. Sighing, she opened one eye,
glanced around the room and fumbled on the night table
for her watch. Six o'clock. An unearthly rising time for
someone on vacation. "Who is it?" She was awake now

and, although the vivid reality of the dream had faded, its languid happiness lingered on. Pleasant dreams were a scarcity in her life right now, and she wanted whoever was at the door to leave so she could close her eyes and try to recapture it.

"Room service."

"Room service?" What a great time for a mix-up. You'd think that they would be more careful this early in the morning. "You must have the wrong room," she grumbled. "I didn't order anything."

"Room one eleven. That's you, isn't it?"

"Yes." Meli pulled on her robe and padded to the door. This man wasn't going to give up until he got a personal explanation. "But there has to be some mistake." She kept the safety chain in its socket and slid the door open. Her brief experience with Jud had taught her the value of being cautious.

"Good morning."

"Jud." He was standing outside holding a large cardboard tray from which a heart-shaped red antherium in a slender milk-glass vase sprouted incongruously amid waxed-paper packets and Styrofoam boxes and paper cups.

"Breakfast?" The question was a beseeching invitation. "For two?"

"I don't think so." Too awake now to confuse her dream with reality, she recalled how they had parted last night and remembered how angry she had been. If there was anything that didn't interest her right now, it was an early morning rehash. She turned away and started closing the door.

"Don't," Jud pleaded, holding the door ajar. He searched his mind for the words that would convince her to forget last night, but he couldn't think of any. How could he explain his feelings to her when he didn't understand them himself? Why did he keep pursuing her when he knew she could never be his? Was he developing masochistic tendencies? He knew that wasn't it, knew that he was hoping he'd find a way to work things out. "Please, Meli?"

Meli studied his face and felt her resolve weakening. If she had slept last night, he obviously hadn't. The lines on his cheeks were etched deeper, and his eyes were tinged with red. She couldn't turn him away. "I appreciate the thought, Jud, but it's a bit early, isn't it?" she said, opening the drape while he set the cardboard tray on the table by the window and began unpacking it. She tightened the belt on her robe. Two nights ago she had felt no shame when he had caressed her naked skin, yet now her robe seemed too suggestive. The mood, their relationship, everything had changed once Jud had held her in his arms and called her Carrie. She wasn't about to enter into a relationship with a man who was already involved with another woman.

"I thought we'd get an early start." Jud placed the milk-glass vase with the antherium in the center of the table, then stepped back to admire the setting.

"It's early, all right," she said, yawning as she fingered the collar of her robe. "But exactly what is it we're getting started on?" She might be tired, but she wasn't completely irrational. She wasn't ready for a continuation of last night's argument.

"Tom Hazlet, an agent from our Hawaii office, has a sailboat, and he's offered me a private tour of the islands. I thought you might enjoy coming along." He was making a peace offering and hoped that she would accept.

"You've invited me? Don't you think your friend might have some thoughts on the matter?"

"Guest of my choice, he said. And you're my choice."

Jud folded a paper napkin over his arm, then held out one of the green barrel chairs beside the table and motioned her toward it.

"You look ridiculous." Actually, he looked better than he had when she'd first seen him outside her door; the tired lines on his face disappeared when he smiled, making him appear younger, almost boyish. She found it difficult to maintain last night's anger when Jud was trying so hard to make amends.

"Maybe." His gaze swept slowly over her. "But then again, you're not exactly formal."

Looking in the mirror, Meli noted her rumpled robe, her sleep-tousled hair, straight in some places and curling into ridiculous angles in others, her freckled complexion, no makeup, not even lip gloss. God, she looked awful. Well, she wasn't about to start scrabbling around like a headless chicken. Jud would have to accept her as she was. It was his fault for waking her up. "I wasn't expecting company," she said. "Mornings I'm not human until I've had my coffee."

"I'll remember that," he said, his eyes rising to lock with hers. "It might come in handy."

His voice held a seductive tone which Meli noted but tried to ignore. "Not unless your breakfast delivery area includes Maryland. I'm leaving in three days." She walked to the slider and stared into the garden.

"Three days? Not much time."

"I've been here for two weeks. Except for some reefs off the smaller islands, I've seen most of what I had planned on seeing."

"I wasn't thinking about reefs."

"Oh? Us?" Meli met his suggestive innuendo head-on. "What would more time accomplish? Our relationship seems to have been stormy enough during the short while we've had together, wouldn't you say?"

"Stormy? Perhaps, but two nights ago when I needed a safe haven, you were there. I can't forget that."

At this point Meli wasn't at all certain of what she wanted from Jud, but it definitely wasn't gratitude. "You don't owe me anything."

"A cup of Kona coffee?" he offered, lifting the lid from the paper cup. "To make you human? How can you resist?"

"How, indeed?" Meli agreed, reaching for the coffee. The pungent scent was absolutely irresistible. "Mmm, that smells good."

Along with the coffee, Jud had brought orange juice, scrambled eggs with Portuguese sausage, and sweet rolls. Now, with the exaggerated pomposity of a supercilious waiter, he set one Styrofoam-encased portion in front of her.

"A veritable feast," Meli said, lifting her coffee cup and inhaling the rich, fragrant aroma. "I've always wanted breakfast in bed. This is a close second." She scooped some eggs onto her fork.

"I aim to please," Jud said, disregarding his own food while resting his chin on his hands and watching her. He liked the way she looked, sleepy and tousled. Right now bed seemed like a very appealing idea—minus the scrambled eggs. But he didn't think Meli would appreciate the suggestion. Her anger had erupted very quickly, but it was slow to fade, and he could still hear it in her voice, see it in her eyes. He thought about making some excuse for his behavior, then decided on the truth. She wasn't the kind of woman he wanted to lie to. "Meli, I'm sorry about last night. I didn't mean to upset you, but I'm so tied up inside that there are some things I just can't talk about, not anymore. Can you understand that? Accept it?"

"It's over, Jud, let's forget about it. You don't have to

tell me anything.'' How could he comprehend her resentment at being shut out, her need for acceptance. ''What I
did the other night . . . anyone would have helped you.''
Cradling her cup between her palms, she stood and
walked out to the terrace. ''You don't owe me a thing.''

''Great. Then how about coming on this boat ride with
me? No strings attached. I told Tom and Linda Hazlet
about your job and they offered to dock at some of the
smaller islands so you can dive for specimens.''

Meli thought for a moment. She wanted to explore
some of the reefs off the smaller islands, but the cost of
chartering a boat was prohibitive, and if she went with a
tour group, she'd have neither the time nor the privacy her
work demanded. Jud's offer was too good to turn down.

He waited on the terrace while she showered and
dressed, and by eight o'clock they were boarding the
Topaz Mist, a twenty-eight foot sailboat.

Tom Hazlet, a lean, ruddy-faced man in his early
thirties was lifting a cooler onto the boat. ''So you're the
lady who helped us out,'' he told Meli when Jud introduced them.

''Anyone else would have done as much,'' Meli said,
her face warming beneath his friendly gaze. She didn't
want them setting her up as some sort of heroine. After
all, Jud had borne the brunt of the danger.

''Maybe so,'' Tom said thoughtfully. ''But I'm glad
you were there.''

''That makes two of us,'' Jud said.

''Make it three.'' A tiny redhead, whose pixie haircut
and flat, hipless physique reminded Meli of Peter Pan,
bounced out of the cabin and offered Meli her hand. ''Hi,
I'm Lin Hazlet.'' Standing on tiptoe, she flung her arms
around Jud and kissed his cheek. ''We've grown real fond
of Jud and, ornery as he is, we'd hate to see anything

happen to him. Come on downstairs,'' she said, turning her attention back to Meli. ''We can unpack while these two mess with the sails.''

Although Meli would have preferred staying on deck and helping with the sails, she followed Lin into the cabin. Somehow she got the feeling that unisex duties hadn't made it to the *Topaz Mist* and the men wouldn't welcome her help. Once they were downstairs, Lin confirmed her suspicion.

''Sit down,'' she said, motioning to a striped blue and white bunk and reaching for a thermos. ''There's really nothing much for us to do down here. I've prepared everything at home. It's just that the men need some time alone.'' She handed Meli a tumbler of iced tea.

''Jud asked me to come.'' Meli didn't want Lin thinking that she had invited herself. ''I hope it's all right.''

''Of course it's all right; Jud wants you here. We all do. Listen, when I said they have to be alone, I didn't mean to make you feel unwelcome. It's just that sometimes, with their job, they need some time together; they're the only people who can understand the tension they're constantly under. They can relax with each other in ways that they can't when an outsider is around.''

''Jud's mentioned some things about his work.'' Not much, she thought. ''It must be rough.'' Meli felt like a snoop, and she hated pumping Lin for information about Jud, but she wanted to know more about him and she knew he wasn't going to be the one to tell her.

''Rough?'' Lin's chuckle was humorless. ''Can you imagine how it must feel to work undercover, knowing you could be discovered at any moment? There are times when Tom comes home so wound up that he can't talk without exploding, not even to me. So rather than say things he'll regret later, he just locks himself in his study and listens to music, for hours sometimes. It's torture, torture for them and worse for the women who love them.'' Lin peered into her tea morosely.

Worse for the women who love them, Meli thought as Jud's voice whispering ''Carrie'' echoed in her memory. Obviously Carrie was someone who mattered to him. Why else would he call out her name while he was groggy with sleep and holding another woman in his arms. So why wasn't Carrie here with him? Meli had seen how tense and nervous Jud was last night. Was that why he didn't want Carrie around? Was he using her as a substitute? She was just about to ask Lin about Carrie when Tom poked his head into the cabin and asked if they were going to spend the day hibernating.

''No,'' Lin said, winking at Meli. ''We just needed some time alone. You know, girl talk.'' Standing up, she brushed off her shorts, and from that point on, everyone stayed on deck, helping with the sails and steering, or just sitting and relaxing. Jud sat near the stern of the boat watching Meli flip her hand through the water while Lin and Tom busied themselves at the prow. Four adult and one baby dolphins began trailing the boat, spinning and leaping out of the water.

''They're fascinating,'' Meli said as she whistled softly and tried to mimic the sounds they were making while their long beaks and heads circled above the water's surface. ''They're trying to communicate with us, you know. I did a study project in New Zealand during my master's program. We shouldn't think of them as merely another dumb animal. They're practically our equals, and I get so angry when I read about them being trapped in fishing nets that I could—Sorry,'' she murmured, catching herself. ''Why didn't you remind me that this wasn't a lecture class?''

''Go on,'' Jud said softly. ''I like listening to you. It's

the nicest lecture I've ever had. You really care about them, don't you?''

''Yes. They're so friendly and intelligent that I can't bear the thought of anyone hurting them. Look.'' When the baby dolphin saw a chance to swim away, two adult dolphins pursued him and steered him gently back to the center of the group. ''They don't want him to get hurt. They use a form of sonar to communicate and warn each other of dangers and to swim through waters that are often too murky for visual navigation.''

''What are they doing now?'' Jud asked as the adults began rolling over and nudging each other with their beaks.

''It's an expression of affection.'' The dolphins lingered behind and Meli looked away.

''Affection, hmm? Well, you did say they were almost human in their mannerisms.''

The bristling warmth flaming up Meli's arms wasn't caused by the late morning sun. When Jud spoke to her in that soft, intent voice, it was almost as if he were touching her, caressing her. ''Better than human,'' she said, forcing a light tone she didn't feel. ''Dolphins are always helpful, and they can be trusted.'' Despite the attraction she felt toward Jud, the unseen Carrie hung between them like a shroud. Why hadn't Tom waited a few more minutes before calling to Lin? Why hadn't he let them hibernate just long enough for Meli to ask about Carrie?

''Hey, you're drifting away from me. What's happening?''

''It's nothing. I'm just tired.''

''Got you up too early, did I?''

''Mmm,'' Meli said, spreading a towel on the deck and plopping down on her stomach. ''I enjoy my work, but when I'm on vacation like this I realize that I could definitely adjust to a life of leisure.''

"You'd be bored after a month."

"Maybe, but I'd love to give it a try. Ah, if only I didn't have to pay the rent or eat, or—" Pouring some suntan lotion into her palm, she squirmed uncomfortably and tried to reach around to her back.

"Here, let me help you," Jud said, squatting down beside her. "Just lie down and I'll take care of everything." He lifted her hair away from her neck and began applying the lotion, small circles with his fingertips, stroking slickly over the tense cords in her neck down to her curving shoulder.

"Oh." Meli sucked in her breath. His touch was tender yet erotic, just as she had known it would be. Although she wanted him to go on forever, she knew she had to stop him. Jud belonged to another woman.

"We'd better untie this," Jud said, his voice husky as he loosened the straps on her bikini top.

"No." Meli reached around, clapping her hands over his to stop him. Her flesh hungered for his touch, but her mind forbade it.

"Lie still." Turning his hand to capture hers, he began stroking between her fingers, using his thumb to smooth the lotion. "You don't want to get strap marks, do you?"

Closing her eyes, she shook her head, then rested it on her elbows, sighing as he massaged the lotion into her back, first lightly with his fingertips, then a firmer pressure with the heel of his hand. His touch was subtle yet determined, and she reveled in it, wanted more. How could something that felt so good be so very wrong?

His thumbs walked down her spine, gliding over the ridges while his long, questing fingers cheated at the sides of her breasts, probing the burgeoning curves. "The most important thing about suntan lotion," he whispered, leaning closer, "is to cover every exposed part of your body and to rub it in . . . very thoroughly."

Flames flickered within her, their crackling warmth licking at her senses. Her nipples tautened and tensed. So fervid was her need that she had to stop herself from turning onto her back and cupping his hands to her breasts.

His palms slid over her sleekly lotioned back from her sloping shoulders to the curving waistline above her bikini bottom. His slow, controlled movements made her body tremble with desire as, in this warm, sunny world where they alone existed, she ached for him to press lower, to touch her more intimately. Her sigh hovered between contentment and need.

"Feel good?" Jud asked, his ragged tone as erotic as his touch.

"Mmm." She didn't want to think; she just wanted his hands to continue weaving their magical spell.

"Your legs," he said huskily. "I'd better get to your legs. If they burn, you won't be able to use them. You've got to use your legs."

He started with her toes, curving in between them, then stroking over her soles, ankles, calves. He lingered at her knees, circling toward the center, up to her inner thighs. His fingers brushed her tender flesh, grazing at the edges of her swimsuit. The intimate femininity covered by the fabric quivered in eager anticipation, and Jud was too observant not to notice.

Meli wanted him to continue more than she had ever wanted anything in her life, yearned for him with every tremulous inch of her body, yet her conscience warned that he wasn't hers to take. She had to stop him, had to stop herself.

"Hey, you guys," Lin called from the prow, "how about some lunch?"

Lin's voice was a pin pricking Meli's bubble of dreams.

Fumbling for her bikini straps, she scooted to her knees and stared at Jud.

"I didn't mean for that to happen," he said. "But I can't seem to keep my hands off you, and even when I touch you, it's not enough."

He didn't mean for that to happen. How familiar those words sounded. Exactly what her mother had said when she had explained that she was leaving Meli's father for a man he had always considered one of his dearest friends. I'll never do that, Meli had sworn silently, and she had meant it. "You put on some lotion and saved me from a bad sunburn," she said, turning away from Jud. "That's nothing to be sorry about." Shrugging, she sidestepped him and headed for the prow. We haven't done anything wrong yet, she told herself, and we're not going to.

"I hope you're starving," Lin said. "I packed a ton of food."

Ton might have been an exaggeration, but the food was certainly plentiful. They chatted while they ate, and two hours later, after finishing the cold chicken and fruit salad, they anchored near a clear, shallow underwater garden just off a small island.

"This is the world's greatest snorkling spot," Lin said, slipping on her flippers and flexing her feet. "And we get to use up our leftovers." She tore some French bread and handed half to Meli. "Be sure to wear those heavy gloves if you don't want to get nipped by some ravenous fish."

Meli pressed her earplugs in place, slipped her face mask over her head, adjusted her breathing tube and draped her canvas sack over her shoulder. "See you later," she told Lin. Her flippers slapped across the deck as she plodded to the side and lowered herself into the water.

A school of fish responded to her movements, and

within seconds the bread had vanished. Then, standing quietly, Meli surveyed the cove. It was calm and shallow, a serene watery forest brimming with life, both plant and animal—a marine biologist's dream. She swam through the garden, concentrating on the numerous varieties of seaweed and kelp, samples of which would prove useful in the lab studies she was conducting to see if they could possibly be an untapped source of food.

A coral reef jutted into the garden, and Meli decided to follow it to shore so she could collect some samples of island plants for comparison with the ones she had acquired on Kona. When she reached dry land she dropped her snorkling gear on the beach and walked into the brush. Growth on the island was limited mostly to common varieties of coconut palms and ferns, but Meli cut off some samples, labeled them and put them in her sack.

She had just completed her search and was returning to the beach when Jud came stomping through the thicket, his features a complex blend of anger, concern and relief.

"Where the devil have you been? Didn't you hear us calling you?"

"Wait a minute, I can't hear you," Meli said, pulling out her earplugs. "There, that's better."

"I'd better let the others know I've found you. We thought something might have happened to you." He jogged back to the beach, pulled a handkerchief out of his pocket, waved it toward the boat, then stretched out on the sand and rested his back against the trunk of a large palm tree.

"Why were you worried?" Meli asked, dropping her specimen sack on the sand and kneeling beside him. "You knew I was in the cove. What on earth could have happened to me?"

"What could have happened to you?" He questioned her through hooded eyes, then, looking down, scooped up some sand and idly sifted it through his fingers until only a sand dollar, perfectly round and unblemished, rested on his palm.

"That's beautiful," Meli said. She had found sand dollars before; they weren't a rarity, but they were so delicate that they were invariably chipped or broken when she found them. This one was a beautiful specimen which she would have loved adding to her collection. She waited for Jud to offer it to her, but he studied it thoughtfully, then slipped it into his bathing-suit pocket. Meli tried to hide her disappointment. He had found it and it was his to keep if he wanted to. After all, he didn't owe her anything.

"What could have happened to you?" Jud asked, repeating her question of moments ago. "Do you want the entire list that ran through my mind? Getting tangled in seaweed. Falling against some coral. Crab bites. A lonely shark. A—"

Meli leaned forward and placed her index finger across his lips. "That's quite a bit of worrying from a man who spends his time dodging bullets."

"That's my job," he said, capturing her hand and tracing her fingers with his thumb. "It has nothing to do with how I feel about you." A thick screen of dark masculine lashes veiled the intensity of his half-closed eyes as he pressed her palm to his parted lips and drew small tantalizing circles with his questing tongue.

"How *do* you feel about me?" Here's his chance, Meli thought. He can explain about Carrie or he can be evasive and pretend she doesn't exist. Oddly enough, Meli wasn't certain which response she preferred.

"You're too small, light as a feather," he said, pulling

her down on top of him and stroking his hand over her back. "But when you're close to me like this you feel so right that I wouldn't change a thing, not one little thing." He turned slowly, rolling her beneath him.

"You really mean that? That you wouldn't change a thing?"

Grinning, he levered himself to his elbow and looked down at her. "Maybe I'd better refresh my memory," he said, running his hand over her shoulder, then down her arm to her waist. "No," he said, "everything seems just perfect, exactly right." He slid his hand along her bare waist and cupped the bottom of her breast. "There's not one thing about you I'd want any different."

Meli trembled with uncontrollable desire, and for a moment she was bewildered by the intensity of her reaction. Staring silently down at her, Jud held her gaze with ease. It was pointless to deny her response when she was so certain he could sense it, but emotions weren't all that mattered; morality counted, too, and Jud was hiding something from her—Carrie.

"You wouldn't change anything about me," Meli said, covering his hand with hers and moving it away from her breast. Her intentions were admirable, but they wouldn't last very long if he kept touching her, and she didn't want to do anything that she'd regret. "I don't like being used as a substitute for another woman."

"Another woman?" Looking at her quizzically, he shifted her hand to the back of his neck and returned his own to her breast. "I don't know what you're talking about." Soft, he thought, she felt so soft. He wanted to lose himself in her.

"I'm talking about Carrie, Jud. I'm not going to let you use me just because she's not around."

"Who told you about Carrie?" Jud's voice was cold

and hushed as he flung himself away from her. "And what makes you think you could ever replace her?" he asked, turning his back to her and staring out over the water. "You're nothing like Carrie, nothing like her at all."

"That may be, Jud, but I do have principles of my own, and I don't intend to be used just because I'm convenient."

"You're right," Jud said, hunching his shoulders and clasping his arms in front of him. "You shouldn't be Carrie's replacement. That's too much to ask of any woman. Thanks for stopping me from making a terrible mistake." Without glancing at her, he raced into the water and began swimming toward the boat.

Stunned by his unexpected response and his hasty departure, Meli sat up and drew her knees to her chest. She watched until all she could see was the forceful splash of him cutting through the water. The beginning and end of their relationship. Well, at least Jud had been truthful, and he hadn't tried to lie or tell her some tall tale about not knowing a woman named Carrie.

Resting her chin on her knees, she closed her eyes and inhaled the warm moist air. From the moment Jud had held her in his arms and whispered Carrie's name, Meli had known that this was the only possible end to their relationship. Better now than later, she told herself. This was one wound that time would have deepened, not healed, and lately time had become her enemy.

With a lethargy that mirrored the heavy ache in her heart, she gathered up her gear and walked slowly into the water. Whoever Carrie was, she meant a lot to Jud—probably his steady girlfriend, maybe even his wife. Meli didn't want to see Jud again, but she had no other way of getting back to Kona and she wasn't going to spend the rest of her life on this island.

She scanned the deck as Lin helped her board. Jud was helping Tom adjust the sails; he glanced in her direction, then looked immediately away.

"What happened out there?" Lin asked. "Jud's steaming. I can't remember ever seeing him this upset. What on earth did you do to him?"

Shrugging, Meli began stowing her snorkling gear in her canvas carryall. "I asked him about his wife." It was a wild guess, but Lin's response would tell her if she was correct.

"Carrie? You asked him about Carrie? Oh, Meli, how could you?"

So she was right; Carrie was Jud's wife. Although Meli had been almost certain, she had continued to hope that she was wrong, that perhaps Carrie was a casual girlfriend, and that the ties between them were not permanent, not binding. "How could I? I don't understand you, Lin. You're married. How would you feel if Tom became involved with another woman?" She remembered all too well how her father had felt—completely destroyed. He had never recovered.

"It's not the same."

Not the same? Meli stared at Lin and shook her head in disbelief. Was Lin trying to tell her that Jud didn't have a strong marriage? That Carrie wouldn't mind him having an affair with another woman? Great, she thought, then let him have it with someone else, because I'm not interested in that kind of relationship. "I think I'll go change," she said, walking toward the cabin. She was too annoyed by Lin's attitude to continue the conversation. A homewrecker was a homewrecker, and she had no intention of becoming the other woman.

She closed the cabin door, then went to the head to strip off her bathing suit and towel herself dry. What was wrong with her? Why did she feel so deprived at the prospect of never seeing Jud again? She barely knew him, and yet she knew him so well. Wasn't there some proverb about being responsible for someone once you had saved his life? If she hadn't saved Jud's life the other night, she had certainly helped him out of a tight spot. Was that the catalyst that kept drawing them together?

Regardless of the reason, the attraction existed and she had been a fool to come here with Jud. Ever since he had held her in his arms and called her Carrie, she had known that he belonged to another woman. All right, so she had wanted to see him again to convince herself that he was safe. But she had known that last night. Why was she here now? Not because of the snorkling. That might be the excuse she gave him, but she had to be truthful with herself; she was here because she had wanted to be with Jud. Although she knew she had to accept it, she couldn't bear the thought of his belonging to another woman, of never seeing him again.

Leaning over the sink, she checked herself in the mirror. She was certain that the freckles sprinkled on her nose had doubled in the hot Hawaiian sun. What did Carrie look like? Meli wondered as she let the water run and sponged off her face. Was she very beautiful? Exotic? Probably. Jud's wife would have to be exotic. She frowned at her own homespun reflection and reached for the body powder on the shelf beside the sink. What difference did it make how Carrie looked? She was the woman Jud had loved enough to marry. He belonged to her and nothing else really mattered.

Meli looked for her clothes and remembered that she had left them on the bunk. Draping the towel around her toga-style, she opened the door, strode across the cabin and saw Jud just as she reached the bunk. He was kneeling before the open refrigerator, but his attention was riveted on her.

If, once before, his eyes had touched and caressed her, they now devoured her, hungrily watching her breasts as they rose and fell beneath the skimpy terry-cloth covering. His body betrayed the dictates of his mind, and he could feel his blood throbbing through his temples. Forbidden fruit, he thought; Meli Fancher was one pleasure he didn't dare pursue, yet here he was gaping at her like some gangly teenager. Maybe if he made love to her just once he would get her out of his system. He had nearly taken her on the beach, but she had mentioned Carrie. As he recalled the incident his anger returned. "I came to get some beer," he said. "I didn't know you were here." He should have asked Lin to get the beer. He didn't want to be alone with Meli, not anymore.

"I wanted to get out of my wet suit." Furrowing her brow, she glanced at the sunlight streaming through the open door. "I thought I had closed it."

"You did. I knocked, but no one answered. You probably didn't hear me in there."

"I had the water on. I was washing." At the moment she was too nervous to be concerned about explanations. Why was the towel upsetting her so? Actually it covered more of her body than her bikini had. Still, just knowing she was bare beneath it . . . that if it loosened . . . considering the way she and Jud had parted, the situation seemed much too intimate, too embarrassing. Why didn't he just take his beer and leave?

Rising slowly to his feet, Jud kicked the refrigerator door closed and set the beer on the shelf above it. He stared at the top of the towel and the gently swelling breasts beneath it. Lowering his gaze, he followed the towel to where it ended just at Meli's thighs. The bunk was right behind her and he couldn't stop the scenario winding through his thoughts: lifting Meli into his arms, setting her on the bunk, peeling off the towel . . . His groin tightened as the images became too powerful to ignore.

Much as he wanted to forget her, he couldn't. The rigidity of his body was mute but graphic testimony to her power over him. Still, he couldn't disregard their conversation on the island. *I won't be Carrie's substitute.* As if he'd ever ask her to, as if he'd ever ask any woman to endure what Carrie had. But what he couldn't comprehend was Meli's callous attitude. How could he have misjudged her so? What was her reason for mentioning Carrie? To turn him off? If so, it had succeeded admirably. "Who told you about Carrie?" Probably Lin, he thought, remembering how she and Meli had been talking in the cabin before lunch.

"You did." Meli looked over her shoulder at the bunk. Sitting would make her feel less exposed, yet the towel was so short, it would hike above her thighs, hardly more modest. She remained standing.

"I did?" he challenged her. She was lying; she had to be. He wouldn't have told her about Carrie. Even with his closest friends he couldn't discuss Carrie; the subject was too painful.

"That night in my hotel room," Meli explained, trying to clear his confusion. "You were talking in your sleep." He obviously didn't remember holding her in his arms and she wasn't about to remind him. "You mentioned Carrie. She's your wife, isn't she?" Although she had already learned Carrie's identity from Lin, she wanted to hear Jud confirm it.

Turning away, Jud gripped the overhead railing until his nails whitened. Carrie . . . his wife . . . had he called for her in his sleep? Probably. Her plaintive image came to him whenever he allowed himself to relax. And those nightmares, horrible nightmares. Why had he ever married her?

"Look, Jud." As Meli watched his straining muscles flex across his bronze shoulders, she realized that despite her well-meaning intentions, she couldn't stop herself from remembering his touch, the hard strength of his arms, the stroking silk of his palms. "Look, Jud, I like you." Why bother lying? She was the one who always insisted on the truth, wasn't she? Besides, she told herself, Jud's senses were too keen not to have noted her reactions. "I just don't want to get involved with a married man."

"And if I weren't married?" Jud pivoted quickly, and the lines on his face deepened as if he were thinking, trying to make a decision.

Here it comes, Meli thought, remembering the excuses her mother had made when her father had begged her not to leave him. "We have nothing in common anymore. I've outgrown you. Ours is a marriage in name only."

"What about the children?" her father had asked. "How can you do this to them?"

"They'll adjust," her mother had replied. "Children are amazingly resilient."

But neither Sue nor she had ever really adjusted, and nine months later her father had died. Did Jud have children? she wondered. As far as she was concerned, none of it made any difference; she wasn't getting involved with a married man. "I'm not married," Meli went on, "and if you weren't married . . ." What was the point in contemplating might-have-beens. The reality of the situation was all that mattered. Jud was married.

If he weren't married. Meli's words echoed in Jud's ears. He had known her for such a short time, yet only this morning she had called it a stormy relationship, stormy and intimate. He felt he knew her so well, well enough to realize that she wasn't the type of woman to be satisfied with the casual affair he was prepared to offer. His conscience told him what he had to do, but his body dictated other needs, and if he stayed in this cabin any longer, he couldn't be sure which demands would win. Turning away from her, he picked up the beer. "I'd better get back. Tom's waiting for these."

Lin and Tom were both at the wheel when Jud came up on deck. He handed Tom one beer and offered the other to Lin.

She shook her head. "You'd better have it. In fact you look as if you can use something stronger."

"I'm all right," Jud said, popping the can open and looking out to sea.

"She's very nice," Lin said.

"Back off the matchmaking, Lin. You know I'm not interested."

"That's not how it looks to me. You're interested all right, but you're cutting her off because of Carrie. Why did you tell her anyway?"

"Lin," Jud said, smiling to take the edge off his words, "that's really none of your business."

"You don't scare me, Jud—"

"You heard the man," Tom said firmly. "Let it alone."

"Hmph, men." Lin wrinkled her nose in disgust and walked away. "So damned pigheaded. I'll never understand—" Her words broke off as she rounded the cabin entrance and nearly collided with Meli.

"Sorry," Meli said.

"Forget it. It's my fault. I'm so angry, I can't see straight. Jud broke off with you, didn't he?"

"I'd say it was mutual," Meli said, walking to the prow. "I don't know what Jud had in mind, but I'm not getting involved with a married man."

"Married man?" Lin put her hand on Meli's shoulder. "I don't understand. Jud's a widower. Carrie's dead."

Chapter 5

IF JUD WASN'T MARRIED, WHY ON EARTH DID HE WANT her to think he was? When Meli had asked Lin that question, the titian-haired woman had responded with a noncommittal shrug.

"Jud's the one to answer that," Lin had said, remembering how he had told her to mind her own business. "but when you find out, I wish you'd let me know."

Why did Jud want her to think he was married? The question kept reeling through Meli's thoughts long after Lin had retreated to the cabin. Hadn't she told him how she felt about his being married? That she wouldn't get involved with another woman's husband? Clearly stated that if he weren't married . . . Of course! The answer was obvious. She had given him an out and he had taken it.

His nonexistent marriage was his protection, a method of precluding any serious relationship with her. Hadn't he avoided her at the pier? Met her only after she had phoned his office? Then asked her to dinner to make certain that she wouldn't mention his name to anyone?

She knew he was attracted to her; inviting her on this boat and his behavior on the island was sufficient proof of that. But, apparently, that's all it was—a brief, meaningless attraction—one warm, languorous afternoon of love-making, and then nothing. She could hear him now. "It was nice while it lasted and I'm sorry I can't offer you anything permanent, Meli, but I'm already married." A marvelously convenient excuse even if it wasn't true.

Closing her eyes, she let the sea mist spray gently over her face, and she remembered the beach, how Jud had looked at her and touched her. She wasn't totally naive. He had wanted her just as she had wanted him. She hadn't imagined that, and even more confusing was the nagging suspicion that he was fighting himself as well as her. But why? None of the reasons she considered made any sense.

Her thoughts returned to that first frightening night when he had apologized for touching her and had told her that he hadn't been near a woman in a long time. Was that why he had held her on the beach? Taken her in his arms and caressed her lovingly? Was he merely hungry for the touch of a woman? Any woman? It was entirely possible, and somehow she found that conclusion more devastating than any of the others. She didn't want to be just any woman; she wanted to be special.

In any case, what was she supposed to do now that she knew the truth? Confront Jud with it? No, that would be too embarrassing for both of them. The best thing would be to pretend she had never spoken with Lin and make a clean break with Jud. That, after all, was what he wanted, wasn't it? His reasons didn't really matter.

When the boat docked, Lin invited Jud and Meli to dinner. "Nothing special," she said, "just some salad and spaghetti. Then Meli and I can chat while you and Tom go to that briefing.''

"Thanks," Meli said, "but I'm really tired." She turned to Jud and smiled. "That doesn't have to stop you though. I'm sure I can catch a cab back to the hotel.''

'It seems we've played this scene before,'' Jud said wryly. "And my script hasn't changed since yesterday. No cab. You came with me and you're going back with me.'' He cupped Meli's elbow possessively and nodded at Lin. "Thanks for the invite, but we'll have to take a raincheck.''

"Any time," Lin said. "You know you're always welcome.''

"You're angry again," Jud told Meli when they were in his Mustang riding back to the hotel.

"Not angry, just tired," Meli countered, leaning her head back and closing her eyes. The less said, the better. She didn't want to listen to any more of his lies.

"You're withdrawing behind that shell, blocking me out, just like you did last night.''

"I guess we're incompatible. I hate liars and deception seems to be a way of life with you—undercover on the job and off. One chance meeting doesn't necessarily make for a lifelong friendship.''

"Forget about how we met. I'm interested in now. What are you feeling now? Right at this moment?''

"Tired. I told you I was tired.'' She closed her lips as tightly as her eyes and wound her arms around her chest. No good. Her protective shell wasn't working. She couldn't block out either Jud or his words, yet how could she admit what she was feeling? That one part of her wanted to scream and rage at him, call him a fraud and tell him she hated him for lying to her, while another, less self-respecting part of her wanted him to complete the lovemaking he had started on the beach. She said nothing.

Jud could think what he wanted about her, but she hadn't come to Hawaii for a brief vacation fling.

"I'm sorry for what happened back on the beach. Not for everything, just for blowing up at you," Jud said, turning the car into the hotel parking lot. "I shouldn't be taking my tension out on you."

"No, you shouldn't," Meli agreed, opening the car door and swinging her legs to the pavement. She remembered what Lin had said about the tension, the pressure of Jud's job. Obviously she wasn't as understanding as Lin. She would never be able to tolerate the lonely silences Lin had described. She didn't need any reminders of how it felt to be shut out by people close to her; some experiences were too painful to forget. "Good-bye, Jud." She leaned back into the car before closing the door. "Take care of yourself."

"I'll see you inside." Jud slammed the car door and fell into step beside her. "No point in letting you walk in alone."

"No." Turning abruptly, Meli faced him, arms akimbo. "I meant what I said, Jud. I don't want you walking me anywhere and I don't want to see you again. This is good-bye." She strode quickly away and trotted up the steps.

For a moment he set his jaw and watched her silently, then he started after her and caught her just as she put her key into the lock. Leaning against the doorframe, he imprisoned her with his arms. "And if I refuse to accept that?"

"You have no choice."

"That's for me to decide, isn't it?" He followed her in and closed the door behind him.

"No, Jud. This is my room, my decision." She spoke with her back toward him, not wanting to look at him. "Get out."

"Why? You let me stay when it was much more dangerous, so why do you want me out now?" He came up behind her, crossed his arms over her waist and pulled her toward him. "Because you found out I was married?" His lips whispered softly against her temple and his breath warmed the curve of her ear. "Stop being so prudish. I don't want you to be angry with me."

Meli felt his splayed fingers flexing into her abdomen, and for a brief moment she yearned to turn herself into his arms and feel the lean strength of his body hardening against hers. No, she told herself. She had her pride. She wasn't going to let him placate her with meaningless kisses. Jud Thompson was a deceitful fraud.

"Stop lying to me." She pulled herself out of his arms and turned to face him. "Lin told me the truth. You're not married."

"You know?" One black eyebrow arched quizzically. "Then why?"

His implication was clear. Why are you rejecting me if you know I'm not married? "Because I know that you're trying to protect yourself. Right now you're in the mood for a brief fling, but you want to make sure you have a convenient excuse in case I begin to expect something more. Well, forget it. I'm not as fragile as you think. I can take the truth. You don't have to make up lies about a nonexistent marriage just because what you feel for me isn't serious enough for anything more than a one-night stand."

"Not serious enough? Are you blind, Meli? Can't you tell how I feel? What I've felt since that very first moment I held you on the cliff and you refused to desert me?" He stepped forward, closing the inches between them and cupping her chin with his hand. "Oh, Meli." He brought her lips close to his and kissed her tenderly. "My sweet, brave Meli. How could you ever think I wasn't serious, that I didn't want you more than I've ever wanted any other woman?''

His whispered words parted her lips to the tormenting explorations of his tongue, and when she gasped he became more demanding, sucking hungrily until he felt her trembling in his arms.

"Easy, sweetheart," he murmured, lifting her onto the bed. "I've been a fool, trying to fight what we both wanted, needed.'' One hand opened his shirt buttons while the other caressed her breasts. "We've both been fools. Let's live for the moment and take what we can get.''

When he touched her like that Meli found it difficult to think, and if her racing heart was any indication, within a few minutes she would be too caught up in the magic he was weaving to concentrate on anything other than the movements of his hands. Much as she wanted him to continue, she knew she had to stop him now, while she could still think straight.

Curving her palms over his shoulders, she pushed him away. "No, Jud, you're wrong. We don't want the same thing. I don't want you to make love to me out of gratitude or pity.''

"Pity?'' Jud murmured. "You may be an authority on dolphins, sweetheart, but you don't know very much about men.'' He rolled swiftly onto his back and caught her in his arms before she had a chance to escape. Cupping her buttocks firmly, he pressed them against his hips. "Does that feel like pity, Meli?'' His eyes were dark with desire as they gently caressed her face. "And as for gratitude, little love, well, that comes later.'' He smiled as he raised himself and kissed the tips of her breasts. "Much later.''

"No.'' Meli rolled away from him and sat at the side of the bed. "Whatever you're offering, I don't want it. We don't want the same things, Jud.'' Crossing her arms over her breasts, she strode to the glass slider and looked out over the ocean. "I don't want what you want." Her emotions went too deep for a casual relationship. They always had.

"You make it sound like a business deal," Jud muttered, swinging his legs to the floor and sitting up. "I offer this, you accept that, reject something else. Arbitration? Compromise? Good grief, I only wanted to make love to you." He combed his fingers through his hair.

Make love. Had the word *love* ever been more abused? Did what Jud felt for her have anything to do with love? Could he have lied to her if it had? No, Jud was talking about sex, casual sex, and she didn't want it.

"I'm not what you think I am," she said, trying to tell him that she wasn't interested in a quick vacation romance. Perhaps that's all it would turn out to be, but she couldn't enter the relationship with that expectation. "I don't want you to make love to me when . . ." She couldn't continue. How could she explain that much as she was physically attracted to Jud, trust and commitment were equally important to her?

"Go ahead," Jud prodded. "Finish it. You don't want me to make love to you when what?"

"When I know it means nothing to you." There, she had said it, voiced her doubts, laid them bare for him to see. "Nothing more than a physical release."

"Ah, so you're a mindreader, and all this time I thought you were a marine biologist. How do you know what anything means to me? You barely know me."

"Exactly," Meli agreed. "And I don't make love with people I barely know."

"What better way to get acquainted?"

Silently, Meli frowned her disapproval. This wasn't a joking matter.

"I'm sorry," Jud said. "That crack wasn't called for." He'd spoken out of habit; sarcasm was his usual method of avoiding pointed questions about his personal life, things he didn't want to talk about, think about. "What do you want to do?"

"Talk."

"Isn't that what we've been doing?"

"I've been talking, but you've been fighting me. Every time I ask a question, you cut me off. You've used sarcasm, anger, jokes, but in all the time we've known each other, you haven't told me anything about yourself."

"I don't blurt out my life's story to everyone I meet."

"And I—"

"Shh." He held up his hand to silence her. "I know. You already told me. You're not just anyone. All right, Meli, maybe you deserve some answers. What do you want to know?"

"About you, about Carrie." Meli hesitated for a moment. "Why you wanted me to think you were still married."

"You're not asking for very much, are you?"

"Please, Jud." How could she explain that she wanted more from him than casual sex; she wanted his friendship and trust, and for that he had to open up to her. "I'm not asking any more than I need. I care about you, Jud. I'm trying to understand, but you have to help."

"All right." Leaving the bed, Jud opened the slider, walked to the terrace, and stretched out on the chaise. "I met Carrie while I was stationed in 'Nam. She was a sweet, scared kid. I don't suppose we had very much in common except for our loneliness. In the States I probably wouldn't have given her a second glance, but things were different there and she became the only refuge I had in that damned inferno. She was so frightened when I told her we were pulling out." He stared up at the sky and clasped his hands behind his neck. "I couldn't leave her there. So I married her and brought her back to the States where she'd be safe. Safe, ha! Some joke. Within a year she was dead, blown to bits by some drug dealers who were trying to get to me."

Meli stepped behind the chaise and put her hands on Jud's shoulders. "I'm sorry, Jud." Her fingers flexed, massaging away the tension in his shoulders. She remembered back to their first meeting when he had pulled away from her, saying that he bloodied everyone he touched. Now she understood what he had meant. He'd been talking about Carrie. He blamed himself for her death. What a horrible guilt to have to live with. No wonder he welcomed excitement and found the terror in his mind more threatening than a hail of bullets. Was he so miserable that he wanted to die? she wondered. Was that why he exposed himself to danger? "I shouldn't have made you talk about it."

"It's all right, Meli. I suppose I owed you an explanation." Reaching behind him, he caught her hands in his and pulled her down beside him. "Now that you've heard the true life story of Jud Thompson, what about you?"

"What's to tell?" Her life seemed dull by comparison, her problems meaningless. "You know almost everything, where I live, my job."

"But not the most important thing." Narrowing his eyes, he studied her with a strange intensity. "Like what you want out of life."

"I don't know. I guess we don't have much choice about that, do we?" How could she tell Jud that devoted as she was to her career, she still yearned for a home and family? A family which she now knew might well be an impossibility. Closing her eyes against Jud's mind-probing scrutiny, she visualized dark-haired children with his features playing on a farm somewhere. The images were vivid enough to touch, but too unreal to discuss. Jud had given her no reason, no right, and yet— "My job takes up most of my time, and for the rest . . . I haven't thought about it that much."

"Marriage?"

Meli shrugged. "That depends." Her disrupted childhood had taught her not to make plans that were dependent on other people. She could control the course of her career, but marriage wasn't up to her, and as for a family, well, time wasn't on her side there either. "My career is pretty demanding." That had been her stock answer for so long that it rolled off her tongue with consummate ease, yet now she knew it was as much an excuse as the truth.

"That makes two of us," Jud said. "Agents shouldn't be married. If Carrie hadn't married me, she would still be alive. I'll never do that to any other woman, never let myself become seriously involved, never get married again." He was trying to be truthful with Meli, to tell her that much as he enjoyed being with her, nothing permanent could ever come of their relationship. If she wanted to continue seeing him on those terms, the choice was hers.

"You must have really loved her."

"She was a scared kid. All she wanted was to be safe."

"You can't go on blaming yourself, Jud."

"Don't worry about me," Jud said, squeezing her hand for a moment before he swung his feet off the chaise and stood. "I'm tough enough to survive, but I know now that I have to be alone. Love makes a man vulnerable, and agents can't afford that. I can't make any promises to a woman . . . nothing binding."

So that was his reason for avoiding her, his guilt over Carrie, his fear of endangering someone else. Meli showed him her hands, palms up, palms down. "Empty," she said. "No chains, no ropes, nothing to tie you up with."

"Just so you understand." He wasn't going to lead her on, give her false hope for something that could never be.

"I'm the most understanding woman you'll ever meet," she said, standing beside him and placing a hand on his shoulder. At this moment she wanted more than anything to hold him in her arms and comfort him. Once he gave their relationship a chance, she was sure he would change his mind about making it permanent. If two people loved each other, they wanted to be together, didn't they?

He hesitated for a moment as if he were trying to reach a decision. "You said that you're going to be here for three more days. Suppose I take you to breakfast tomorrow and then we drive up to see Pele. Kilauea's been acting up, so we might be lucky enough to see some fireworks."

"I wasn't aware that we needed to visit a volcano for fireworks." Pele was the Hawaiian volcano goddess who, when she was angry, supposedly spit fire. "I thought we were managing just fine in that department all by ourselves."

"Such an understanding woman," Jud said, smiling. "And a sense of humor too. How lucky can a man get?"

"It's nice to be appreciated."

"Oh, you are. Have no doubts about that." His hands framed her cheeks as he brought her face close to his, and he kissed her on the forehead. "I'll see you in the morning. Walk me to the door, then lock it after me."

Meli watched him walking away and realized that she didn't want him to leave. "Jud, um, look," she paused, trying to find the courage to voice her desires. "You don't have to go. I don't want you to go."

"And I don't want to go, but I can't stay, not tonight.

You were right about us needing more time together, and time is what I don't have now. Remember my briefing?" He checked his watch. "Less than two hours from now." He opened the door and stepped into the corridor. "Lock up tight. I'll see you tomorrow. Seven o'clock. And be sure to wear something warm. It gets chilly up in those mountains."

Following Jud's directions, Meli pressed the doorknob lock and hooked the chain into its socket. Then, leaning against the door, she listened to his footsteps fading down the hall. They paused and she heard him speaking with someone. Whom was he talking to? she wondered. Curious, she put her ear to the door, but the faint voices had disappeared.

True to his word, Jud picked her up at seven the next morning. "Close your eyes," he said. "I have a surprise for you."

"Oh, no." Meli shook her head. "I know all about your surprises, Jud Thompson. They're more like bomb-shells."

"This one you'll like. No explosions, I promise. Come on, close your eyes. It's nothing bad, unless you don't like presents."

"A present? Well, why didn't you say so? It's a characteristic I'm not particularly proud of," she admitted in a stage whisper. "But I'm terribly greedy." She pressed her eyes tightly together, then covered them with her hands.

"A confession like that shouldn't go unrewarded," Jud murmured, stepping behind her and standing so close that his breath feathered her temples. "Now I wish the gift were more impressive."

His hands rested lightly on her shoulders, and she shivered as the chill of a smooth round object fell just above her breasts. Then Jud's fingers moved to the back of her neck, lifted her hair and fumbled with the fastening of a chain. "I don't usually give women presents, but this is a special gift for a special lady." He kissed her nape gently before releasing her hair. "You can open your eyes now."

Meli lowered her hands and glanced down. The sand dollar Jud had found yesterday was suspended on a thin gold chain that brushed the edge of her dark blue halter. It had been polished to a pearly white glitter.

"It's beautiful," Meli said, fingering the striated circle. "But how did you ever do it? I mean when?" Last night he had left her to attend a briefing and now it was only seven in the morning. "Where did you find the time?"

"After I left you last night I dropped it off at the jewelry shop in the arcade, told them what I wanted and asked them to leave it at the desk so I could pick it up this morning."

"Thank you."

"It's not much. I'm glad you like it. I wanted you to have something to remember me by."

"Something to remember you by?" Meli stopped examining the sand dollar and studied Jud's face. Nothing. His features were completely inscrutable. "You make it sound as if I'm never going to see you again." A chilling knot tightened in the pit of her stomach as she crossed to the dresser and picked up the brown velour sweatsuit she was planning to take with her. Was he saying good-bye? Had he received another assignment at last night's briefing? Was he canceling their plans for today.

"No such luck. You can't get rid of me that easily. We have a date with Pele, and I intend to stick to you like glue." His arm circled her waist as they left the room, and he wondered if Meli realized how literally he meant that remark.

Hawaii Volcanoes National Park, at almost the opposite end of the big island, was a two-hour drive from Kona. "Not very interesting," Jud said. "Unless you're into coffee farms, cattle ranches and sugar plantations."

"Cattle ranches? Hmph, I'm a water baby, remember?" The road looked wet, but she knew it wasn't. Just a mirage, she mused, sunlight on asphalt.

"A Circe calling to me from the shore. How could I forget?"

"Hardly a Circe," Meli protested. "I didn't turn you into a beast, did I?"

Jud's hands relaxed on the steering wheel as he turned to look at her for a moment. "There are times," he said softly, "when you bring out the animal in me."

"Really," Meli said, shifting herself closer while silently cursing the car's bucket seats. "Could this be one of those times?"

Reaching over, Jud caught her hand and brought it to his lips. "This road is deserted, but not that deserted." He glanced up to check his rearview mirror. "In fact, there's someone coming up behind us right now." He released her hand, his concentration now divided between the car behind him and the road before him. Probably Nick and Kenny, he mused. They were supposed to be tailing him just in case Sam Adams's unapprehended cohorts took the bait.

Meli looked over her shoulder. A blue Datsun with two men in it was barreling up behind them. "He's doing more than sixty," she said. "That's crazy on a narrow mountain road like this. Doesn't he see us?"

Jud's gaze shifted to the mirror once again. Why the devil were they speeding like that? He peered into the mirror intently, trying to see the men's faces and identify them. "He sees us all right." His hands tightened on the steering wheel as he slowed to round a hairpin curve. Whoever was in that car wasn't very friendly. His initial supposition about them being from the F.B.I. had been dead wrong, and if he didn't do something fast, that wasn't all that was going to be dead.

The blue Datsun screeched along behind them. The distance between the two cars was diminishing. Close. They were getting too damned close. Closing in for the kill. Unbidden, the words flashed through Jud's mind.

"What's wrong with him? Is he insane?" Meli waited for the car to slow down, but it just kept coming; in fact the driver seemed to be speeding up. "He's going to cause an accident. Let him pass, Jud."

"He doesn't want to pass us, Meli." Jud pressed the gas pedal and the Mustang bucked, then sprinted forward. "At least not while we're still on the road." He reached for his car phone. No response. Nothing. Dead. They must have fooled with it while he had been in Meli's room. Damn. Why hadn't he remembered to check it? He held it against his ear again, hoping he had been wrong. Dead. Dead. Dead. The word echoed in his ears, but he rejected it. He couldn't let anything happen to Meli.

"But why?"

"The fish swallowed the bait, but the bait doesn't want to be eaten." Jud frowned and his lips tautened. "Don't worry, Meli. We'll be okay." His voice was firm and reassuring. No point in letting Meli know how frightened he was, more frightened for her than for himself.

The Datsun lagged behind, but only briefly. The road straightened and the coffee farm gave way to a lava desert with barren, moonlike craters.

Desolate, Meli thought, totally desolate. If they force us

off the road here . . . She was more frightened than she had been on the night when she had first met Jud. This time the men were directly behind them. They couldn't conceal themselves in darkness or flee to the safety of her hotel room. She didn't share Jud's optimism. How were they going to be all right?

The Datsun edged forward, hitting their bumper and jolting the car. Jud steered toward the center of the road and crossed over the dividing line. Cars coming from the opposite direction had been few and far between, and Meli now prayed that they would stay that way.

"Where the devil are they?" Jud asked, glancing in his mirror once again.

"They're right in back of us," Meli answered. How could Jud not see them? "Good grief, they're practically on top of us," she said as the Datsun swerved across the road and fell in directly behind them.

"Practically, but not quite." Jud checked his mirror once again. He knew where the Datsun was, but where was his backup? Where were Nick and Kenny? "Not another car in sight. Damn, you can't count on anyone but yourself."

A grove of acacia loomed in the distance. Starting level with the road, the trees tapered down, hanging along the edge of the cliff. If their pursuers forced them off the road at that point . . . Meli blocked the thought; the conclusion was too appalling.

"Okay, Meli, hold on tight," Jud said. "I'm about to do some fancy driving." Flooring the gas, Jud sped away from the Datsun, then slowed briefly and executed a U-turn.

For a few terrifying seconds the left front wheel skidded along the edge of the pavement. There was less than a foot of soft shoulder and then a drop—ten, twenty feet. What difference did the exact distance make? Meli thought, grasping the edge of her seat. If they went over, what difference did it make? Either way they would be killed.

They didn't go over. Just as Meli felt the car begin to dip, Jud straightened the wheel and set them back on the road. They were speeding in the opposite direction now, away from the blue Datsun.

It didn't take long for their pursuers to realize they were now chasing air, that the car they had been following was now behind them, heading back toward Kona. Within minutes they were turning too.

"They're coming after us," Meli said, looking over her shoulder and watching as the Datsun turned. "Too wide." Covering her mouth with her hand, she gasped as the Datsun's tires screeched, skidded onto the shoulder, teetered for one nerve-racking moment, then tumbled over the edge of the cliff.

Chapter 6

MELI WATCHED THE DATSUN PLUNGING DOWN THE cliff. Horror, relief, guilt, and then, finally, nothing, just a deadly numbness.

She heard the car door open and saw Jud sprint to the side of the road. Seconds after he had started toward the Datsun it exploded and burst into flames. For a moment he stood there, staring and shaking his head, then he walked slowly back to the car.

"Are you okay?" he asked, opening Meli's door and holding her arm lightly.

"I'm fine," she lied. Her chest was so taut with fear that she could scarcely breathe.

"That's good, honey." Leaning into the car, he stroked her hair back from her face and kissed her forehead. But she looked anything but fine. Drained, scared out of her wits, anything but fine. Still, she wasn't letting go; she was fighting her fears, and he knew what that was like. Even after the agony of 'Nam and the day-to-day stress of his job, the terror of being pursued never left him, not completely. In his line of work experience helped, but it didn't cure. He had been a fool to involve Meli, but he had been more afraid to leave her alone, unwilling to entrust her safety to anyone but himself.

"Talk about exciting dates," Meli said, gasping audibly as she tried to check her rampaging emotions.

"No one could ever accuse us of being dull." Jud felt like a total heel. He should have sent her back to the mainland. She would have been safe there. But he had wanted to see her again, to be with her for just a little longer. Now this. He wasn't surprised. He had expected some action from Adams's pals; that's why Nick and Kenny were supposed to be following him. So where the devil were they? "Come on," he said, cupping her elbow. "I think you could use some air."

Stepping out slowly and mechanically, Meli cast a brief glance at the fiery wreck, then she turned away and rested her head against the car window. The early morning sun beat down on her back. Although it was chilly here in the mountains, it was going to be a hot day in the valley, another scorcher. She hunched her shoulders as she visualized the scorching heat in the flaming Datsun, then inexplicably she shivered. Her breakfast was rising in her throat, and if she didn't control herself . . .

"Meli?" Jud touched her shoulders lightly and kissed the top of her head. "Everything's okay. It's all over. Here, you'd better put this on." He slipped her sweatshirt over her shoulders, then waited while she stepped into the matching pants. "You're shivering."

"I'm all right. I just need to be alone for a while." She knew that if their pursuers had had their way, the car burning in the canyon would have been Jud's Mustang, and no matter how many jokes they made about their exciting dates, she couldn't stop shaking. Those poor men;

she knew they were evil, but what a horrible way for anyone to die.

Jud walked slowly to the back of the Mustang, then watched her as he opened the trunk and took out some warning flares to set around the car. Meli was brave, he thought, a real fighter. He understood her need to be alone because that was his own method of dealing with pain and confusion, but he had always attributed that to his Navaho heritage—Indian stoicism. Meli shared that stoicism, was like him in so many ways, but by now he knew that compatible as they were, she was too gentle to share the dangers of his world. He was walking back to set the last flare in place when he spotted a gray Chevy coming over the hill. "It's about time," he muttered, crossing his arms over his head and waving at the car.

The two men in the Chevy returned Jud's wave, then pulled to a stop in front of the Mustang.

"Who are they?" Meli asked, coming up behind Jud and linking her arm through his. They looked like local surfers to her, tall, tanned and wearing jeans and eye-popping Hawaiian shirts. *Sam Adams had worn that kind of shirt*. The fact that three-quarters of Hawaii's male population wore exactly the same attire didn't alleviate her apprehension; Sam Adams's image lingered in her mind, and she connected these men with him. Had Jud and she survived one attempt on their lives only to be caught up in another?

"Friends," Jud said, smiling. He could tell she was wondering if they were a backup for the duet in the Datsun. "Local agents, they should have been here long before this." His arm circled her shoulder casually as he approached the two men getting out of the car. "Lucky for us we made it without them."

"Some protective cover you guys are," Jud said calmly.

The thinner of the two men brushed his hand over his blond-streaked mustache and shrugged. "Our car blew a radiator hose. We had to wait for a replacement." He walked to the edge of the cliff. "Looks like you managed all right on your own."

"Fortunately," Jud replied wryly. Then he introduced Nick and Kenny to Meli. "Can you call this in, Nick? My phone's out. They must have blown the batteries while I was inside."

"I know. We tried to reach you. We figured something was wrong, but there wasn't anything we could do."

"Well, it turned out all right for us, but I can't say the same for them." Jud motioned to the burning Datsun, then switched his attention back to Meli. "I don't suppose you feel much like continuing up to the volcano." He could feel her trembling; she wasn't in any condition to go sightseeing. He'd take her back to her hotel, stay with her for a while.

Meli shook her head. Jud and the other two agents were so calm and unemotional. She didn't doubt that the rigid control was part of their job, keeping their inner tension corked until it was released in another, more private moment. Was that what Lin Hazlet had meant when she had said that Jud and Tom had needed some time together? She wrinkled her nose as acrid fumes from the burning Datsun permeated the air. "No volcano," she said. She'd seen enough fireworks today to last her a lifetime.

"Back to the hotel?"

"That will be fine." Right now all she wanted to do was curl up in bed and pull the covers over her head.

"Are you sure you're all right?" He didn't like her insipid behavior, her succinct, monotone replies. It was out of character. Brave woman or not, she couldn't be this calm. She was holding something back, and when the dam broke . . . Better if she let it out now.

Nick held his hand over the car telephone and motioned to Jud. "Charlie's waiting at the army base. He wants you to check in there. We'll clear things up here and take her back to the hotel," he said, indicating Meli.

Jud looked at Meli. She didn't say anything, but he could feel her stiffen and he realized he couldn't leave her. He was the one she knew and trusted, not Nick or Kenny. "She'll come with me." Pulling her closer, he headed back to the Mustang without waiting for Nick's reply.

"Thanks," Meli said. She didn't relish the idea of staying around here one minute longer than was necessary. Somewhere safe and quiet, that was where she wanted to be. Somewhere safe and quiet.

"We're a team," Jud said lightly as he helped her into the car and closed the door. "Besides, I'm beginning to think you're my lucky charm."

Meli shook her head. "Luck had nothing to do with what happened back there." She recalled how skillfully he had maneuvered the Mustang. "You knew exactly what you were doing." Incompetence just wasn't part of his makeup, she decided. "You always know exactly what you're doing." So why had he lied to her about being married?

"Do I?" he asked. "I wish I shared your confidence." Sometimes when he was around Meli he found himself doing the opposite of what he had planned. Like now. Why was he taking her back to the base with him? Why couldn't he bear to leave her? She would have been perfectly safe with Nick and Kenny, but he had wanted her with him.

"Those men, Jud, were they the last?"

He flinched as if she had pricked a nerve end. "There's never any last," he said caustically. "If there were, I'd be out of a job."

Meli's hands tightened into fists. She wished he were

out of a job, at least out of this job. Don't say anything, she warned herself. Hadn't Jud told her that any discussion of his working arrangements was off limits? Now they seemed closer than they had ever been, and the last thing she wanted to do was provoke him into retreating behind his shell and cutting himself off from her. Still, she couldn't stop herself and the words were out of her mouth before she could control them. "There are other jobs," she said. Less dangerous jobs, she meant.

"Not for me." He looked at her for a moment, his eyes burning with a hidden message she couldn't quite read. "I am what I am, Meli. Don't let that tender heart of yours fool you into thinking I can be anything else. I'm not going to change, Meli."

But for Meli Jud's eyes shrieked louder than any words he had spoken. *I'm not going to change for you. Don't fall in love with me*. Pointless. It was too late. He had already become an irreplaceable part of her life. Still, he didn't have to know how she felt. She wanted his love, not his pity. "My tender heart doesn't fool me at all. I'm a scientist, Jud."

"That's good. I wouldn't want to see you hurt." He watched the muscle in her cheek tense, and suddenly he knew that she had been hurt before they met, and that the pain still throbbed in her memory. Without understanding why, he wanted to comfort her. More than anything he wanted to comfort her.

Then don't hurt me, Meli wanted to shout. But what good would that do? She remained silent as they drove through the gates of the military camp. Love was one emotion that couldn't be forced. She had learned that long before she met Jud.

Jud showed his credentials to the guard, and after explaining that Charlie Cobberly was expecting him, he arranged for Meli to stay in one of the guest houses.

"Try to rest," Jud told her. "I'll get back as soon as I can."

The spartan two-room suite located in the officers' facilities reminded Meli of an unoccupied college dormitory. She entered through a small sitting area with green vinyl furniture and drab brown carpeting which continued into the bedroom, where a double bed occupied the space beneath the window and a small walnut dresser stood against the opposite wall. The same green vinyl chair sat to the right of the night table.

The M.P. who had accompanied her upstairs mentioned that lunch was available in the dining hall, but Meli didn't think she could eat anything; her breakfast still hovered close to the surface. After he had left she kicked off her thongs, slipped out of her sweatshirt, stretched out on the bed and listened to the lawnmower droning outside her window. She felt odd—exhausted, drained, but somehow not tired. She didn't want to sleep; she wanted to think. She inhaled deeply and arched her neck toward the open window. The clover-sweet scent of freshly cut grass filtered through the louvers and, sighing, she closed her eyes.

She couldn't deny that she was shaken by what had just happened. If only Jud's work weren't so dangerous. It didn't have to be. He could do something else, take a desk job in Washington. But he didn't want to. He had told her to accept him as he was or not at all, that he wasn't looking for a serious relationship. Yet she remembered how gently he had held her in his arms when he had wanted to make love to her. She was certain that he couldn't have done that if she didn't mean something to him.

So what were her choices? Take Jud at his word? Continue pretending that she didn't really care about him and return to Maryland to lick her wounds in silent pride?

Or extend her vacation in Kona and try to convince him to change his mind?

The lawnmower seemed to have established a pattern: a set number of paces in one direction, then a reversal and retracking in the opposite. The steady whir was like a restful sedative. She rolled over onto her stomach and ran her fingers over the nubby cotton bedspread, tracing the bold plaid pattern. She had never been a quitter, never hesitated to go after something she really wanted, and she wanted Jud, didn't she? Pride or no pride, she wasn't about to pretend that Jud was unimportant to her and just get on a plane and fly back to Maryland. She'd stay in Hawaii, spend more time with him and see if she could change his mind. Or maybe he was right, maybe he wasn't for her. Either way, there was one best method of finding out—getting to know him better.

The lawnmower's drone merged with her thoughts and she found herself drifting into sleep. I'm not really tired, she thought, but the room was so quiet, so calm and peaceful. I'll nap for a few minutes, she mused, just a few minutes.

When she awoke and looked at her watch she found she had been napping for nearly three hours and the room seemed different. She held her breath for a moment and glanced up at the window. The shutters were closed and the lawnmower's buzz had been replaced by chirping birds. She sniffed and wrinkled her nose. No scent of grass. Instead, she smelled coffee, the pungent aroma of coffee.

Her tousled hair waving back from her face flowed over her ears and onto the pillow and, as she brushed her fingers over it and stretched herself awake, the skin on her bare neck prickled. She wasn't alone. Someone was watching her. She could sense it. Slowly she rolled onto her back, and glancing at the dresser saw Jud's reflection in the mirror above it. He had pulled the chair close enough to the bed to prop his feet on the mattress, and his hands cradled a steaming mug while he studied her with pensive eyes.

"Jud?" She lifted herself on one elbow while smoothing her hair with her other hand. "How long have you been sitting there?"

"A few minutes." He had been there for a half hour, watching her and trying to sort out his feelings. Asleep, she looked younger than ever, almost like a teenager, but his feelings for her were definitely not filial. Now, as he watched her sleep-softened face and listened to her husky voice, he wanted to make love to her more than ever. Yet would it be fair to her when she had told him that she needed more of a commitment than he was able to offer. "They said you didn't eat anything. I brought some cola, sandwiches, brandy and a thermos of coffee." He pointed to a tray on the dresser. "Are you hungry now?"

"No. Just a little groggy." She sat back against the headboard and straightened the straps on her halter top. "Coffee would be nice."

"Coffee it is." Swinging his feet off the mattress, he crossed to the dresser and poured some of the steaming brew into a mug. "How about some brandy?" he asked, holding up a bottle. "It does wonders for army coffee."

"No thanks. I need a waker-upper, and brandy would only put me back to sleep."

"Anything you say." He carried the mug to the bed and tried not to notice the lush curve of her breasts as he handed her the coffee, but despite his well-intentioned effort, his eyes and his mind were inexorably drawn to them.

Meli followed his gaze and was embarrassingly aware of her décolletage. Ridiculous, she told herself. There wasn't anything wrong with her outfit; it was a replica of what she and millions of other women in Hawaii wore every day. Yet here in this room, alone with Jud, she somehow felt too bare, too exposed. She looked for her sweatshirt and found that it had fallen to the floor. When she reached for it, her mug tilted, spilling hot coffee on the bedspread and on her sweatpants as well. Shrieking, she dropped the mug and tugged the pants away from her leg.

"Take them off." Setting his mug on the night table, Jud trotted to the dresser and grabbed some ice from the bucket where the cola was cooling.

"It's not bad; I think the velour absorbed most of it." She fumbled with the waistband tie while trying to keep the damp fabric away from her leg. Damn, the bow had tightened into a knot.

"Here, let me do that." Jud settled himself beside her on the bed, cupped the ice cube in his palm and began picking at the knot. "What were you trying to do? Leaning over like that while you were holding hot coffee?" He released the knot, then gripped the waistband.

She arched her hips while he pulled down the sweatpants and tossed them on the floor. "I was trying to get my sweatshirt." The cool air offered some relief and she massaged the angry red circle coloring her thigh. Not really painful, thank God, just hot and tingly, like the beginnings of a sunburn.

"Ice will take away the sting and stop it from swelling." Gently he rubbed the ice cube over the burn.

"That's not necessary. My pants absorbed most of the heat and now that they're off—" Meli bit back the remainder of her protest. The ice felt cool and soothing. "You're right. That does feel good. Thanks."

"You're very welcome," Jud said softly, continuing his tender ministrations until the cube had melted and only the gentle strength of his palm was stroking over her flesh. "It feels good to me too." He stretched out beside her and his hand edged higher, brushing over her cotton shorts, her bare midriff, teasing the undersides of her breasts. "You feel good." Her skin felt like satin, so fragile and feminine; he wanted to run his hands over her body, all of it.

"Jud." Shifting onto her side, Meli molded herself to his lean length and clasped her hands behind his neck. Death, the burning car and their escape were so vivid in her mind that she wanted to be held and comforted, restored to life by love, Jud's love. "Hold me, Jud, please hold me."

"Shh, honey." Jud cradled her face against his chest and gently stroked her hair. Nice, he thought, very nice. Holding her in his arms was so peaceful, like a summer shower or a brook rippling over its pebbly bed. He drew her curtain of hair aside and kissed her nape. "Did I ever tell you how sweet you are?"

"No," she murmured against his chest. "But it's never too late to start. I love compliments almost as much as I love presents." She lifted her head and glanced down at the sand dollar. "Maybe this was the lucky charm that saved us today."

He followed the direction of her gaze, but he barely noticed the sand dollar. Her halter top draped loosely, exposing the swelling cleavage between her breasts. "Beautiful," he whispered, slipping his hand beneath the halter. "So soft and beautiful." Cupping one breast, he caught the nipple between his fingers and nudged it gently until he felt it tauten to his touch. "If I had my choice of lucky charms . . ."

"Oh, Jud," Meli moaned as her body shivered in response. "Let me be your lucky charm," she whispered, feathering her fingers across his chin. Keep me with you, she added silently. Let me protect you. "I couldn't bear it if something happened to you."

"Don't." Rolling her onto her back, he silenced her lips with the pressure of his. "Don't talk about anything happening, not now."

Briefly Meli chided herself for mentioning the constant danger of his job, then his lips parted hers and she was lost in the penetrating warmth of his mouth—brandy and coffee and Jud. She caught her breath, and rational thought became impossible as Jud's kiss deepened and turned her into a mass of quivering sensuality. She needed him so much; they needed each other.

Lifting his head, Jud fanned her hair out over the bedspread. "I'm not reliable, Meli. Can't stay in one place. Have to keep moving." He knew he was all wrong for her, but he wanted her more than he had ever wanted any other woman, and right or wrong, he couldn't keep himself from touching her. "Stop me, Meli, you have to. I want you too much to do it myself. Oh, but you're sweet, so very sweet."

"You know what they say about sweets, Jud; they're habit-forming." Her fingers were meshed behind his neck, holding him close. "One taste leads to another, and after a while you can't stay away."

"Weren't you listening, honey?" Jud asked, nuzzling his cheek against hers. "I can't stay away right now." He loosened the ties on her halter, then tossed it to the side of the mattress. "You're beautiful," he murmured, "so soft and delicate, so very perfect." His fingers drew feathery circles around the nipple of one breast while his mouth closed around the other.

Sighing, Meli arched her torso, lifting her body closer to his warm, questing lips. She felt as if all her senses were tensed, concentrated, drawn to the erogenous vortex of Jud's sucking mouth. Her hands combed through his hair as she held him to her. She wanted to prolong this moment, to make it last forever, yet the quivering bud at the core of her femininity blossomed beneath his touch and demanded more.

Perceiving her need and responding to his own, Jud released the fastening on her shorts and eased them down. Lifting himself on one elbow, he studied her nakedness and brushed lightly over her breasts, her waist, her hips. "Have I ever told you how often I've dreamed of this moment? How many times I've imagined the way you'd look?"

"Are you disappointed?" Her voice was a throaty whisper. "Do I meet your expectations?"

"Some." He lifted a curling tendril off her cheek and tucked it behind her ear. "I thought about your hair, loose and ruffly. Do you know that when the sun hits it, it turns red?"

"There's no sun here." She traced the curve of his jaw and remembered when he had warned her not to touch him. He wasn't denying her now; she began unbuttoning his shirt. His chest hair matched the tousled ebony of his head, but she already knew that, had made that discovery on their first night together, when she was cleansing his wound.

"No sun," he said, "just a hazy light filtering through the shutters." His index finger drew small half moons beneath her eyes. "Your eyes are green like the sea. When you're angry they get dark . . . storm clouds."

"Are they dark now?"

"No. Kind of dreamy. Like liquid emeralds." He probed gently at her lips, urging them apart.

Her tongue flicked over his finger and she drew him to her. "Guess what I'm fantasizing about." She kissed his finger, sucked the tip.

"Is it your fantasy or mine?"

"Does it matter? I'd be more than willing to share."

"Sharing, soft and accepting, just as I dreamed you

would be. So full of promise." His voice was a husky whisper.

"And I always keep my promises." Meli slipped his shirt off his shoulders and flinched when she saw the scars on his chest.

"Do they upset you?" He framed her face with his hands and his fingertips caressed her cheeks lightly, as if they were made of fragile china.

"I don't want to see any more. I don't want you hurt again."

"Ah, Meli. Sweet, soft, Meli." He kissed the side of her neck, tracing the pulsing vein down to the hollow of her collarbone, worshipping, tantalizing, but not satisfying. "What do you want with a man like me?"

"Everything, Jud, I want everything." Meli ached for him; she wanted to be held, touched, loved, but Jud was treating her delicately, almost as if she were breakable. "Jud." She grasped his shoulders so tightly that her nails bit into his skin. "I'm not a porcelain statue, Jud. I'm a flesh-and-blood woman." Frantically she pulled him toward her. "I need you, Jud."

She trembled as his arms tightened around her and this time when their lips met there was no tender hesitation, just a raw, demanding hunger that Jud could no longer conceal. "You're driving me wild. I've never wanted any woman as much as I've wanted you. Can you tell how much I want you?" He cradled her buttocks and lifted them closer until she felt his surging desire straining against the denim fabric keeping them apart.

"No more than I want you," Meli said, remembering the expectant thrill that had shivered through her body when she had first seen him in the moonlight.

He lifted himself for a moment and shrugged out of his jeans. Then they were together, no barriers between them, just skin caressing skin. "Hold me, Meli, hold me tight."

His legs slid between hers, baring the core of her femininity, and his torso ground, seeking, surging, finding. He wanted to possess her, to make her irretrievably his.

The raw, unleashed power of Jud's masculinity was a thunderbolt, electrifying Meli, dominating her; she arched herself, moving closer, wanting to envelop and control his body just as he was controlling hers. "Oh, Jud, I want you, need you so."

He levered himself away and looked down at her. Her eyes were misty, her lips parted as she ran her tongue across them; he was overwhelmed by an odd mixture of throbbing devotion and unrelenting lust. He wanted to protect, please, possess and dominate her all at the same time, yet he had no right, no right to anything. He was perilous to women, poison for Meli.

"Please, Jud." Her palms squeezed his buttocks, urging him toward her. "Now, Jud." Her agonized plea voiced the passionate yearning imprisoned within the silences of her writhing body. Only Jud held the key to release, and if he turned away from her now . . . He couldn't, he just couldn't.

"Oh, Meli, my darling Meli," he groaned as her hands clasped and drew him closer. He couldn't stop, not now, and with one swift downward motion he plunged into her moist enveloping warmth. "Oh, my love."

"Ah." Sighing, Meli closed her eyes as she felt the force of him filling and claiming her. "Oh, Jud, dear Jud."

His hips rotated with a maddening slowness as her lips parted and his tongue tantalized hers with the same leisurely torture. He wanted to make the pleasure last, wanted to make it as thrilling for her as it was for him.

Meli responded hungrily, holding him closer, arching her body toward his. She felt herself soaring, reaching for a pinnacle just inches away, almost touching, but not quite. Faster. She had to move faster, had to get there. She gasped and moaned in her need.

Jud increased his pace, forging deeper in response to her unspoken plea. In a frenzied surge of passion he kissed her cheek, an ear, her neck. Then, fighting for control, he buried himself in the curving sweetness of her shoulder. "Oh, my sweet love." He closed his eyes as he inhaled the clean scent of her skin, certain that if he saw the exquisite yearning in her features he would explode, and he didn't want to, not yet, not until he had brought her to the apex, not until she had experienced the euphoric joy that he knew would soon be his.

"Jud, Jud." She gasped his name as her nails bit into his back. "Oh, Jud." Her voice broke in low, unrestrained whimpering. "Now, Jud, now."

He felt the tremored contractions deep within her body. They surged toward him, clutched at him, driving him beyond the point of control. He grasped her tightly as, thrusting deeper, he felt himself rush joyfully into her, losing himself, yet feeling more whole than he had ever been.

Sighing, he collapsed against her breasts. Ecstasy, he thought, sheer ecstasy. If he could choose one moment of his life to last forever, this scintilla of bliss would be it. Meli shivered in release as he held her closer and covered her face with kisses. Drained, he shifted onto his side, carrying her with him. He couldn't bear the thought of losing her, yet he knew this joy couldn't last, that his love for Meli would endanger and possibly destroy her. And he wouldn't let that happen.

For several cloud-soft moments only the ragged rasp of their breathing broke the passion-spent silence, and it seemed to take forever for Meli's heartbeat to steady and return to normal. She lay beside Jud quietly, her fingers toying with his damp, curling chest hairs. Nice, she thought, so very nice. She was too content to move, too satisfied to speak and, as she drifted toward sleep, she knew only that she wanted to stay with Jud forever. "Forever," she murmured, her warm breath searing his flesh, branding him and making him hers. "Forever."

Chapter 7

MELI TOSSED RESTLESSLY IN THE BED, THEN BURROWED her face in the pillow. Scents of morning were drawing her toward consciousness and she didn't want to wake, not while she was still filled with the hazy delight of last night's memories.

Smiling to herself, she reached across the mattress for Jud. She wanted to touch him, to have him hold her, to reassure herself that last night had really happened, that it hadn't been a dream. As she patted the pillow her heart pounded apprehensively. Jud wasn't there, and all she felt was the pristine chill of rumpled linen.

Reluctantly she blinked herself awake. She smelled freshly brewed coffee and heard hushed movements in the sitting room: footsteps, papers rustling. Her clothes, which had been haphazardly strewn over the mattress and floor, were now neatly folded on the green vinyl chair. Jud must have put them there. It had been considerate of him to let her sleep, but now she was up and she wanted to see him.

Flinging back the blankets, she slipped out of bed and began getting dressed. The phone rang in the other room and she heard Jud answer it. Although she had no intention of eavesdropping, she couldn't avoid hearing Jud's portion of the conversation.

"That's all right, Tom. I was up. No, she's still sleeping."

Jud must be talking to Tom Hazlet, Meli decided as she reached behind her to tie her halter straps. Maybe tonight she and Jud would take Lin up on that standing dinner invitation.

"I thought Adams would be the one to crack," Jud said. "So he admitted everything once you told him about the car crash? Led you right to Emerson? Who would have thought he'd be mixed up in something like this? His family is old island. Missionary stock."

Emerson? The name sounded familiar to Meli. Of course. The Emerson family owned a good deal of property on Kona; they leased it to others, but never sold it.

"Well, then I guess that wraps it up. Meli's fine, just a little shaken, but she'll get over it once she returns to the mainland. No, it wasn't hard on me at all. Just part of the job. I told you I'd stick with her, make sure that nothing happened to her until the case was solved."

An ominous chill shivered up Meli's spine as she heard Jud say good-bye and drop the receiver back in its cradle. Her hands froze over the clasp of her shorts. *Just part of his job? Stay with her until the case was solved?* It couldn't mean what she thought, yet somehow she was certain that it did. There weren't many other possibilities.

Stiffening her shoulders, she slipped into her thongs and walked into the adjoining room. Jud stood by the window, one hand cradling a steaming mug, the other resting on the telephone. He turned at the sound of her footsteps.

"Good morning," he said, his dark eyes sweeping over her in a contemplative gaze. "How about some coffee?" He motioned to an electric carafe on the table at the side of the room. "You did say that you needed a cup of coffee first thing in the morning."

"I heard you on the telephone," she said, ignoring his offer. This was one morning when it would take more than coffee to put her in a good mood.

"Then you know we've caught them all."

Meli was glad that the criminals had been caught but, at the moment, that part of Jud's conversation didn't interest her. "What did you mean about staying with me until the case was solved?"

Jud turned away, avoiding eye contact, as if he were embarrassed or ashamed. "You shouldn't have listened."

"Don't change the subject, Jud. What did you mean?"

Setting the mug on the table, Jud plunged his hands into his pockets and stared out the window. "We didn't want to panic you, but Adams suspected that you'd helped me and we didn't know how much he'd told the others, whether they'd try to track me down through you. So we put you under round-the-clock surveillance."

That explained the man in the hotel room across from hers. Now she had to know about Jud. Had everything between them merely been part of his job? Just another assignment? "Mostly by you?" she asked, forcing the question over the lump in her throat. Was that why Jud had stayed with her?

He nodded. "I watched you during the day, then at night someone else took over." He tried to sound casual. He didn't want her to know how afraid he had been for her, how unwilling to entrust her protection to anyone else.

"But not last night."

"Now, wait a minute," Jud said, turning from the window and coming over to grip her arms. "You don't think . . ."

Meli's insides were churning and, at this moment, although the pain wasn't physical, she was more afraid of being hurt than she had been up on the ridge. But she hadn't panicked then, and she wasn't going to panic now. "You know what I'm thinking, Jud." *Tell me it isn't so* was the unspoken message in her eyes. Please, Jud, tell me it isn't so.

Silently Jud brushed the sleep-tousled hair back from her face and framed her cheeks with his hands. Meli thought he was going to kiss her, but he didn't. He just looked at her tenderly and his long fingers traced her arching eyebrows. "You're beautiful in the morning." He wanted to lift her in his arms and carry her back to bed, but he knew he couldn't. Maybe it would be best to let her go on believing what she thought, to break it off now.

"Tell me, Jud, was staying with me last night part of your job?"

"No. You weren't in any danger. You couldn't be hurt here on the base." He couldn't lie to her. Not about last night.

"So why, Jud? What did last night mean to you?" If it was too soon for him to love her, then at least let it be something stronger than casual sex, not just a one-night stand.

Releasing her, Jud retrieved his mug and cradled it in his hands. "What happened last night had nothing to do with my job. You're an attractive, intelligent woman, Meli, and I like you a lot. . . ." Too much, he told himself, much too much. He should never have let last night happen, but he hadn't been able to stop himself. There was something about Meli—a strong attraction that sometimes occurred between a man and a woman. He'd heard about it, but had never before experienced it.

Meli's stomach completed the somersault it had started when she overheard his conversation with Tom. "But? There's more, isn't there? Go ahead. Finish it, finish what you were going to say."

"Last night should never have happened. I should have been able to stop myself, but I just couldn't." Turning his back to Meli, he slammed the mug down on the table and plunged his hands into his pockets. "I wanted you too much." He hated losing control, and he hadn't before, not until Meli. "What can I say except that I'm sorry."

That guilt again, that horrible guilt. "There's nothing to be sorry about, Jud." She went to him, put her hands on his shoulders and rested her head against his back. "I wanted you too, Jud. I wanted you to make love to me, to love me. I want to be with you."

"No." His shoulders tensed as he jerked away from her and walked stiff-legged to the window. "You don't know what you're saying. Yesterday you had just a taste of what being with me is like. Don't you know we could have been killed out there? *You* could have been killed?" He turned to her, his expression as wretched as the misery tightening around her heart. "Is this how you want to spend the rest of your life? Running? Worrying? In constant danger?"

"I don't know how I want to spend the rest of my life," Meli said softly. No point in asking for a commitment that he wasn't ready to give. "Right now I know only that I want to spend more time with you."

"No. There's no future in it. I was a fool to let things go this far."

"But they have. So what are we going to do about it?"

"I've arranged for you to be taken back to the hotel. I'll be receiving a new assignment."

"You mean this is good-bye? That we won't be seeing each other again?"

"It's the best way, Meli. The only way." He stared at her as if he were memorizing her features. The images he formed now would have to last him for the rest of his life.

"It's not the only way." Guilt or no guilt, she was tired of having Jud think only about his feelings. What about hers? Didn't she matter at all? "That's a lot of garbage," she shouted, her anger overriding her fear. "You're afraid. You talk about facing danger and living on the edge of death, but you're afraid to take a chance on love."

"Meli—" He reached for her.

"No. Don't touch me. You've spent so many years behind the safety of that isolating shield that you're scared to come out."

"I'm thinking of you."

"Right." Meli laughed humorlessly. "You're tearing out my heart to protect me from being hurt. Forgive me if I don't thank you." Hot tears welled behind her eyes, and she ran into the bedroom. She wasn't going to play on Jud's sympathies, wasn't going to let him see her cry. He might like to envision her as some delicate porcelain doll, but she had more strength than he credited her with.

Jud followed close behind her. "Meli, you don't understand."

"You're right, and this is one time when I don't want to understand. Your reasoning is ridiculous. You're ripping me apart, and I don't want to understand. Okay? If you want absolution, you're not going to get it from me." She picked up her shoulder bag and folded her sweatsuit over her arm. "Now, who's driving me back to Kona?"

"I'm not letting you go, not like this."

By now Meli's seething anger had boiled into breathless rage. What he was doing to her was bad enough, but to ask

for her approval . . . "If you try to stop me, I'll scream."
Arms akimbo, she glared at him, her eyes blazing with the
fury storming within her. "Let me go, Jud. Let me go
now or I'll bring the whole damned army down on you."

Jud hesitated for a moment, then plodded into the other
room. Through the open doorway Meli heard him speaking on the phone. She wanted to go after him, to talk to
him, to try to work things out, but pride and indignation
wouldn't let her. She wasn't about to grovel at his feet and
beg for his love. She was damned tired of having to plead
for love and acceptance, and she wasn't going to do it
again.

A few minutes later she heard the outer door open. A
young M.P. stuck his head through the bedroom door and
announced that he would drive her back to Kona. When
she walked into the sitting room, Jud was nowhere in
sight. He hadn't even cared enough to say good-bye.

During the ride back to Kona her baby-faced driver
made some attempts at conversation, but he gave up when
he saw that Meli was too distraught to respond with more
than a few politely brief answers. Indeed, Meli's thoughts
were anything but pleasant; they vacillated between a
desire to pummel Jud while ridding herself of all her
pent-up anger and a need to kiss and touch him, to feel his
strong but gentle hands stroking and caressing her body
until once again they were as close as any two human
beings could be, to hear him say that he had been
mistaken, that everything would be all right. She was
totally confused.

She knew that Jud was attracted to her, that he wanted
her. I like you a lot, he had said, but love—he wouldn't
even allow himself to think, let alone mention the word.
"He's so damned afraid to be human," she mumbled.

"Excuse me?" the driver said, half turning to her.

"Nothing. I'm sorry. I was just thinking out loud."
Great, Meli thought. Now he's got me talking to myself.
She pressed her lips tightly together, as if by doing so she
could confine her anguish to the privacy of her mind.

She accepted that she loved Jud. In the short time that
she'd known him he had become a part of her life and she
acknowledged that realization as something that had to be
dealt with like her flyaway hair and quicksilver temper.
But what could she do about it? Nothing. She had
practically thrown herself at him, offered to take him on
any terms at all, and he had rejected her, sent her away.
She had risked the humiliation of admitting her feelings
for him and nothing had come of it. Unrequited love. The
phrase sounded like something out of Victorian romance,
yet that was exactly what she was experiencing. Unrequited love. So what choice did she have, except to return
home, lick her wounds and resume her life as a not-so-
swinging single?

Sue and Bobby were waiting for her when her plane
landed at Dulles Airport. She hugged Sue, kissed her on
the cheek, then swooped Bobby into her arms, and, for the
first time since she had left the military camp, she felt the
paralyzing numbness ebbing from her body.

"I'm too big for that, Aunt Meli," Bobby protested,
wriggling himself free.

"Oops, sorry," Meli said, tapping her temple. "I keep
forgetting. You're almost seven, aren't you?" She
couldn't very well explain to Bobby that the hug had been
more for her sake than for his. Never had she felt the need
for family more than she did at this moment.

"What did you bring me?" Bobby asked as they
walked to the baggage area.

"Bobby," Sue said, rolling her eyes toward the ceiling.
"What did I tell you about that?"

"Bring you?" Meli repeated in mock surprise. "I thought you were too old for presents." But her teasing grin told him that she wasn't serious.

"Oh, Aunt Meli."

Meli had parked her car at Sue's Georgetown home, where she was planning to have dinner and spend the night before returning to Maryland. Sue and David had bought the house ten years ago and they had been renovating it ever since. The old red brick exterior had been carefully cleaned and the window shutters and front door had been painted a glossy black enamel. The interior had been restored as closely as possible to its original state—parquet floors, Oriental rugs, pale blue wainscotting, gessoed ceilings and reproductions of original colonial wallpapers. The furniture, much of it inherited from David's wealthy family, was antique—English, French and American.

The house was perfectly suited to Sue's classic blond beauty, but much as her sister tried to make her feel at home, Meli always felt as if she were visiting a museum. Her first act, upon arrival, had been to open her luggage and give Bobby his present. Now he was padding around the house in a wet suit, flippers and face mask, looking like an extraterrestrial touring a colonial mansion. Meanwhile his mother and aunt were sitting in the kitchen having coffee at a round clawfooted oak table.

"You look as if you need another vacation," Sue said, eyeing Meli quizzically as she poured cream into a dainty Limoges cup. "It's Ingrid's day off, so I'm serving."

Meli shrugged. Sue might miss Ingrid, but she didn't. The stern-faced maid only added to her discomfort. "You know how it is. Packing, specimen hunting, running around, never a dull moment. Not to mention jet lag."

"Ah." Sue nodded and tapped her tapered nails on the buffed tabletop. "So those puffy red eyes are just the result of too much partying and traveling through time zones?''

Eagle-eyed Sue, Meli thought. She had tried putting on heavier makeup, but apparently the extra coverup hadn't fooled her sister. "That's right." Meli glanced around the room, searching for a change of topic. "Your herb garden looks nice and healthy," she said, carrying her coffee to the greenhouse window. Sue, a gourmet cook, insisted on fresh herbs. From the flower pot to the cooking pot was her motto. Ingrid took care of the serving and cleaning up.

"If that's a polite way of telling me to mind my own business, it's not going to work. We've been too close for too long. You've been crying, Meli. You look awful. You haven't looked this bad since Daddy died. Now, are you going to tell me what happened, or am I going to worry myself sick imagining all sorts of terrible things?''

Meli nodded and carried her coffee back to the table. Her insides were so tensely knotted that she felt she would burst if she didn't talk to someone and, whenever her mother hadn't come between them, she had always been able to confide in Sue. "I met him about a week ago," she said, continuing her monologue until they had consumed a pot of coffee and she had told Sue everything about her relationship with Jud—almost everything. Some things were too intimate to relate even to Sue.

"Well, that's a new line if I ever heard one," Sue said. "I've heard about men making up stories, but this is really unbelievable. I mean, not wanting to become seriously involved with you for your own good. If you ask me . . .''

"I believe him, Sue. That's the worst part of it. I think he's telling the truth.''

"But it doesn't make any sense. Look, I'm older than you, and take it from me, when you love someone, you can't just break off a relationship. I can't even begin to imagine a life without David.''

"Which is exactly the way I want it," David Linton said as he walked into the room and bent to kiss his wife's cheek. "Hello, Meli. How was the vacation?" He loosened his tie and took a coffee cup from the china cabinet.

"Fine," Meli said.

"Miserable," Sue corrected her, dumping out the old grinds and preparing a fresh pot of coffee. "Because of a man."

"Oops." David leaned back in his chair and made a surrendering gesture with his hands. "That sounds like an indictment of the entire species. Maybe I ought to go out and come in again."

"Oh, you," Sue said, offering him some cheese and crackers. "You were never like that. Why, you asked me to marry you on our second date."

"Smartest decision I ever made," David said, snaking his arm around her waist and hauling her into his lap. "I'd do it all over again if I had to." He brushed back her hair and kissed her neck.

"Hmm." Meli stood and carried her cup to the sink. "I think maybe I'll go upstairs and freshen up." She felt like an intruder as she watched the love flowing so easily between them, and she envied her sister.

"Oh, come on, Meli," Sue said, slipping off David's lap while he still grasped her hand. "Sometimes David just doesn't think. We didn't mean to embarrass you."

"Don't apologize," Meli said. "What you and David have is really beautiful. I just wish . . ." She sighed, then smiled. "I'd better get upstairs. That time change is a real killer."

The door to Bobby's room at the top of the stairway was open, and Meli peeked in on her way to the guest room. The red lantern lamp shed a soft light on the dark blue carpet and the long lines of minutemen marching across his draperies and bedspread, but there was no sign of

Bobby. Then she heard splashing in his bathroom. Bobby taking a bath without being coerced into it? Impossible. Unless her nephew had undergone a startling change of personality during the short time she'd been in Hawaii. She peeked into the bathroom and called to him.

"Hi, Aunt Meli." Bobby, sporting all his scuba gear sat in an overflowing tub while an equal amount of water puddled on the white tile floor. "This is a great gift. It really works. Watch, I can see underwater, and breathe, and—" He ducked beneath the surface and a few more gallons of water surged over the tub's edge and onto the floor.

"Oh, Bobby, your mother's going to kill you." And probably me, too, for buying you that scuba gear, she added silently. Sue's immaculate housekeeping and her active little boy were the only discordant notes in this otherwise harmonious home. How many times had Sue declared that Meli was better suited to be Bobby's mother than she was? "A nice quiet little girl, that's what I should have had," Sue would say. "If he wasn't the spitting image of David, I'd swear the hospital had switched babies on us." "Come on, Bobby, get out." Meli released the drain stopper and Bobby stood, creating additional puddles on the already sopping floor.

"You won't tell my mom," Bobby said while he pulled off his mask and began unzipping his wet suit. "She's not like us, Aunt Meli. She doesn't understand about scuba diving and things like that."

Meli stared at Bobby as an image from the past threaded through her mind. Her father and her on a fishing boat. "I'm lucky I have you, Meli-girl. Sue and your mother just don't enjoy this sort of thing." Her throat tightened and she found it difficult to speak. "I guess we could mop it up with some towels, but what will we do with the wet evidence?"

"I could run them through the washer," Bobby said with such confidence that Meli was certain he had done it before.

"Okay," Meli said, dropping to her knees and soaking up a puddle with a towel she had dragged from a stack on the baker's rack beside the tub.

Five minutes and five towels later both the floor and Bobby were dry, but Meli felt as damp as if she had been caught in a sudden downpour.

"Thanks, Aunt Meli," Bobby said, "you're the greatest."

"Right. I'm the absolute greatest. And the feeling is mutual." Meli loved Bobby as much as if he were her own child. "Now," she said, ruffling his hair. "You take care of these towels, okay?"

Meli watched Bobby start downstairs with the towels, then she continued down the hall to the guest room. At least someone thought she was the greatest, she mused wryly, even if it was only her six-year-old nephew. But as far as Jud was concerned—she blocked the memory. Summer was over and she had to forget about him, had to get on with her life, a life without Jud.

Six weeks later, in mid-October, Meli stood at her classroom window overlooking the quadrangle. The brittle brown lawn was littered with red and yellow leaves, and the trees were nearly bare. Autumn had arrived, winter was near, and still she found herself unable to concentrate on her work.

Memories of Jud lingered on, intruding on reality. Every time the phone or doorbell rang, she thought of Jud, prayed it was he. But it never was. Nothing seemed to help; she couldn't get her mind off him. Unbidden, his image appeared among the sea of student faces while she was speaking in a large lecture hall, and then at night—

nights were the worst. How many times had she dreamed of Jud only to awaken and search for him in the darkened shadows of her room? Too numerous to count.

Now, as she walked through the lab checking the temperatures of her kelp beds and adding the proper nutrients, she wondered if she'd ever forget him, ever stop trying to fill the empty spaces in her life with conjured images of Jud. Instinctively her hand rose, fingering the sand dollar nestled in the open neckline of her beige silk blouse. Another reminder of Jud. Why didn't she take it off? Toss it away? She couldn't. It was all she had left of him, all she could really cling to, and she couldn't stop hoping that maybe he would change his mind.

Her thoughts were a jumble of wishes and memories when she shifted the textbooks she was carrying, switched off the lights, locked the laboratory door and headed for the parking lot. Purposefully she banished her problems and forced herself to concentrate on the present as she checked her watch. Four o'clock. She flipped through an imaginary agenda. Her classes were finished for the day, but she had a student-faculty reception at seven. Coffee, tea and dried-out cocktail sandwiches. Past experiences had taught her the wisdom of arriving with a fairly full stomach, but she didn't feel like preparing anything at home. Besides, she thought, mentally reviewing the contents of her refrigerator, except for Sue's frozen doggie bags, there wasn't much to choose from; it was much simpler to grab a bite in the faculty cafeteria.

The cafeteria was almost deserted, just a scattering of people. Meli hated eating alone, so she stood by the cash register near the entrance and surveyed the room, looking for someone to sit with.

Then she saw him. It was happening again. Her mind was conjuring up Jud. Right there, seated next to an attractive brunette at a table near the coffee machine. She blinked to clear the vision. No help. It still looked like Jud. It *was* Jud. He was wearing a brown corduroy jacket and his Hawaiian tan had faded, but this time he was real. The impact of seeing him stunned her and, as she groped to regain her composure, two of the bulky texts slid out of her arms and tumbled to the tile floor, a thudding duet that reverberated through the room.

Jud and the woman with him interrupted their conversation and turned to look at her. Meli found herself staring into Jud's eyes, those smoky black pools that sent erratic spirals whirling deep within her. Her heart soared and, for one whimsical moment, she thought that Jud had reconsidered, changed his mind and come after her. Yet if he had, why hadn't he come to her classroom? Why was he sitting in the cafeteria? And who was the woman with him? She knelt to pick up her books as, from the corner of her eye, she saw Jud rise and start walking toward her.

"Meli?"

The deep baritone resurrected all the erotic memories Meli had been fighting since the day she left Hawaii, and for a moment she remained still and silent, needing the time to gather her thoughts, her confidence. She saw the tips of his shoes—buffed cordovan leather—and noted the smooth drape of his tan worsted slacks. She hoped her face wasn't mirroring the love and longing in her heart.

"Meli, are you all right?" Strong hands reached for her books.

She noticed the twisted silver ring and recalled how smooth it had felt, remembered the chill of it against her skin. Her arms prickled at the memory, and at that moment she knew that much as she tried, she would never be able to forget him.

"Hello, Jud." She shifted her books to his waiting arms and let him help her to her feet. "This is a surprise, seeing you here." Instinctively she was happy to see him, yet she was angry too. This campus was her territory, her home, and it was cruel of Jud to come here flaunting another woman. Still, she couldn't give vent to her emotions. People were watching them, and she fought to keep her tongue under control. "Is there some special reason?"

"Official business," he said, cradling her books in the crook of one arm while his other arm circled her waist.

Official business. The woman with him didn't look very official.

"That Hawaiian incident gave me too much exposure, so the director thinks I should keep a low profile for a while. I've been temporarily reassigned to investigative work in D.C. I'm here on a recruitment program."

"I see," Meli said, swallowing the lump in her throat and trying to keep her voice calm and indifferent. "How long have you been on campus?" With all the colleges in the country, why did the government have to send Jud to this one?

"Two days. I've been meeting with some department heads, talking to individual students."

"I see," Meli repeated tonelessly. Two days, she thought, two days and he hadn't even tried to call her. If she hadn't run into him here, he probably would have come and gone without her knowing it. And she, love-struck fool that she was, couldn't get him out of her mind. Dumb, dumb, dumb, she chided herself. Thank God she had managed to keep her emotions under control. Now if she could just continue it for a short while longer . . .

"Well." She curved her lips in a false smile. "It was nice seeing you again, Jud." She reached for her books.

Jud shifted them beyond her grasp. "We have to talk."

Meli shrugged indifferently. "Talk." Her whole body

ached with a weak, flulike sensation. She felt as if the life were draining out of her. So how could a dead person talk? "I'm listening."

"Not here." Jud glanced irritably around the room. The woman he had been sitting with was walking toward them. "Tonight. Can I see you tonight?"

"I'm busy." Faculty attendance at Dean Jarlman's little tête-à-têtes was de rigueur, yet even if it weren't, there wasn't any way she was going to agree to see Jud again. She might be a fool, but not that much of a fool. All she wanted to do was to get smoothly through this encounter and then go home to recover in privacy.

"I'll be here until Friday. When can I see you?"

"Sorry, I'm all booked up."

"Are you sure?" He reached out to touch her shoulder, then backed off when she flinched.

"I'm positive, Jud. Now, if you'll just let me have my books—"

"You can't be that busy. Just name a time. Tell me when."

The brunette had walked to the end of the steam table and was obviously waiting for Jud.

"Never." Meli held out her hands. "My books, please."

"You mean that, don't you? Have I hurt you that much, Meli, so much that you won't even speak to me?"

"Please, Jud." Surreptitiously Meli eyed the brunette. Her hair hung over her shoulders in thick straight strands of midnight velvet, and there was something about the way she held herself—tall, proud, confident. Who was she? Meli wondered. Jud's latest conquest? Did he have to flaunt her? Couldn't he understand how Meli felt about seeing them together? What it was doing to her?

"All right." He handed her the books and returned to his table. "We'll let it go for now."

Meli watched Jud approach the brunette, who put her hand on his shoulder, looked pointedly at Meli, then whispered in Jud's ear. Jud nodded and chuckled. Meli was certain they were talking about her, laughing at her. She hesitated for a moment, wondering if she should stay in the cafeteria and prove her indifference to Jud. No, she decided. What was the point? There was a limit to her acting ability, and right now her insides felt so queasy, she'd choke on a glass of water. Turning abruptly, she left the cafeteria. Jud could think whatever he pleased, carry on with as many women as he desired. It didn't matter to her. Not anymore.

Chapter 8

"I NEED A DRINK, A REAL DRINK," NED FODIN, THE chairman of the science department, said for the third time. "Why can't they serve anything except this insipid cider at these damned faculty soirées." He ran his fingers through his curly red hair and narrowed his bloodshot blue eyes. "They're hard enough to get through when you're drunk, but when you're sober . . ."

"You keep your job," Meli said.

"Then," Ned said, wrinkling his nose at the cider glass he was holding. "We must question whether the job is worth the sacrifice."

It was 7:15, and after a stop at her apartment where she had fed Muffin, the pregnant cat she had found five weeks ago, and changed into a green silk shirtwaist dress, Meli was standing next to Ned Fodin in the reception room of Dean Jarlman's house. The ivy-covered home was the largest residence on campus. In fact, when the college had welcomed its first ten students more than one hundred years ago, the three-story fieldstone structure had comprised the entire school—classrooms, dorms and faculty quarters. Now the house had been refurbished to meet the needs of the sixty-year-old dean and his silver-haired Bostonian wife. The two upper stories housed their private living quarters while the entire first floor served as a formal entertainment area for college functions such as the autumn social.

Although Meli didn't share Ned's complaints about the tedium of faculty parties, she could sympathize with them. The brilliant analytical chemist had been a Berkeley flower child in the turbulent sixties, and even after being at this staid Maryland college for nearly twelve years, he was still as much at odds with the conservative environment as his red and black plaid jacket. Understandable, Meli thought. Ned would always be mildly rebellious, and nothing here would ever change. Not even the decorations and refreshments, she decided as she surveyed the large pine-paneled room that was dominated by a fieldstone fireplace and gilt-framed portraits of Dean Jarlman's eight predecessors. Year after year, each seasonal gathering seemed to have its own set format, and the autumn social called forth cornucopias of gourds and corn husks accompanied by mulled apple cider and small tea sandwiches.

The atmosphere was festive yet subdued. A dusky brass chandelier and six crystal wall sconces augmented the hearth's shadowy glow while an old English folksong played by the faculty string quartet merged with muted conversation and laughter. The older faculty members held court on chintz-covered chairs and sofas while the student guests remained standing in small conversational groups, and although the muted lighting created a suitably romantic atmosphere, the small oak dance floor was practically deserted; only three couples glided to the wistful music. This wasn't a dancing crowd, Meli noted as she nodded to Dean and Mrs. Jarlman who, along with several other college dignitaries, were maintaining an informal receiving line beside the fireplace.

"Ah, big brother, or should I say big sister, is watching us," Ned grumbled, tilting his head furtively toward the fireplace. "You people should really mingle," he chided in a falsetto Bostonian accent. "Not just hang about with people in your own department."

"Oh, come on, Ned, Mrs. Jarlman's all right. She just wants the faculty and students to get to know one another in a more relaxed atmosphere. And this is the first social of the year."

"Don't remind me," Ned said, gulping down the last of his cider. "You know, I've been thinking of investing in one of those pocket flasks, the kind our alumni bring to football games."

"Two standards," Meli said, shaking her head. "What the alumni do at football games is one thing, but as for faculty members, well, we're expected to be like Caesar's wife. You know, above reproach, pure as the driven snow."

"Speaking of pure," Ned said, motioning toward the fireplace. "Look who just walked in. College jock turned spy. Our friendly F.B.I."

Jud. Meli's heart hammered against her ribs as she watched him shake hands with the Jarlmans. He was dressed in a beige button-down shirt and a brown tweed jacket, yet he looked as virile as he had at their first meeting when he had been bare-chested and wearing jeans. She despised the way her muscles tensed as she observed his languid movements and saw his lips part in that casual half smile that could turn her feelings inside out. Trying to keep control over her emotions, she forced her gaze away from him, and only then did she notice that the brunette who had been with him in the cafeteria was standing beside him. Envy overwhelmed her. Jud had found himself a woman better able to meet his needs than she had been.

"Name's Jud something-or-other," Ned said. "He spoke to the department heads this morning. He's here to recruit some of our brighter students. Needless to say, I wasn't very cordial."

"Really?" Meli said in mock amazement. Ned believed that all government agencies were worthless at best, and as for the F.B.I., he enjoyed comparing them to the gestapo or the K.G.B. "That's so unusual for you."

"Damn," Ned said. "Don't look now, but he's heading toward us. Probably wants to bend my ear a little more. As if I'd ever encourage any of my students to join up with that group of white-collar thugs."

"He's not a thug," Meli said, remembering how gentle Jud could be, how he had risked his own life to protect hers. "He's probably a very decent person."

"Right. And I'm the tooth fairy. Come on, it's time for some very discreet maneuvering." He gripped Meli's arm and led her toward the punch bowl at the back of the room. "We'll get lost in the crowd."

Jud watched Meli walk quickly away from him. Obviously she had meant what she said about never wanting to speak to him again. But he was just as determined to change her mind, and he was going to do it now—tonight. "This way, Paula," he said, putting his hand on the brunette's waist and starting after Meli.

"Are we in hot pursuit?" Paula asked as she elbowed her way past a pipe-smoking student who didn't look old enough to shave.

"You better believe it."

"The lady from the lunchroom?" She snatched two

cups of cider from the tray of a passing waiter and handed one to Jud. "Do you want me to handle her gentleman friend?"

"How'd you guess?" Jud asked, accepting the cider.

"Feminine intuition or superior detective skills. I possess both. Take your pick. Besides, you told me all about her, remember?"

"Not all," Jud said as he joined the lineup in front of the silver punch bowl.

"Well, the parts that were suitable for public consumption. By the way, Jud, don't you think we look a bit foolish, lined up for punch while we're drinking cider?"

"Right. Why don't we just get to the heart of the matter." Jud left the line and stepped in front of Ned and Meli, who had just filled their cups and were walking toward the French doors at the back of the room. "Dr. Fodin." Jud smiled and offered Ned his hand.

"Mr. . . . I'm sorry," Ned said, "but I've forgotten your name."

"Thompson, Jud Thompson, and this is Paula Stamford," Jud said as the brunette shook hands with Ned and then turned to Meli. "She's an important part of my recruiting team. We're very eager to hire more female agents."

So, Meli thought, the brunette was an F.B.I. agent. Someone who could understand Jud's work. Someone he could relax and talk with. Someone as used to danger as he was. A woman with whom he could share his life. An ideal couple, Meli mused as she fought back an urge to pummel them both.

"Meli Fancher," Ned said.

"Miss Fancher and I have already met," Jud said, clasping Meli's hand.

"Oh?" Ned's sharp eyes flickered from Jud to Meli, then back to Jud again. "More recruiting? Or is the F.B.I.

hunting for underwater treasure. Let me assure you, there's nothing at all subversive about Meli. She goes a little overboard on kelp and algae, but outside of that I can vouch for her.''

And who's going to vouch for you? Meli wondered, remembering Ned's colorful past. A recommendation from him was tantamount to an indictment. ''We met in Hawaii,'' she explained quickly. ''Jud helped me find some of the plankton I brought back to the lab.'' Miss Fancher indeed. She wasn't about to start calling him Mr. Thompson. Was he afraid to let Paula find out that they had been more than mere acquaintances?

''I see,'' Ned said. ''So you've been helping Meli with her seaweed experiments, trying to find a cheap, available food for the hungry masses. Exactly the type of thing a decent person would do. It's your job that's got me all confused. I've never been too fond of that agency. Speaking of which, how's your recruitment campaign going?''

''Not too well,'' Jud replied. ''Some people have a closed mind. They won't even listen to what I have to say.'' His gaze settled on Meli.

''Well, you know how it is,'' Ned said. ''Some people aren't too turned on by your tactics.''

''Perhaps they're basing their judgments on past experiences,'' Jud said, his voice low and serious. ''Our views may have changed. They could at least hear me out, listen to my side of the story.'' He kept his gaze fastened on Meli and his scrutiny was making her uncomfortable.

Talk about basing judgments on past experiences, Meli thought. Jud was the last person in the world who could point a finger at that. Wasn't he letting his past control his present and his future? But if he wanted to play a game of double entendre . . . ''Some people are so set in their ways,'' she said softly, ''that they cling to their beliefs even when they're wrong." Why did his eyes have to be so warm and appealing, like the velvety depths of a moonlit night? "Dead wrong."

"But you're not like that, are you?" Jud questioned.

"We're scientists," Meli said, including Ned and trying to steer the conversation away from the one-to-one basis Jud had adopted. "We deal in facts." And the facts were that less than six weeks ago Jud had told her he had never wanted to see her again, and that up to this very moment he hadn't made any real attempt to contact her. Two chance meetings didn't mean a thing, and despite his protests to the contrary, no one could accuse him of having gone out of his way to see her. "Only facts, Jud." Pointedly, she eyed the brunette standing at his side. "Just what we can see and hear."

"I hear music," Jud said softly. "Will you dance with me?"

His question caught Meli by surprise. "What?"

"Will you dance with me?" He indicated the dance floor, now occupied by five couples.

"Only students dance," Meli explained. "Instructors are supposed to look sedate and authoritative."

"Trust me. I do a very sedate and authoritive step, nothing rash, just a slow waltz or fox-trot," Jud said, cupping her elbow. "If you'll excuse us for a few minutes?" He nodded congenially to Paula and Ned, then led Meli to the small oak square below the platform where the string quartet was playing.

The last thing Meli wanted was to be in Jud's arms. It was also what she wanted most, and as his arms closed around her she felt them tremble. "Are you all right?"

"Never been better," he said. "Sorry if I forced you into this, but I couldn't think of any other way to get you alone."

"I'd hardly call this alone," Meli said, indicating the other people in the room.

"Close your eyes." His lips feathered her cheek as his fingertips brushed over her eyelids. "Now there's no one here, just us."

Meli opened her eyes and stared at him defiantly. She wasn't about to let Jud cajole her into a romantic mood. He found it as easy to leave as he did to love, but she was still living with the pain, and she was definitely not in the market for any new wounds. "Dean Jarlman is here, and the students, and my colleagues. We're not alone, Jud."

"They're all too busy to notice us." His voice was low and husky as he caressed her hair and pressed her head against his shoulder. "I've found that most people are so wrapped up in themselves that they're usually unaware of anyone else."

If anyone was wrapped up in himself, Meli mused, it was Jud. Overwhelmed by guilt, behaving as if he were the only one with problems, as if everyone else lived in a picture-perfect world. "Don't judge others by yourself, Jud."

"I've never done that, Meli. Never demanded of anyone else what I expect of myself."

They drifted in a slow, languid circle, floating in each other's arms as if the floor were a cloud. Jud's hands splayed across her back and waist, holding her close, and as they swayed in time to the music, she could feel the taut ripple of his muscles, sense the urgent response of her own. We feel so right together, she thought. Our bodies, our movements, as if we were one person. Yet Jud didn't share her sentiments. Even now she could recall the harsh cruelty of his words. "There's no future for us, Meli, no future at all." Then why was he dancing with her? Holding her in his arms?

The music's tempo increased, and as Jud whirled her swiftly across the floor, she felt the demanding strength of his masculinity. His body wanted her as much as hers wanted his. Yet she wanted more. Hadn't she told Jud that? And hadn't he rejected her? She couldn't tell him again. She had her pride. The music slowed to a protracted coda, and leaning above her, Jud eased her into a dip. Meli opened her eyes and looked up at him.

His obsidian gaze seemed to devour her, absorbing her flesh, uniting it with his. Nothing physical, just a pure emotional tugging that mirrored the passion in her heart. The music had ended, but Jud held her in his arms for a moment longer. When he straightened, he kept one hand clasped with hers and slipped his other arm around her waist.

"Can we leave now?" His question was a husky whisper. "Suddenly I find this room much too crowded."

"You can leave any time you want to." That was the kind of relationship Jud wanted, wasn't it? One where he could come and go as he pleased. No commitments. No permanent ties.

"I want to leave when you leave. With you."

"Why?" Meli was tired of all this pussyfooting. She looked over at Paula and Ned. They seemed very interested in each other. Apparently the brunette wasn't above playing the field. Jud had turned to her because she had been such an easy conquest. He had decided to try for a blasé replay of their last night in Hawaii.

"I told you I have to talk to you."

"We said everything we had to say to each other in Hawaii. You don't have to make polite overtures to me just because of a coincidental assignment to this college . . . just because we happened to run into each other." And, she added silently, just because Paula isn't as gullible as I am. Turning away from Jud, she hurried to the refreshment table. She had no intention of admitting Jud back into her life and having him destroy the wispy thread of tranquility she was still fighting to regain.

Listlessly she surveyed the buffet. As usual, the canapes had as much appeal as warmed-over appetizers from an airline dinner. Still, she wanted to get away from Jud, needed some time alone with her thoughts.

"You left the cafeteria without eating," Jud said, coming up behind her. "Did something . . . someone . . . make you lose your appetite?"

"Not at all." Jud could think what he wanted, but no way was she going to admit that she had left because of him. "I simply remembered another appointment." She wasn't about to acknowledge the misery she had experienced when she had seen him whispering with Paula.

"Ah, yes. How could I forget your busy schedule?" His tone was taut and angry. "Not one spare moment. Not for me anyway. Isn't that what you told me in the cafeteria? No time to rest, to talk . . . eating on the run. But you haven't chosen anything yet." He surveyed the table. "Now, let's see." His gaze flickered over the canapes, then came to rest on her face. "I'm sure I can find something I like . . . something we'll both enjoy."

Meli had controlled her temper for as long as she could. Just who did Jud Thompson think he was, flitting in and out of her life at will, traipsing around with another woman, then making cute remarks to her as if she were some empty-headed paper doll? Well, she could be just as cute. "I'm sure you can. Something quick. Just enough to hold you for a while. Nothing too substantial, nothing lasting."

"What if my tastes have changed? What if a snack won't satisfy me anymore? Maybe I want more now. Maybe I want it all."

"Whatever you want, you'll probably have to go

somewhere else," Meli said, glancing toward the back of the room where Paula was chatting with Ned. "I don't think there's anything for you here."

"Miss Fancher?"

"Hello, Eric." Meli turned to the gangly teenager on her left. Eric Harrison was both a dream student and a teacher's nightmare. Two years ago, when he was fourteen, he had entered college with an I.Q. that went off the charts and the social graces of a piranha. Classrooms were his milieu; parties an alien territory, and since the other students weren't intelligent enough to satisfy his conversational interests, he usually socialized with his instructors. "Are you enjoying yourself?" Quickly Meli shifted her attention from Jud to Eric.

"It's okay." He tilted his horn-rimmed glasses higher on his nose, looked at Jud for a moment, then apparently decided that what he had to say was more important than anything he had interrupted. "But I've been thinking about that oil spill problem you mentioned."

"Yes," Meli said, taking Eric's arm and stepping aside to make room for some others approaching the buffet table. Through the corner of her eye she saw one of the group begin talking to Jud. "And what did you decide, Eric?" She led him to some chairs at the side of the room and listened intently while Eric consumed most of the next hour explaining his ambition to develop a chemical compound that would turn salt water and oil into a harmless biodegradable substance. Some of his ideas went beyond what even she could understand. Her attention was waning. She glanced around the room and noticed that some people were beginning to leave. Ned and Paula came by to say good-night. Apparently Ned's views were changing and no longer were all F.B.I. personnel on his most unwanted list, at least this particular brunette wasn't. Ned seemed more interested in Paula than in almost any other woman Meli had seen him with. Odd, Meli had assumed that Paula would leave with Jud, but he was still there. He had joined the chairman of the economics department at the side of the fireplace and was speaking with some students. Obviously she had been mistaken about his relationship with Paula. Had she been equally mistaken about other things?

Meli turned so she could glimpse Jud surreptitiously. Until this moment she had looked at him, but she hadn't really allowed herself to see him. She'd been too afraid of the effect he'd have on her, the effect he'd had ever since the very first time she saw him poised on the prow of the trawler. Then he had been bare-chested and in jeans; now he wore a button-down shirt and conservative tweeds. She found herself stripping them away, remembering how he had clung to the sleek black rocks, his shoulder muscles flexing as he climbed toward her, his damp jeans revealing the contours of his masculinity, his lean hips and long sinewy legs. The image faded, returned—those legs entwined with hers—Jud's passion-flushed face searching, tantalizing, sweeping her off in a whirlpool of love. She couldn't forget, wanted him again, wanted him even as she hated him for rejecting and hurting her.

"Now, the important thing," Eric was saying, "is to find a substance that breaks down the oil without disturbing the ecology. I've been working on some compounds, but I'm just not sure of them."

"You know, Eric, this subject is really too deep for a casual discussion. Why don't you prepare a research paper? Get it started and then if you run into trouble, I'll be glad to help you." Research was Eric's favorite occupation, and when Meli stood and held out her hand, he smiled as if she had handed him a present.

Jud was smiling too. The smile that she remembered when he had given her the sand dollar. Unwittingly her hand reached up to touch her neck. She could leave now, go home without speaking to Jud, get even with him for the way he had hurt her, or she could stay and talk to him, hear what he had to say.

She missed Jud. She might succeed in concealing it from him, but what was the point in trying to deceive herself? How much was her pride worth? Was it worth cutting Jud out of her life? Never seeing him again? That last day in Hawaii she had accused Jud of being afraid to take a chance. Yet today, was she really being any different? And what was she afraid of? He was, after all, only a man, and she was a mature, educated woman, certainly capable of caring for herself. Forcing herself to make the effort, she crossed the room to Jud and edged into the space between two students.

Surprise flickered in Jud's eyes when he saw her, but he continued speaking. "Put in the simplest terms, it's a matter of good guys and bad guys and I like to think we're the good guys. I'm working to keep us on top." Reaching into his pocket, he pulled out some business cards and handed them around. "If any of you are interested in discussing a future with us, you can reach me at this number."

Glancing at the card, Meli noted that it listed a Washington phone exchange. Of course, Jud had mentioned that he'd been reassigned to Washington.

"You don't need that number," Jud said, coming up beside her. "We can talk right now."

Talk, yes, but can I reach you? Meli wondered. Can I really break through that barrier and reach you? "You wanted to talk to me, Jud?"

"Very much." He looked around the room, checking the dwindling crowd. "Not here. Can you leave now?" He helped Meli on with her coat and, after saying good-night to the Jarlmans, led her out the door.

A chilly mist shrouded the night, an icy drizzle that oozed through Meli's bones and made her shiver. She drew on her gloves and pulled her plaid wool scarf over her head.

"I think we could both do with a hot drink and something to eat," Jud said, hunching his shoulders and raising his jacket collar. "I'm parked over there." He pointed to a bumper-to-bumper row of cars parked along the driveway. His arm circled her shoulder as they trotted to a dark blue van with government license plates. "We keep most of our recruitment information in here," he explained, sliding back the door and helping Meli in. "It's more convenient than a car." He turned on the motor and adjusted the heater. "It will take a few minutes to warm up."

"How long have you been in Washington?"

"Two weeks."

"I see." Meli felt a queasy knot tightening in her stomach. For the past two weeks Jud had been just a short drive away and for the last two days he'd been right here on campus. The queasy knot began spinning, rising into her throat. She knew what to expect—some honeyed words to soothe her feelings and ease Jud's conscience. Thanks, but no thanks. She had rejected them in Hawaii, and she didn't want to hear them now.

"I don't think you do," Jud said. "You're reading the situation entirely wrong. Before, when we were inside, you mentioned that this was a coincidental assignment, that we just happened to run into each other." He shook his head. "Not so. I requested this assignment because I knew you were here. I told myself that I just wanted to see you again, to make sure that you were all right."

"I'm all right." She stared into her lap, unwilling to expose her emotions to the scrutiny of his gaze. She was functioning, wasn't she? Back at work, doing her job.

What did it matter if her emotions were drowning in a pool of unshed tears?

"So I've been watching you for two days now, and it's not enough." He lowered her scarf, combed his fingers through her hair and tilted her face toward his. "I want to hold you." He brushed lightly over her cheeks, down her neck. . . . "Touch you." He opened the top button of her coat. "There's been an ocean between us, Meli, but you've never been away from me." He reached into his pocket, drew out the white scarf he had taken from her that first night in Hawaii and gently folded it around her neck. "A small part of you has always been with me. Since that first night I held you in my arms I couldn't forget the way you look, the way you feel."

Meli touched the scarf and her fingers stroked over his. He hadn't forgotten her. She did mean something to him. But what? Exactly what?

"Meli? Honey?"

He was so close, so very close. For a moment Meli felt as if she couldn't breathe. She had wanted Jud so much for so long. Now she could have him. If she moved a few inches closer and put her arms around his neck . . . then what? *There's no future with me, Meli.* Forget the scarf. No commitment was what he meant, just a series of one-night stands, and she would be there waiting whenever the mood hit him. No. She had humiliated herself once and she wasn't going to do it again.

She backed away from Jud and rebuttoned her coat. The drizzle dripping down the windshield had become an icy rain. "There's more than an ocean separating us, Jud. You hurt me in Hawaii. I'm not a masochist. I don't want to be hurt again."

"I didn't mean to hurt you. I—" A horn blared behind them and Jud straightened to check his side mirror. "The car behind me can't get out. I'll have to move." He shifted into drive and pulled out of the parking spot. "I promised you something to eat. This is your territory. Any suggestions about a restaurant?"

"Along there," she said, pointing to a two-lane highway just outside the campus gate. "They're mostly fast food, pizza, burgers, tacos. This is a college town."

"Not very impressive. Isn't there anywhere else?"

"Not unless you want to drive into Baltimore, and in this weather . . ." She indicated the rain streaming down the windshield. "Turn right at the gate and let's see what we can find around here."

Jud drove slowly past Punji's Pizza and The Taco Hut. Their garish neon signs flashed eerily in the rain and they were both crowded with students. Meli knew that The Burger Barn wouldn't be any better. Hardly the place for a serious discussion.

"Go to the drive-in window," she said. "We can take some hamburgers back to my apartment."

Chapter 9

THE YELLOW AND WHITE VICTORIAN HOUSE WHERE MELI lived had originally been built for one family; now its eighteen rooms were divided into four apartments. Meli's was on the top floor. Jud's hand slid smoothly over the polished mahogany bannister as he followed her up the narrow stairway, dark oak at the edges with an Oriental carpet trailing down the middle.

Surprising, he mused, glancing behind him down to the marble-floored entryway from which they had just come. Flickering electric candles in a sparkling copper and glass lantern played muted shadows on the striped yellow wallpaper. He had never given much thought to where Meli lived, but he now realized that he had expected her home to be more modern, functional somehow, not an aerie atop a gingerbread castle.

"Quite a hike," he said as they rounded the second landing.

"Keeps me in shape."

Jud studied the slender legs climbing in front of him. Her shape looked fine to him, at least the little he could see of it. Even hidden behind the folds of her thick camel-hair coat, her body sent his on a rampage, and although he was managing to control his hands, he couldn't control his imagination. In his mind he was taking off her coat, unbuttoning her blouse. His memory was good, but reality was better.

Meli opened the door and walked inside. The minute she stepped over the threshold she knew something was wrong. Muffin wasn't meowing, wasn't stalking across the living room to chide her for being away.

"Muffin," she called.

A weak meowed response came from the kitchen.

Leaving Jud to close the door, Meli trotted across the living room. The pearl beige Siamese cat wasn't in her basket by the kitchen window. A soft night light glowed over the sink, illuminating rattan-wrapped pots of Boston ferns, the white appliances and the blue Delft tiles. Meli called Muffin again. Another frail meow emerged from behind the partially open door of the broom closet.

Kneeling, Meli opened the door. Muffin, surrounded by detergent boxes, cleansers and sponge mops, was huddled on the bottom shelf atop a pile of folded dustcloths. Two honey-gold kittens nestled beside her. Muffin's blue eyes narrowed with effort as she looked up at Meli and struck out with a feeble paw. Meli left the door slightly ajar, got some milk from the refrigerator and poured it into two dishes.

"Something wrong?" Jud asked, placing the hamburger sack on the glass-topped kitchen table. There were plants and flowers everywhere, hanging from the ceiling, climbing up the trellised walls and bunched along the corners of the room. Sweet and fresh, Jud thought, just like Meli.

"Muffin's having her kittens," Meli said, returning to the closet as the meowing became a plaintive call. She opened the door tentatively. Maybe she should move the mop and take out some of the cleansers.

Muffin snarled as Meli reached for the mop.

"It's all right, Muffin," Meli said, pulling away. The cat was still in labor. She'd better not disturb her. As best she could, she checked to see that everything was normal, then she stepped back. "You're doing fine, aren't you? And don't worry about your kittens. I'm not going to touch them." Meli closed the door and placed one dish of milk just outside it. She put the other dish in Muffin's basket, then picked up the hamburger sack. "We'd better go into the living room; I think we're making her nervous."

Jud hesitated for a moment and motioned toward the closet. "Don't you have to do something?"

"Not now," Meli said, walking into the living room. "Muffin wants to be alone. That's why she chose the closet." She knelt to light the white brick fireplace, then as the flames flared around the logs, she settled herself on the sofa.

Jud frowned and drummed his fingers against the doorframe. His brow was creased in concern and he looked as if he doubted Meli's judgment. "It doesn't seem right. If the cat's in pain—"

"Come on, sit down." She patted the sofa seat beside hers. Any man who worried about pregnant cats couldn't be all bad. She opened up the sacks and began taking out the food—cheeseburgers, fries, onion rings, cola. "Having a baby is a very normal function, and animals like to handle it themselves." Jud's disbelieving gaze seemed to be accusing her of callous indifference. "Did you ever have a pet, Jud?"

"When I was five," Jud said, perching himself on the

arm of the sofa. "My grandfather gave me a puppy. Jax was a scraggly little mutt, but I loved him. We had to leave him behind when my father got transferred overseas."

He pressed his lips together and tried to mask his emotions, but Meli could see the remembered pain of separation flickering across his face. She understood how that small boy had felt, recalled her own misery when she had had to join her mother in a New York apartment after her father had died. No pets allowed. Brownie had had to go.

"I thought about Jax for two years, couldn't wait to get back to him, but when we' finally returned he was gone. He'd been hit by a car. You can't count on anything. Nothing lasts." Jud blinked as if clearing his mind of the past, then smiled sheepishly as if he regretted having revealed some private part of himself. "Funny, the things you remember." His inscrutable mask was back in place.

Watching him, Meli recalled her first impression of Jud—an independent man who cherished his privacy and hated asking for favors. A swell of empathy flooded her thoughts, not for Jud, but for the small, vulnerable child he had been. Words didn't seem necessary; she reached up and touched Jud's hand.

When he smiled and covered her hand with his, Meli felt that his touch was as intimate as a kiss. Just sitting here with him in the dimly lighted silence . . .

"*Rrrow, rrrah, err—*" A snarling uproar from the kitchen ruptured the silence.

Meli sprang up, but Jud reached the kitchen before her. Muffin had climbed out of the broom closet and was lifting one small amber kitten by the neck. A box of detergent had overturned; blue and white granules were sprinkled over the closet, the dustcloths, Muffin, and her kittens.

Jud squatted and lifted out the two remaining kittens.

They looked small and fragile in his large, callused hands. Muffin looked up at him and frantically scratched at his pant leg.

"Don't put them down," Meli said, grabbing a handful of soft tissues. "She'll try to lick them off and a stomachful of detergent is the last thing she needs right now." She rubbed the tissue gently over the kittens until all the detergent was brushed away.

Jud cupped the kittens protectively, as if they were rare crystal and his hands were their cushion. "It's all right, old girl," he said, speaking softly to Muffin. "We're not hurting them."

"Put them in her basket," Meli said as she knelt to brush off the kitten beside Muffin.

Muffin's blue eyes shifted from Jud to Meli and back to Jud again as if she couldn't decide what to do. Then with one last quick glance at Meli she trotted after Jud.

Meli added the third kitten to Muffin's basket and cleaned up the broom closet. She watched Jud while she washed her hands. He was stroking Muffin's pearly fur as she lapped the milk. Muffin eyed him warily, but she wasn't snarling, and Meli wondered how a man who was so gentle and caring with an animal could have been so indifferently cruel where her own feelings were concerned.

"I guess some soap and water wouldn't hurt me either," Jud said, rising to his feet and stepping to the sink.

The wind shifted, sending sheets of rain splashing across the kitchen window. Lightning crackled and the streetlights flickered, dimmed, then brightened again. Beneath their glow, watery streamers glistened like holiday tinsel. The lights flickered and dimmed once more, then they went out. The refrigerator and clock radio stopped humming, leaving the kitchen dark and silent.

Muffin mewed softly.

"The power's gone," Meli said.

"Just the lights," Jud said, "not the power, not the special electricity I feel whenever I'm near you."

"Jud, please."

Jud put his hands on her shoulders. "I'm not afraid of the dark. Are you afraid of me? Still angry about what happened in Hawaii?"

"You hurt me. I won't deny that. But you have a right to live your life the way you want to." She wasn't going to beg him to stay with her, wasn't going to succumb to the passion that yearned mindlessly for his touch.

"And if I want you in my life?" He pulled her back against him, and his chin grazed the side of her temple.

"For how long?" Meli asked, angling herself away from him and leaning back against the sink. "Until the storm passes? Until it's time to go back to Washington and on to some new assignment?" Slipping past him, she hurried into the living room. She hated scenes, and she really had no right to be making one now. Jud was free to do as he pleased, but not at the cost of her self-respect. Sinking down on the sofa, she tucked her legs under her and crossed her arms. Flickering shadows from the fireplace danced along the walls, lighting the room with a dim, eerie glow. A stale oily odor of cold french fries and beef permeated the air. There goes dinner, Meli thought. Not that it mattered to her. She was too upset to eat, and any anger she felt was definitely self-directed. From the very beginning Jud had warned her not to build her dreams around him. It wasn't his fault that she hadn't listened.

"Meli." Jud called to her as he fumbled his way across the kitchen. "Where the devil are you? I can't see a blasted thing." Meli knew where everything was, could find her way around in the dark, but Jud was at a definite disadvantage with only the firelight to guide him. He bumped into her Tiffany lamp, then swore under his breath as it thudded to the floor.

"Wait a minute. Just stay put." She slid off the sofa and wove her way through the furniture. "I've got a candle somewhere." She opened a refinished oak icebox at the side of the sofa, groped inside, pulled out a bayberry candle in a china holder and lit it. "Where are you?" She held up the candle and peered into the darkness beyond the fireplace.

"Over here." He was kneeling on the floor, grappling with the lamp, which had separated into two pieces. "I think it's broken."

"Let me see." Meli set the candle on the dry sink behind them, then traced down his arm to where he was holding the two pieces of the lamp. "It's not broken," she said, "it's just come apart. That's the way—"

Jud released the lamp and caught her hands in his. "If the lamp's not broken, then it must have been my heart I felt crumbling in pieces."

"Jud, please."

"That's what I'm asking you, Meli . . . please. Give me another chance. Forget everything I've told you. Make believe we're meeting for the first time. Let's start again." Leaning forward, he backed her down onto the floor.

Even in the darkness she could see him staring down at her. "I don't want to be hurt."

"And I don't want to see you hurt. That's why I sent you away." He had been so certain he was doing the right thing when he told her to leave, yet he hadn't been able to forget the misery he had seen on her face. Over the past six weeks he had thought of her constantly, until finally he couldn't bear the loneliness and had volunteered for the recruitment campaign just so he could see her again. "Do you remember what you told me in Hawaii about not being sure how you wanted to spend the rest of your life, but just knowing that you wanted to spend more time with me?''

"Yes." She remembered. She had been trying to persuade him to let her stay with him. Her pride had been meaningless at that point. Being with Jud had been all that mattered. She would have said anything to convince him.

"And you accused me of being a coward, afraid to take a chance on love?''

"Yes." She had been so eager to persuade him, had been searching for a way to change his mind. Out of her head with love, she had groped for a convincing argument.

"The recruitment campaign was just the means to an end. I came here specifically to see you, Meli. And if I tell you now that I can't promise you a lifetime, but I want to spend more time with you, to get to know you better, to let you get to know me . . ." Resting on his elbows, he leaned over her and stroked her hair back from her forehead. "Is that enough of a commitment, Meli? Is it enough to know that I've never said that to any other woman, that I never thought I would?''

"What about Paula, Jud?''

"She's a friend, Meli, a coworker, just like Ned Fodin is to you. I'm right in assuming that's all he is, aren't I?''

"Yes." Looking up at him, Meli traced the tiny creases at the corners of his eyes. She knew that Jud was telling her the truth, that he was trying to scale the walls he had built between them, to get to know her better and, more important, to let her get to know him. There were no guarantees in life. She, of all people, knew that. But there had to be a willingness to try, and that's what Jud was saying, that he was willing to try.

"All I ever wanted was for you to talk to me, Jud.''

"Talk?" he repeated, his voice low and husky. He

framed her cheeks with his palms, then ran his fingertips down her throat to the open collar of her blouse. "Would it ruin things between us if I told you that right now, at this moment, I'm not really interested in talking?" Ever since she left Hawaii he had been dreaming about holding her again, loving her again. He couldn't forget the softness of her skin, the way her eyes had misted over or her breathless gasps as she had clung to him and writhed in his arms. He hungered for a reunion more intimate than words could offer.

Meli's flesh blossomed beneath his fingers, and her pulse raced to the heat of his touch. "You know, Jud Thompson, for an uncommunicative man, you sometimes talk too much." Meli ran her hands over the front of his shirt and flattened her palms against his chest. "Entirely too much."

"Do I now?" His eyes had grown accustomed to the darkness and he could see her breasts rising against the silk, her nipples so clearly outlined that the clinging fabric might have been sheer. "Sounds like you're a difficult lady to please." His hands trembled as he cupped her breasts, sliding the smooth fabric over them, flexing and massaging the burgeoning flesh.

"Not that difficult," she murmured as she began opening the buttons on his shirt. "It's not hard at all."

"Um, that's where you're wrong." His lips nuzzled her neck and he tasted the clean powdery scent that had now become a part of his most erotic dreams. "It's very hard, my love." He kissed the hollow below her neck and shifted his hips gently over hers. "For you, my love, all for you."

"All of you? Nothing held back?" Her lips brushed lightly over his ear and she caught his earlobe between her teeth. She knew what she was asking, but wondered if Jud understood. Much as she yearned for the languorous pleasure of his body merging with hers, she also wanted more. She wanted him to confide in her, to share his deepest secrets, trusting her to understand.

"I couldn't if I wanted to." Her moist breath warmed his blood, sent it rushing to his head, pounding in his temples. He lifted himself and looked down at her, an awesome desire darkening the depths of his eyes. His hands trembled as, lovingly, he unbuttoned her dress. Candlelight flickered over her, pale and glowing, casting a honey-gold sheen over her skin, smoother and more delicate than the silk he had just removed. "You're beautiful," he said, lowering his lips to her breasts and tantalizing their tips with his tongue, first one, then the other. He was holding himself back, trying to go slowly. She was so soft and delicate, almost breakable beneath his large, callused hands. He closed his eyes, blocking her from his view while he tried to calm himself, to regain his control. Careful, he told himself. He wanted this to be beautiful, didn't want to hurt her.

A knowing smile wreathed Meli's lips. Jud was fighting to maintain the very control she sought to destroy. If they were really to be one, united spiritually as well as physically, then she had to overcome his restraint and make him love her with as much abandon as she loved him. Her hands circled his back, then moved lower and slipped beneath his belt. She wanted to see just how long he could retain his composure.

"Meli." He was losing control. If she didn't stop touching him like this, he wouldn't be able to hold himself back. "Don't do that." He opened his eyes and reached behind him to stop the probing fingers that were driving him past the point of distraction.

"Why? Don't you like it?" Her hands slid to the front

of his waistband and released the snap. "Do you really want me to stop?"

His answer was a muffled groan as his pulse leaped out of control and rational thought became an impossibility. All intentions of gentleness and waiting fluttered into meaningless wisps as his mouth captured hers with an impatient ferocity that left her breathless. He was burning with desire, mad in his need for her. "I love when you touch me. I don't want you to stop, not ever."

Hurriedly and haphazardly discarded, her clothing tangled with his on the floor. A log crackled in the fireplace and briefly flared with fiery life, but the heat of their bodies was more blazingly intense.

He needed to be part of her, to feel her body surrounding his, to merge and blend and bury himself deep within her moist, receptive warmth. His tongue pressed into her mouth, touching, twining, caressing. He had stopped thinking. His passion for her was raw and elemental, beyond the range of lucid comprehension.

He worshipped her with his hands, floating them over her breasts, her abdomen, her inner thighs, and then the center—moist, dewy, silken, feminine folds.

She began moaning softly, beseechingly. "Oh, Jud. Please, Jud." She whimpered, clutching him with her legs, grinding her hips into his. This was torture, tantalizing torture.

Resting on his elbows, he held himself above her and looked into her eyes, misty green emeralds, liquid with desire, her lips, parted, gasping. And suddenly his hands weren't enough, touching wasn't sufficient, not for the physical and emotional intensity blazing within him.

He entered her with a demanding ferocity that rippled through her body, trembles that he felt in the velvety moisture that now surrounded and clasped him to her. She rose to meet him, then matched her movements to his—wild and tender, frenzied and strong.

Her hands explored his back, flexing, clutching, embracing, his sinewy strength and urging him to continue. She felt herself melting, then bathing him in the molten liquid she had become. She clasped him tighter, writhing beneath him as together they climbed and soared toward a height that was just beyond her reach. She wanted this moment to last forever, and yet she couldn't stop pursuing the journey's glorious end. "Oh, Jud . . . I . . ." She felt herself tauten, then rupture, exploding in a kaleidoscope of color and sound that merged with the heated rush of Jud's release.

He lost himself in her, floating, drifting beyond his body, eclipsing his essence and becoming someone new and complete. For the first time in his life he felt whole and fulfilled. Exhausted, yet exuberant, he held her closer, nuzzling his face between her breasts, and at that moment he knew that Meli's love had made him complete. He had been searching for her all his life, and without her he was nothing. He would never let her go.

He raised himself to his elbow and looked down at her. "Are you all right?" He had meant to be gentle, but in the end he had been so desperate to possess her that he had thought only of himself. "I didn't mean for it to be like that." He brushed the damp, clinging hair away from her face and fanned it out over her pillow. God, but she was beautiful. All pink and flushed and so seductive. "I've missed you so much. I've been dreaming about this ever since you left. I'll be better next time. I promise."

"How can you improve on perfection?" Meli asked, glowing in the aftermath of his love. She knew that at last she had broken through the shield he had built around himself, that this time he had been hers, totally and completely, with nothing held back.

"We could try," Jud said. He wanted to love her again, a slow and gentle expression that mirrored the depths of his emotions. She had taken him to the heights of ecstasy, drained and exhausted him, yet he wanted her again.

"Try again?"

"Um-hm." His fingers feathered the curve of her cheek, then trailed along her neck to draw tender circles on her breasts. "Would you like to try again, Meli?"

"Why not," she said, pulling his head down to hers. "I'll try anything twice, or three times, or four—" His lips closed over hers and she stopped counting.

Afterward, she rested in his arms, reveling in her own contentment. How could two bodies be so perfectly tuned to each other's needs, their lovemaking so exquisitely orchestrated? Never had she felt so fulfilled, so utterly relaxed.

"Happy?" Jud asked, running his hand down her back and over the curve of her buttocks. This was what he had been missing, the warmth of her body against his, the feeling of contentment and wholeness that enveloped him whenever she was in his arms.

"What do you think?" She flattened her palms against his chest and toyed with the curling hair, soft and slick with perspiration.

"I think that I've never been this happy." He felt behind him for his jacket, then covered her with it. "I know I haven't."

Meli realized that he must be feeling the chill as well, but she didn't want him moving away from her and getting dressed. "I'm not complaining about perfection, but my bed might be more comfortable. It's right behind you." When Jud glanced quizzically at the blue linen sofa she explained that it opened into a bed. "Housing in the area is pretty expensive, and I fell in love with this studio apartment. I couldn't bear living in one of those concrete monoliths they have on campus. I like things that are different, unique. Like you.''

She slipped her arms into Jud's jacket, then stood and began taking the pillows off the sofa. ''The table has to be moved,'' she explained, noticing the take-out food still congealing on it. ''We never did get to eat,'' she said. ''Are you starved?'' Suddenly she felt ravenous.

''I could do with something,'' Jud said. ''But that stuff didn't look too appealing when it was warm, and now that it's cold . . .'' He stopped and smiled as the lights flashed on and an electric hum filled the apartment once again. ''Back to civilization.''

''Primitive living wasn't so bad,'' Meli said, stepping up to him and putting her hands on his shoulders.

''It definitely has its strong points,'' Jud agreed, slipping his hands beneath the jacket and pulling her against him. ''We can always turn off the circuit breakers.''

''But with the electricity back on I can heat something in the microwave.''

''We can heat something up right here. Using our own electricity. We've done it before.''

''I know, but we're talking about restoking your energy, not depleting it.'' She reached for his hand and led him into the kitchen, determined to feed him before he made her forget about food.

Jud put on his pants and shirt while Meli slipped into her green velour robe. Then she opened the freezer and peered inside. ''I have lasagna, turkey divan, beef Stroganoff, chicken chow mein—''

''T.V. dinners?'' Jud asked, his tone indicating that he'd probably prefer the cold cheeseburgers.

''T.V. dinners indeed. You insult my good taste, Jud Thompson. This is all homemade, gourmet stuff.''

"She's loving, beautiful, intelligent and she can cook; my cup runneth over."

"Three out of four isn't bad. I'll settle for the loving, beautiful and intelligent, but my sister did the cooking." Meli went on to explain that Sue was a five-star housekeeper and cook while she herself found both activities extremely boring. "Now, how about the beef Stroganoff? It's one of my favorites."

"What made you change your mind about seeing me?" Jud asked as he uncorked a bottle of Burgundy and poured some into her glass. Meli's emotions were such an intense part of her personality that for a while he had been afraid she would never forgive him for hurting her, never let him make amends.

"I don't think I ever gave up the idea of seeing you again." She wondered if she should tell him how, during her first few weeks back from Hawaii, she had seen his face each time her phone or doorbell rang. No, she decided. He hadn't promised her anything permanent, just said that he wanted to get to know her better. For the present she would keep her love to herself. "I'm glad you're going to be in Washington for a while." She wished he were staying there forever. Washington was close to Maryland, and what could be safer than a college campus? "Did you ever find the top man behind the espionage ring in Hawaii?" The minute the words left her lips she wanted to swallow them. Hadn't Jud told her that he hated discussing his job?

"We got them all this time." Speaking freely, he told her that because of diplomatic immunity, they had had to release the foreign agents involved, but they had been asked to leave the country and they wouldn't be allowed to return. "That doesn't end it," he said. "Someone else will try again, and we'd better be prepared to stop them."

His tone was determined, but held none of the tension that she remembered from Hawaii.

Meli smiled to herself, reveling in the realization that he trusted her enough to confide in her. If he had changed his mind about discussing his job, he could change his mind about a permanent commitment, couldn't he? Her heart was smiling as they did the dishes and returned to bed.

Chapter 10

MELI OPENED HER EYES TO THE AROMA OF FRESHLY brewed coffee. Inhaling deeply, she ran her tongue across her lips. The scent seemed strong enough to taste.

"Good morning." Jud was standing beside the bed, wearing only his trousers and holding a tray with a carafe of steaming coffee, orange juice, toast and scrambled eggs.

"What are you doing?" Meli sat up, drew the quilt over her breasts and combed her hands through her hair. It was no use, she could feel it springing wildly in all directions. She'd been born too late; her morning looks would have been improved considerably by the sleep caps people used to wear.

"Shh, don't say anything, not one word." Jud poured some coffee into a mug, then handed it to her. "I told you I'd remember . . . coffee first, breakfast in bed."

She cradled the mug in her hands and stared at him in amazement as he set the tray across her knees and sat beside her on the bed. She felt special, pampered, and she didn't know if it was because Jud was serving her breakfast in bed or because he had remembered that she had told him it was something she had always wanted.

"Thank you," she said softly.

"I aim to please, and since you don't cook and I do—"

"You please me very much." The steaming mug warmed her hands, but Jud's gaze warmed the depths of her soul.

"Do I?"

"Mmm." Closing her eyes, she inhaled deeply, enjoying the coffee's rich aroma before holding it to her lips and sipping.

"Pleasing you pleases me." He stroked his hand over her bare back and shoulder, then bent to kiss the side of her neck.

Meli set the mug down on the tray and combed her fingers through his hair, holding him to her. Waking to find Jud beside her like this added a new intimacy to their lovemaking of the night before. She recalled the casual ease with which David had kissed and touched Sue—desire blended with love and trust. Was that what she was experiencing now? The comforting awareness that the joy they had known last night hadn't disappeared but was growing into something new and wonderful.

"A penny for your thoughts?" Jud said, tucking his thumb under her chin and turning her face toward his.

"I know now why I never had breakfast in bed before."

"Oh?"

"Up until this morning the most important ingredient was missing . . . you, Jud."

"Is that an invitation?" Jud lifted the tray and set it on the floor. "Breakfast in bed with you?" As his mouth closed over hers he shrugged off his pants, and Meli decided that coffee wasn't necessarily the best thing to have in the morning, which was very fortunate, because by the time either of them thought of food again, everything on the tray was as cold as last night's cheeseburgers.

"If we keep this up, we're going to starve to death," Meli said, sighing in sleepy contentment. "But I can't think of any way I'd rather go." Her head rested on Jud's chest and her fingers traced the muscles in his arm.

"Don't," he said, rolling over, covering her body with his own and pressing her shoulders into the mattress. "Don't talk about dying because we've made love." His gaze was intent, fearful yet menacing.

She reached up to touch him, but he held her firmly and wouldn't let her move. "I was only joking, Jud." So Jud's wretched conviction hadn't been completely vanquished. He still believed that by loving a woman he was placing her life in danger, courting death.

He closed his eyes for a moment and Meli felt his tension ease as he rolled away from her, swung his feet to the floor and pulled on his pants. She followed after him. The quilt was too heavy to drag off the bed, and her clothes were folded on the rocker across the room, so she stood before him naked. She felt no shame; it was as if she had been with him forever and had no secrets, not from Jud.

"Jud, I want you . . . always . . . just because you're you. Without you I'd be miserable." She wanted him to know how much she needed to be with him. "If I could live forever and never see you again, it wouldn't be worth it. Do you understand, Jud?"

"And if something happens?"

"I'm not afraid, Jud. I love you and I want to spend—" She had been about to say, the rest of my life with you, but she swallowed the words before she spoke them. Jud wasn't ready for that strong a commitment. "As much time as we can together. We both have our careers, Jud, but whenever we can see each other—"

"And if something happens?" he repeated.

"I'll feel the same, Jud. I always will, no matter what happens."

Nothing bad is ever going to happen to you, Jud thought, not if I can help it. He relaxed as he drew her into his arms and felt her body easing his own fears. His lips curved into a smile that reflected the joy of just being near her. "Speaking of careers," he said, "I'm supposed to be addressing some students less than an hour from now."

"Oh, my gosh, what time is it?" She had a nine o'clock lab.

"Seven." He kissed the tip of her nose, then crossed to the chair and put on the rest of his clothes. "I have just enough time to get back to the hotel, shower and change. Luckily I've already had my breakfast." He grinned, then caught her face between his hands and kissed her. "That was dessert." He squeezed her hand tightly, then walked to the door and left.

She stared at the door and felt, for the first time, the chill of her nakedness. Jud hadn't said anything about seeing her again. She had assumed that he had meant what he had said about spending more time together and getting to know each other. Now she realized that she had been mistaken, regardless of the passion that had passed between them, to believe that he was ready to make that much of a commitment. Shame and humiliation filled every crevice of her thoughts. She walked slowly into the bedroom, and the doorbell rang.

"About tonight," Jud said when she opened the door. "I'll be finished at four. What about you?" He had taken it for granted that they would be seeing each other; exact planning was merely a matter of meshing schedules.

She thought for a moment, running a mental finger over her Wednesday calendar. "It's a short day. My last class is at three."

"I'll make dinner reservations for seven. Somewhere nice, linen tablecloths, crystal, candlelight." He looked at her with quizzical concern. "Is something wrong?"

She shook her head. "No, it's just that when you left I wasn't sure if—oh, forget it." She was embarrassed by her lack of faith in him and reluctant to admit it.

"No ifs, Meli. I meant what I said about giving us a chance, and as long as there's a chance for us, we're going to be together. That much I can promise you." He kissed her forehead and left.

Meli smiled all through her shower. She felt like singing. If she had had the time, she would have crawled back under the covers to think about how happy she was, how fortunate, how in love.

Her blissful contentment lasted until just before lunch, when her teaching assistant charged into the lab with news about an oil spill near the wildlife refuge. A cruiser had sprung a leak, and although the refuge itself wasn't in any danger, a nearby island was being threatened. Whenever something like this happened which, in Meli's opinion, was far too often, her classes took a field trip.

After changing into jeans and a ski jacket, she thought about contacting Jud and telling him that she would be late for their dinner date, but she had no idea of where to reach him and finally left a note on the windshield of his van. Then she piled some students into her car and headed for the refuge.

Once she got there she didn't have time to think about Jud or anything else; she was too busy washing oil off the birds that were floundering helplessly on a beach strewn with dead fish. A dismal mist surrounded Meli and the students, slicing through their clothing and chilling their bones.

"It's like tar," one of her students said, carefully dunking a mallard into some detergent and stroking the sticky substance off the feathers.

"That's exactly what it's like," Meli agreed, rinsing off a gosling and putting it into one of the cages the wildlife society had provided. The icy water seeped through her rubber gloves and she shivered. "Poor birds. Their feathers stick together, their wings are useless and they can't fly or swim. What a miserable, helpless feeling."

"If I can come up with that compound I'm working on," Eric said, handing her another gosling, "we should be able to eliminate the problem."

If it could be done, Meli thought, Eric would probably be the one to do it, but in the meantime they had a lot of bird-bathing to do.

When Jud's van pulled behind the row of cars parked at the side of the road, Meli was rinsing off another duck and handing it to Eric. She promised Eric that she would be right back, pulled off her rubber gloves and walked up the beach to greet Jud. She hadn't expected him to meet her here, hadn't even told him exactly where she would be, yet he had found her and had cared enough to come after her. She was so happy to see him that the ache in her arms lightened and she was barely aware of the dampness that permeated every pore of her skin.

"Hello, Jud." She pulled off her gloves and offered him her hand.

"Ned told me where you were." Jud caught her hand between his, held it for a moment, but made no move toward a more intimate greeting. He had seen the students watching them and could wait until they were alone. He thought too much of Meli to risk embarrassing her. "I got your note," he said, still holding her hand as they began walking back toward the shore. "You're a very charitable person."

"Charity has nothing to do with this. When I want to be charitable, I write out a check. It's only when I really care that I give of myself." She pushed her hair back from her face. Useless. The damp sea breezes had made it coarse and sticky. She frowned as she remembered her plans to go home directly after her three o'clock class and spend the time pampering herself so she'd feel beautiful when Jud came to pick her up. Right now she felt about as glamorous as a leather-skinned Cape Cod fisherman. "I guess this puts a crimp in those plans you made." How had he described it? Linen, crystal, candlelight? "But this was an emergency and we had to help out."

"I understand." He rubbed his index finger across her cheek and brushed away some sand. "I changed the reservations, made them for later. I still intend to take you to dinner. To save time I brought my clothes with me so I can change at your apartment. Now, what can I do to help?"

Meli explained that they were catching all the waterfowl they could, washing them in detergent, then rinsing them off. "We put them in cages," she pointed to the poultry crates stacked on the back of a truck, "take them to a nearby nonpolluted area and release them." She spoke softly, almost apologetically. If Sue thought she was a bleeding heart, what would Jud say? Considering the significance of his assignments, washing off ducks must seem very unimportant to him.

But he didn't criticize her. He tilted her chin gently and looked into her eyes. "You're one of the good guys," he said. "Even if you are a girl."

And Meli smiled up at him, forgetting her chilled,

sticky skin and feeling as beautiful as if she had spent the last three hours in a frothy bubble bath.

"Now, stop looking at me like that unless you want your students to get an unexpected lesson in sex education. Tell me how I can help."

By the time it got dark, Jud was as soggy the rest of the duck bathers. Meli drove her students back to the campus and told Jud she would meet him at her apartment. When she got home he was waiting outside holding a leather-trimmed suit bag and a matching piece of luggage.

"I should have given you my key," Meli said, slipping out of her shoes. No way was she going to bring those sandy clumps into the house. She fumbled in her purse, found the key, and unlocked the door. When they walked into the kitchen, Muffin looked up from her basket and purred; her kittens, their eyes still closed, snuggled beside her.

"Well, isn't she the proud mother," Jud said, kneeling beside Muffin and rubbing her behind the ears while Meli poured some milk into her dish.

"All mothers are proud. Unfortunately it's not going to be that easy to find homes for these kittens. Unless, maybe some of the students—"

"Can't the vet do something? So this doesn't happen again?"

"Yes, of course," Meli said, her eyes growing suddenly somber. "We'll have to do something." And the ache in her heart returned as she remembered another decision that she might have to make.

"Is anything wrong?" Jud asked. "It's the humane thing to do, isn't it? Spaying a cat?"

"Yes, of course."

"Well, then why do you look so upset? What's bothering you?"

"Nothing, except that I'm greasy and chilled to the

bone.'' She looked at Jud's oily clothes and windblown hair. ''And you don't look so great yourself.'' Mentally she tried to work out the logistics of this clean-up operation. It would have been much easier, she decided, if Jud had gone home to change. ''Why don't you shower first.'' She could probably use the extra time to cream her face and brush out her hair.

''All right.'' He started walking away, stepped into the living room and paused. Then, turning back to her, he held out his hand. ''Come with me. We can shower together.'' It was as if he had sensed the depression that had come over her and didn't want to leave her alone.

Meli hesitated for a moment. She knew that she had gone to bed with Jud, had held him naked in her arms, yet somehow showering together seemed more private, more intimate. But that's what love was all about, wasn't it? Intimacy, trust, sharing, commitment. ''That's the best invitation I've had all day,'' she said.

''Oh, how many invitations have you had?'' In the bathroom now, Jud had taken off his clothes while Meli still wore her bra and panties. He came up behind her and began unhooking her bra.

''Oh, you know, an attractive woman like me . . .'' She fluffed her snarled hair dramatically and leaned her head back on his shoulder. ''Who can keep count?''

''Who indeed?'' Jud murmured, dipping his head to kiss the back of her neck while his hands cupped and caressed her breasts. ''But you've turned them all down and accepted mine. I'll have to see that you don't regret it.'' Dropping to his knees, he hooked his thumbs into the elastic of her bikini panties and tugged gently until they fell loosely around her ankles. He held her to him as his lips worshipped her bare flesh—her toes, ankles, knees, thighs.

''Jud, no, please.''

"Yes. I want to know you, all of you." His tongue teased and tantalized, driving her into a quivering frenzy of unexpected passion. Moaning helplessly, she tangled her fingers in his hair and slowly rotated her body. Holding her tightly, he drew her to him. He hungered for her, couldn't get enough of her.

"Oh, Jud, sweet Jud." She clung to him, urging him on.

His kisses grew stronger and more demanding as he heard her sigh and felt the pleasure rippling through her body. It was as if she were a part of him, as if her joyful, shuddering release were his own, and his heart swelled as he rose to see her contented smile.

He led her into the shower and turned it on. Warm water flowed over them. They shampooed their hair and then he began washing her body.

She had been thoroughly satiated, languid with the contentment of release, yet now, as his hands slid down her body, she felt the tension building once again.

"Your turn." His voice was husky as he handed her the soap.

She started washing him, soap foaming over his arms and chest, then lower. He stepped closer, pressing her hips against his while gently parting her thighs. Water streamed over them and Meli felt as if they were surging through the rapids, circling, climbing, dipping, until finally they reached the pinnacle and she called Jud's name while they spilled over the falls in a splashing explosion of ecstasy. Open-mouthed, she gasped against his chest. It was as if she were drowning, had drowned, yet never had she been so utterly alive.

The shower stall was filled with steam as Jud reached behind her and turned off the water. Silence seemed to fill the room when he bent to kiss the droplets shimmering on her lashes. "I love you, Meli." He brushed the damp, curling tendrils back from her face and kissed her lips. "I love you, my darling." And the words rang in Meli's ears like the joyous pealing of bells. He loved her. Jud loved her.

He tucked one towel around his waist, then wrapped her in another and carried her back into the bedroom. "I really want to take you to dinner tonight," he said, setting her on her feet and pressing his lips to her forehead. "So go get dressed before I forget my noble intentions."

Dinner at the elegant French restaurant was everything Jud had promised, everything and more; he hadn't mentioned the long-stemmed red rose, or the small gold foil box of chocolates, or the photo he had arranged for.

What a wonderful man he was, thoughtful, caring, considerate, eager for her happiness. If Meli stopped to think about it, that was probably an important part of her feelings for him. He cared about her, really cared. To Jud she was important, very special.

"What are you thinking?" He studied her as he sipped his coffee. The white china cup looked incredibly delicate cradled between his large hands.

How much I love you, she thought. "How happy I am that we met," she said. "Even if the circumstances were rather bizarre." Earlier that evening Jud had told her he loved her, but they had been in the shower then, glowing with fulfillment, and wasn't there a saying about not holding a man accountable for any statement he makes under those conditions.

His lips tilted in a lazy smile as he continued watching her.

She felt a tingling tightness deep within her. "What are you thinking?" I love you was the answer she wanted.

"That we ought to go home." Still watching her, he signaled for the waiter to bring the check. "That I want to be alone with you."

And that, Meli thought, wasn't such a bad suggestion, not bad at all. She reached across the table and covered his hands with hers.

They spent the next two nights together. On Thursday evening they ate at a Thai restaurant and attended a Mozart concert given by the college's music department, and on Friday they saw the drama club's presentation of *A Streetcar Named Desire*. Meli was amazed to find that although their backgrounds were so different they could find enjoyment in the same activities.

Jud was returning to Washington on Monday, which would make it more difficult for them to see each other. But Meli didn't want to think about that; they still had the weekend.

"So now we've got the whole day in front of us," Jud said late Saturday morning as he stretched lazily beside Meli in bed after a night spent exquisitely entwined in love. "What would you like to do?"

"Umm." Smiling, she slid her body sensuously against his. "Do you really want to know?"

"You're becoming a sex fiend," he said, pulling her on top of him and looking up at her.

"Are you complaining?"

"Does it look like I'm complaining?" His fingers feathered lightly down her back, then shaped themselves to her curving hips. "I have a house in Virginia. We could drive out there. Be alone for a—"

The telephone rang, jarring them apart. Meli reached to answer it. "Hello." She tried to slow her breathing, but the husky tone remained in her voice.

"Meli, this is Sue. Are you all right? You sound funny? I didn't wake you, did I?"

"No. I wasn't sleeping."

"I should hope not," Jud murmured.

Meli shot him a silencing glare.

"Well, you should be up anyway. It's after eleven and we're expecting you at two."

"Two?" Meli repeated blankly.

"Bobby's birthday party. Mother's flying in from New York. Don't tell me you forgot."

"No, of course not, how could I forget?"

"How indeed?" Jud whispered, tracing circles over her breasts, then gently lifting his lips to the tautening centers.

Inhaling deeply, Meli tried to arch her body away from him, but that only seemed to make her flesh more accessible. "Stop it," she said, covering the mouthpiece.

An innocent smile wreathed Jud's face as he lifted his hands and clasped them behind his head.

"We're you talking to me?" Sue asked.

"No, I'm just muttering to myself."

"Chicken," Jud mouthed.

"I was wondering if you'd do me a favor," Sue said. "My refrigerator is stacked to the hilt and Bobby's cake has to be refrigerated, so we're leaving it at the bakery as long as possible. Could you pick it up on your way here? It's that little French patisserie."

"No problem," Meli said. "And would it be okay if I bring a friend with me?" She had no idea of how Jud would feel about spending the day with a bunch of seven-year-olds, but not even he could make her miss Bobby's birthday party.

"Sure. Anyone I know?"

"No."

"Male or female?" Sue's voice sparked with interest.

Meli hesitated. She hadn't told Sue about Jud being in Maryland. For the last three days they had been living in their own secluded world—private, special—and she wanted to hold on to that cloistered magic for as long as she could. "Be surprised. I'll see you at two." She leaned forward and hung up the phone.

"Good, she's gone," Jud said, drawing her back into his arms. "Now, where were we?"

"We were just about to get ready for a birthday party," Meli said, pushing him away and swinging her legs over the side of the bed.

"Funny, I could have sworn we were doing something else."

"The memory is the first to go," Meli said, knotting the belt on her robe and stepping into the hallway. "You must be getting old, Jud." Too old to play cops-and-robbers, she added silently.

"Old, am I? Why don't you come back to bed and let me show you just how old I am?"

"Have you ever been to a birthday party with a bunch of kids?" she asked, sticking her head back into the bedroom.

"Not recently."

"I didn't think so. Take my advice, Jud Thompson. Save your energy. You're going to need it." Meli hurried into the bathroom and turned on the shower. She herself wasn't concerned about coping with the children; her mother was the person whose company she anticipated with dread.

Chapter 11

By evening Jud silently admitted that Bobby's birthday party had been as draining as Meli had predicted. David and Sue had been so exhausted that he had offered to drive some of the children home. Actually, he had been happy to escape from Meli's mother. He had never met a more self-centered woman, and her preference for Sue was so blatant that Jud could sense Meli's pain.

At various intervals during the day, Edwina had criticized Meli's clothing, job and lifestyle. She had eyed him pointedly when mentioning the latter, and that was when he had offered to drive the children home. It was obvious that despite all the faults Edwina found with Meli, she still didn't consider Jud suitable for her daughter.

When he returned from taking the children home, Sue had insisted on showing him the family album. Jud made an appropriate comment every now and then, but for the most part he was silent. He found it difficult to connect a freckled, skinny, straggly-haired Meli with the attractive woman sitting beside him. Sue, on the other hand, was like a china doll: clear, pink complexion, flaxen hair, bright blue eyes. Talk about growing up in a shadow, there wasn't one photograph in which Sue's beauty didn't highlight her sister's plainer looks.

"Sue was always so beautiful," Edwina said, echoing Jud's thoughts as she stood behind the sofa and peered over his shoulder. "I had such high hopes for her . . . a model or even an actress."

"I couldn't act to save my life," Sue said. "In fact, Meli had all the theatrical talent. Don't you remember that play she wrote in junior high? Excuse me, Jud." Reaching over, she flipped through the album and stopped when she came to a photograph of Meli sporting a gray wig and wearing a faded cotton housedress. "There she is. She won an award for that. Wrote, directed and acted, some superbrain."

"Yes," Edwina agreed. "Both my daughters were outstanding—in different ways, of course. Sue is sociable and feminine like me, while Meli takes after her father. He was an English professor, you know. Not very ambitious. Preferred fishing to parties. We were so different that it's amazing our marriage lasted as long as it did. I felt like a new woman after I left him."

"I wonder if you'd excuse me," Meli said. "I've seen these pictures at least a hundred times and I'm eager to know how Bobby's doing with his metal detector." The metal detector had been her present to Bobby, and he was currently searching for buried treasure in the small back-yard garden. She grabbed her coat from the closet and hurried outside. How could her mother speak so casually about the divorce that had broken her father's heart and probably killed him? Meli's hands trembled as she stood on the back porch and buttoned her coat.

The garden was a panorama of bare shrubs and evergreens. Bobby, on his knees, was using a hoe to turn the earth in an azalea bed. The metal detector lay on the ground beside him.

"Any luck?" Meli asked.

"Two rusty nails," Bobby said. "I guess this isn't a very good spot."

"The beach is the best place. All sorts of things are buried in the sand. I'll ask your mother if we can go there one day."

"Tomorrow?" Bobby asked, sitting back on his haunches.

"Well, I don't know about tomorrow."

"You could sleep over and we could have a picnic. It's a great idea. I'll go ask Mom if it's all right." He dropped the hoe, wiped his palms on his trousers and trotted into the house, nearly colliding with Jud, who was walking out.

"What did he find?" Jud asked Meli. "A gold doubloon?"

"No such luck. Two rusty nails. Then I was foolish enough to mention that the beach was an ideal spot for treasure-hunting. I'd forgotten Bobby's need for immediacy. Now he's inside pestering Sue about an outing for tomorrow."

"It seems to me that we just came back from the beach," Jud said, reaching into his pocket, then taking the hoe and burying some coins at the base of a juniper tree. "It's not much, but it's better than a rusty nail."

"You're a really nice guy, Jud Thompson," Meli said, moving into his arms.

"How nice?" His arms tightened, drawing her closer.

"The best," she said, standing on her toes and pressing small kisses along the side of his jaw, tantalizing the corners of his mouth. "You worry about cats and birds and little children." He would make a wonderful father, she thought. If she and Jud were to get married, would he want children right away?

"Hey, you guys," Bobby shouted from the steps. "Mom says dinner is ready."

Dinner was served by a tall, middle-aged maid named Ingrid whose eyes never met anyone's at the table and whose lips never parted in a smile. She might as well have been a robot, Jud decided.

"Does your work ever take you to New York?" Edwina asked Jud, her spoon poised above her lobster bisque.

"On occasion. Right now I'm assigned to Washington."

"He's been on our campus for the past week," Meli said.

"What a pleasant coincidence," Edwina said. "After having met in Hawaii, I mean."

"Very pleasant," Meli agreed, wishing her mother would get off the subject. Odd, wasn't it, she mused, all her life she had yearned for her mother's attention and now that she was finally receiving it, she no longer needed it. She had Jud.

"Well, I must be sure to give you my address," Edwina said. "I've always enjoyed entertaining Meli's friends, at least the two-legged kind." She patted her mouth with a white damask napkin. "You wouldn't believe the animals she'd come home with. Why, when we moved to New York—"

"I can just imagine," Jud said. "Pregnant cats, seasick sea gulls."

"Let me tell you about those sea gulls," David said. "They can be damned pesky when you're up in the air."

"So tell me, David," Meli said, "how are you enjoying your new toy?" She had endured being the center of her mother's attention for as long as she possibly could. How did Edwina always manage to sound like a martyr when she discussed her younger daughter?

"Some toy," Sue grumbled. "Do you have any idea what that plane cost?"

"Did I deprive you of anything to buy it?"

"No, of course not," Sue said.

"Then don't complain about the cost. Think of the money we save when we fly into New York to see your mother. Next time we go we can even take Jud and Meli with us. In fact, Jud might be another weekend pilot." David looked at Jud for verification.

"Sorry," Jud said, "I'm strictly passenger material. I never get behind the controls."

"Ah, you should try it sometime." David lifted his wineglass toward the ceiling. "There's nothing like it. After sitting in a crowded courtroom all week it's great to be out in all that open space. Listen, Sue tells me you're staying over. Maybe we can go up for a short hop tomorrow."

"Thanks, but I don't think so," Jud said. "I fly when I have to, to get from place to place, but as far as doing it for pleasure . . ." He waited while Ingrid placed a slice of beef Wellington on his plate. "My father was an Air Force test pilot. He went up in an experimental jet and never made it back down. I was only ten years old, and since then I've never had any interest in flying. I wish my father hadn't. I don't think I've ever stopped missing him. Men with children have no business doing dangerous things. You should stick to your judge's bench, David. It's nice and safe."

"I'm sorry about your dad," David said, "but accidents happen. You know what they say about crossing the street being dangerous. Everyone needs some relaxation, some excitement."

"I get plenty of excitement on my job."

"I guess you do at that," Sue said, pressing a floor buzzer that connected to the kitchen. "Perhaps someone would like some more beef," she told Ingrid, "or spinach soufflé."

After dessert—pears in lemon ice and champagne—Sue suggested coffee in the music room. Bobby said good-night and asked Meli to come upstairs to tell him a bedtime story. "One of your scary ones, Aunt Meli."

Jud followed a few minutes later, then lounged in the doorway and watched them. She's so gentle, he thought. A family person, the kind of woman who should be surrounded by children. The realization wasn't something he wanted to think about, so he forced it to the back of his mind.

Sue's sleeping arrangements were what she considered to be proper but practical. Her mother, as usual, slept in the guest room next to Bobby's, while Jud and Meli were at the opposite end of the hall, in separate rooms connected by a communal bathroom.

Under Edwina's watchful eye, Meli bid Jud good-night at the door to his room and then continued on to her own. The connecting bathroom door was the first thing she noticed when she walked in. Somehow she had expected that Jud would have opened it, but he hadn't. She could hear him moving about, then the flow of the shower.

Hastily she undressed and slipped into the pale blue nightgown Sue had draped across the bed. Would Jud come to her room? she wondered. He had seemed silent and withdrawn after dinner. Was he comparing her to Sue, noticing her inadequacies? Probably. Everyone did. All her life she had lived in Sue's shadow. She never should have brought Jud here.

She frowned at her reflection in the mirror above the dressing table. Her lower lip was too full, her nose too freckled, and her hair was absolutely impossible. She was tugging a brush through the mass of tangled curls when the shower stopped. A few minutes later the bathroom door opened and Jud walked into the room. A blue towel was wrapped around his waist, his hair was damp from the shower and moisture glistened on his tanned chest.

Meli looked into the mirror and saw him walking toward her, but she didn't turn around. Her fingers tightened around the brush and the pace of her strokes slowed when he stepped behind her and placed his hands lightly on her shoulders.

"Put down the brush," he said, his hands lowering to her waist. "I love the way you look all tousled and untamed." Pressing his palms lightly against her waist, he urged her away from the bench. "Let me be the one to tame you."

Turning, she put her arms around his neck. He loved the way she looked, loved her, wanted her just as she was. Her palms flexed over the throbbing veins in his neck, her fingers combing through his hair and drawing his lips down to hers. "You can tame me all you want, but I'll still be wild about you."

"I wasn't sure," he murmured against her lips as he bent to lift her into his arms.

"Wasn't sure of what?" Her tongue traced the inner edges of his lips. Jud's arms tightened around her and she felt the prickling remnants of Edwina's barbs begin smoothing away. "What weren't you sure of?" Her tongue darted, curling around his.

"Mmm." Jud pressed closer, and his mouth opened to inhale her breath, the very essence of her being. He had spent hours watching Edwina crush her, and there hadn't been anything he could do. All day he had kept his passion under control and when Meli had said good-night in the hallway, he had been afraid that Edwina had said something to turn her against him, that she wouldn't want him with her tonight. "I wasn't sure you'd still want me," he said, nuzzling her neck and carrying her to the bed.

"You weren't sure if I'd still want you?" she repeated, her lips quirking in a disbelieving smile.

"You've been so tense all day, so cold." He stretched out beside her and toyed with the straps on her nightgown. "I thought maybe I didn't fit in here, didn't measure up to your family's expectations."

"You fit me perfectly, Jud." Her arms circled his back, her fingers flexing lightly, testing the strength in his shoulders. His muscles were like ribbons of steel, tough and unyielding. "I never felt so right with anyone, but I was afraid that after seeing Sue and hearing my mother, you wouldn't want me." Edwina was the one she didn't fit in with, not Jud. He was as comfortable as her skin.

"Not want you? How could I not want you? You're the sweetest, most desirable woman I've ever known." All afternoon he had been wondering how a cold fish like Edwina could have given birth to someone as warm and wonderful as Meli.

"Then you don't mind that I'm not as beautiful as Sue?"

"Who says you're not?"

"Oh, Jud."

"You don't believe me, huh? Then I guess I'll just have to find some way to convince you." He dropped her shoulder straps and lowered her bodice to her waist. "Do you see this?" He thumbed a beauty mark just above her left breast. "It's part of my most erotic dreams. All through dinner I've wanted to unbutton your dress and kiss it, and now I can." His lips brushed lightly against her flesh, then trailed lower, circling her nipples, first one, then the other, kissing and teasing with his tongue until her hips rose and began moving rhythmically against his.

"Jud, please, Jud." Desire meshed with love, and she ached to be part of him. Her mouth was too dry to speak, and she closed her eyes as her fingers loosened the towel, baring his flesh to her explorations.

He gasped as she cupped his hips and lowered her hands to his thighs. "Oh, yes," he cried. "Do that. I love when you do that. I love when you touch me." He raised himself slightly and slid the silky nightgown down her legs. What was it that made this woman so special, that made his whole body cry out in its need for her.

"The light," she said, motioning to the bisque figurine lamp on the bedside table.

He shook his head. "Let's leave it on. I want to see you." How could he explain the rushing joy he felt when he saw her lips part, her tongue tipping moistly between them, her eyes growing misty with desire. "You don't mind, do you?" If it really bothered her, he would turn it off, but she looked so lovely in the lamplight, which Sue had softened with a pink shade.

"No." She liked being able to see him, enjoyed watching the velvety shadows play across the glistening muscularity of his shoulders. "No, I don't mind. I like looking at you, looking and touching." Her hands stroked higher, flattening against the granite planes of his lower abdomen. She felt him tauten in response.

"Oh, Meli." Her name was a rasping groan as he shifted himself and rotated his hips until his fierce male strength teased at the core of her femininity. "Do you have any idea of what you're doing to me?"

"Is your heart racing wildly?" she whispered. "Does your body hunger for my touch?" She curled her fingers over the bulging muscles in his shoulders and stroked slowly down his arms. "And when we're this close—"

Her breath formed a ragged edge around her words as he buried his face in her neck and nipped gently at her earlobe. "Mmm . . . mmm . . ." She was ablaze, and Jud was a zephyr flaming her higher; for a moment she couldn't speak, couldn't even think.

"When we're this close, what?" he asked, lifting his cheeks away from her neck and trailing kisses along her collarbone to the curving beginnings of her breasts. "Tell me, Meli." His lips circled the full swell of her flesh and closed tenderly over the ripe rosy tip. Then, ever so gently, his tongue teased it to a burgeoning tautness which was echoed deep within the inner recesses of her body. "What happens when we're this close, Meli?"

"It's not enough," she gasped. "I think I'll die if you don't come closer, if you're not a part of me."

"I want to be part of you, want to lose myself in you," Jud said, lifting himself on his elbows, framing her hips and slowly guiding them, fitting them to the searching power of his. "Let me lose myself in you, Meli." His eyes took possession of her face as his body thrust deeply into hers. She belonged to him, all of her, totally and forever. "Let me make you mine."

He clutched her buttocks and set the rhythm, urging her to match it. She moaned softly and yielded, kneading his flesh, pulling him closer. She felt herself leaving her body, encircling and becoming part of him. The pace increased until the merging movements of their bodies soared out of control and melted in the intensity of the heat flaming between them.

Meli gave herself up to the excitement of the moment, arching, clutching, grasping, but she couldn't touch what she wanted, she could only sense it, feel it. It was somewhere near, within her, around her; she could almost find it, almost, but not quite, and then it came, an explosive, fiery moment that shattered her insides and dazzled her with the brilliance of a million shooting stars.

Groaning, Jud collapsed on top of her and buried his

face between her breasts. Then, still holding her tightly in his arms, he shifted to his back and sealed her body to the sheltering length of his. "I love you, Meli, and I've never said that to any other woman." He had lost a part of himself, but with Meli he had found more happiness than he had ever known.

"I think you're beautiful," Meli murmured, kissing the sleek dampness of his chest. "That first time I saw you standing on the trawler I thought you were the most beautiful man I had ever seen, and later, when you were in my room, I wanted to touch you, touch you like I'm touching you now."

"Men aren't beautiful," Jud whispered, feathering his lips over her forehead and wishing this moment could last forever. She had met his needs with such perfect strength, yet now she seemed so fragile. Never had he felt such tenderness for a woman, yearned for her happiness even more than his own.

"You are. Your skin is like burnished leather, smooth and tanned. Your hair is so dark." Rolling slightly away from him, she leaned on her elbow, looked down at him and brushed her fingers over his hair. "Like raven's wings. And your eyes . . . glowing bits of coal that were flaming just moments ago. Now they're like embers, warm and glittery."

"A poetic scientist?" he asked, reaching up to ruffle her hair. "You're full of surprises . . . a very exotic lady."

"And you're a very exotic man. When I first saw you, I thought you were Polynesian."

"One-quarter Navaho."

"Navaho?" She tilted her head back and smiled. "See, I was right. I knew you were special. Now, let's see. If you're one-quarter, then your children would be one-eighth Navaho."

"If I had any children, which I don't."

"I know you don't, not now, but when you do."

"I don't plan on any, not ever."

"Oh." Tiny invisible icicles stabbed at Meli's heart. No children, not ever. A few months ago she might have shared Jud's sentiments, but not anymore, not since she had spoken to Dr. Carrow and not since she had met Jud. Now she wanted children, Jud's children. "I felt like that once," she said, sitting up and crossing her legs in front of her. "But things change, Jud."

"Not for me, Meli. Not on that." His hand circled her foot, his thumb stroking lightly over her sole, then tracing the outlines of her toes. "I'll never have any children."

"But, Jud, how can you be certain?" Was there some medical problem? Meli's stomach felt as queasy as it had when Dr. Carrow had posed that possibility to her. No, there couldn't be. If there had been, Jud wouldn't have been so concerned about taking precautions each time they made love. He had been very subtle, but she had noticed.

"I told you about my father, Meli. Surely you can see that in its own way my job is every bit as dangerous as his was. Bringing kids into this crazy world is bad enough, but when you know that you might not be around to guide them over the rough spots . . ."

"You had your mother, Jud."

"My mother, yes, indeed, I had my mother." Jud's cynical chuckle held not the slightest trace of humor. "The only reason she married my father was because she liked the idea of being married to a pilot—lots of free time, lots of glamour. When he died the glamour vanished and I was a very definite impediment to her freedom. She left me with my grandfather and I heard from her so infrequently that by the time she died in a car crash, I couldn't remember what she looked like."

"I'm so sorry, Jud." She leaned closer and rested her head on his shoulder.

"There's nothing to be sorry about. I've recovered."

Yes, you've recovered, Meli thought, but at what cost? There's such a bitter unhappiness within you. "It doesn't have to be that way, Jud." She stroked his cheek gently, her fingers rasping over the late-night stubble. "If you loved someone, wouldn't you want to make them happy? And wouldn't a family be part of that happiness? We can do better than our parents did."

He caught her hand, held it tightly between his and brought it down to his chest. "There's no place in my life for children, Meli, not ever."

They stayed like that for several minutes—stiff, unmoving, silent. Then Jud sat up and reached for his towel.

"I guess I'd better get back to my room," he said, wrapping the towel around his waist. "Sue might be upset if she sees my bed hasn't been slept in."

Nodding, Meli pulled the sheets over her naked body. In spite of the intimacy they had just shared, she now felt embarrassed by her nudity. Something had changed between them, and Jud felt it as well as she. He wasn't returning to his room because he was afraid of offending Sue; he was leaving Meli because a barrier had risen between them. The word *children* loomed before them in capital letters. She wanted them and he didn't.

Meli watched Jud walk to the door and felt the chill of desertion, of being alone once again. Any hopes that had blossomed during their lovemaking crumpled now beneath the weight of his statement. From the moment she had met him, Meli had been envisioning his children, yet now he was telling her that those dreams would never become a reality because he didn't want children, not ever.

All right, she told herself, so he doesn't want children now, but no matter what he says, things change. Remember when he didn't want to make love to you? She recalled the passion that had exploded between them just a few minutes ago. He had certainly changed his mind about that. Given time, he might revise his ideas about children. Time. Her old enemy time. If time was in her favor when it came to changing Jud's mind, it was certainly against her where Dr. Carrow was concerned. *If you're planning on marriage and a family, Meli. Then do it now.*

After spending the last few days with Jud she knew that she wanted to spend the rest of her life with him, and until a few minutes ago she had been equally certain that he felt exactly the same way about her. He had told her that he loved her, had admitted that he had never said that to any other woman. She knew that Jud wanted to be with her, but she also knew that his willpower was strong enough to overcome his desires, and if she insisted on having children . . . Well, she didn't have to insist. She wanted Jud, wanted him more than anything in the world—more than children. They could be perfectly happy together, just the two of them. But what if Jud did change his mind and then it was too late for her? She would have to speak with him and explain the situation.

Shivering, she pulled the covers tighter and curled her knees up to her chest. It didn't help. The chill wasn't being brought on by the surrounding air; it was lodged deep in her heart. Why couldn't her life be simple just this once? Why did she have to decide between the man she loved and the children she wanted? His children.

The hours crawled by with agonizing slowness while she sleeplessly thrashed through the night. When the first gray hint of a rainy dawn slivered through the blinds, she put on her robe and walked into Jud's room. He wasn't there. The bedcovers were rumpled, and the pajamas he had borrowed from David lay folded on a chair, but Jud wasn't anywhere in sight.

Had he left during the night? Meli wondered. Had her confession about wanting children disturbed him that much? No, she decided, no matter how upset he was, Jud wouldn't run off without speaking with her. He wasn't that type of person.

She returned to the bathroom, showered, dressed in the pearl gray slacks and sweater Sue had lent her, and went downstairs. Jud and Bobby were sitting at the kitchen table. Jud's fingers were curled around a steaming yellow mug as he listened to Bobby's theory that the morning's rain was a temporary situation that would clear before afternoon.

"Good morning," Jud said, placing his mug on the table and standing. His hair was rumpled and his eyes looked tired and troubled. "Coffee?" Without waiting for her answer, he crossed to the counter and poured her a cup.

"Yes, please," Meli said, studying his haggard appearance and concluding that his night had been every bit as sleepless as her own.

When he handed her the cup, their fingers touched, and an electric tingle raced up Meli's arm. Jud's startled expression as he pulled his hand away told her that he had felt it, too, and somehow Meli found comfort in the knowledge that they still had at least that much in common. The attraction they felt for each other was still as strong as ever. "Thanks." She sat down beside Bobby while Jud retrieved his mug and remained standing.

"Jud thinks it's too rainy for our picnic," Bobby said, plopping his spoon back into his cereal bowl. "But I told him that it might clear up."

"I don't think so, Bobby," Meli said. "But even if it

does, the sand would be too wet. We'll have to postpone it.''

"Oh." Staring glumly at his cereal, Bobby dipped his spoon in and out of the bowl. "I wanted to use my metal detector; now I probably won't ever get the chance."

"Not get the chance," Meli said. "Of course you will. I promised, didn't I? Tell you what I'm going to do." Reaching behind her, she picked up the pad and pencil that Sue kept by the telephone and began writing on it. When she had finished, she tore off the sheet of paper and handed it to Bobby.

"Raincheck," he read. "This raincheck is redeemable for one day at the beach with Aunt Meli."

"Now you have it in writing," Meli said. "It's all legal and there's no way I can back out. Just ask your dad."

Which is exactly what Bobby did. David assured him that Meli's signature made the paper a binding document. The rain continued, and after breakfast, Jud suggested that since the weather was so bad it might be best if he and Meli made an early start back to Maryland.

Sheets of rain streamed across the windshield, and the steady click of the wipers punctuated the gloomy silence within the van. Yet even without speaking, Meli knew what Jud was thinking. After all, she had seen the tautened lips and furrowed brow often enough in Hawaii.

"Do you want to talk about it, Jud?" she asked softly.

"Truthfully," he said, hunching over the steering wheel as he swerved to avoid a sprawling puddle, "no. I don't want to talk about it or think about it. I wish I could make the whole damn world go away so we could be alone, just the two of us. But that's the problem, isn't it?" he asked as the light turned red and he hit the brake. "That wouldn't be enough for you, would it? The two of us I mean. You meant what you said last night, didn't you? About wanting children."

"Yes," Meli admitted. What was the point in lying? "I've been thinking about it a lot recently. You see—" She considered telling Jud about Dr. Carrow's diagnosis, then decided against it. Mightn't that be putting unfair pressure on him, playing on his sympathies? She didn't want his sympathy; she wanted his love.

"I see it all too clearly, Meli. I saw you with the kids at the party, then reading that bedtime story to Bobby, and again this morning with the raincheck. You should have kids, Meli, lots of kids."

"But not with you?"

"Not with me."

"And if I tell you that children aren't as important to me as you are?" She spoke slowly, trying to still the quivers in her voice. The truth was that she didn't want children, not if they weren't Jud's.

"You mean that, don't you?"

"Yes."

Jud stared at the road silently. He knew she was telling the truth, that she would deprive herself of children to be with him. But if a family meant as much to her as he thought it did, then her life would always have a void that even his love couldn't fill. He couldn't ask it of her, couldn't take his happiness at the expense of hers.

Quietly Meli waited for his response. She had told Jud that he meant more to her than anything else in the world, so what more could she say?

Jud was equally uncommunicative. A veil of silence hung between them until he turned into the block where she lived and pulled the van to a halt in front of her house. When he shut the ignition and stared mutely through the windshield, she knew what his answer was going to be even before he spoke. She didn't want to hear it. Her fingers closed around the door handle and she could feel the icy chill of the metal seeping through her fleece-lined gloves.

"I can't give you what you want, Meli."

"Can't or won't?"

"I'm not a family man, Meli. You have to understand."

"Maybe I do, Jud. Maybe for the first time I do." She opened the door and hopped out of the van.

"Meli, let me explain." He leaned across the seat and tried to stop her.

Rain streamed down her face as she turned toward him. "Don't bother, Jud. No excuses, no explanations. I can't go through these ups and downs, not anymore. Either you want me or you don't. Let me know what you decide when you decide. Until then leave me alone. For God's sake, leave me alone." Pulling her hood over her head, she ran up the steps and into the building.

Chapter 12

A DISHEARTENING SENSE OF DÉJÀ VU WASHED OVER Meli as she trudged up the stairway and unlocked the door to her apartment. They had played this scene before, at the army camp in Hawaii. Falling in love with Jud, being happier than she had ever been, then having him snatch it all away, insisting that it was for her own good, that he wasn't the man for her.

She unlocked her door and dropped her key back into her purse. Muffin padded across the living room to greet her and rubbed her head against Meli's leg. "It looks like we've both been deserted," Meli said, bending down to stroke the cat's sleek beige fur. "I wonder who started the rumor about women not being able to make up their minds when it's always the men who can't seem to follow through on their commitments?" Muffin purred, then stretched and began walking back into the kitchen.

"Okay, cat," Meli said, following after her. "I guess

neither of us would win any prizes when it comes to choosing a mate." She washed and refilled Muffin's dishes, then knelt to pet the kittens. "I suppose things could be worse," she told the squirming mustard-colored kitten. "At least Jud did the walking before we had a family. He was very definite about that." She put the kitten back into the basket, went into the bedroom and began undressing. "So why don't I feel relieved? Why do I feel so unbelievably miserable?"

And the misery didn't ease with the passage of time. Each day seemed like an eternity, and as one week dragged into the next, she found herself reconstructing that last morning with Jud, revising their conversation, imagining statements she might have made, words which would have convinced him that where she was concerned his fears were totally unfounded.

It was easier in the daytime when she could lose herself in her work, but at night, alone in her apartment, she found herself thinking about Jud, wondering where he was, staring at the telephone, hoping he would call her, wanting to call him. She could if she wanted to, she thought, glancing from the silent telephone to the slip of paper Jud had given her with his phone number on it. But what good would it do? He was the one who had to change, not her. Children represented a commitment. That's why Jud didn't want a family. He was still afraid of a permanent relationship, wanted to be able to leave whenever the mood hit him, didn't want anything tying him down. She stared at the telephone as if by concentrating she could make it ring. Why didn't he call, damn it? Why didn't he call?

When finally the telephone did ring, she jumped, momentarily startled by the sound. Then she reached for it. Maybe there was something to mental telepathy? Jud's image flashed into her mind as she reached for the receiver, but her sister's voice, high-pitched and hysterical, crackled over the wires.

"Have you heard from Bobby?" Sue asked.

"No," Meli replied, frowning into the receiver. Who better than Sue knew that Bobby had to ask his mother's permission before using the phone? "He always checks with you first, doesn't he?"

"Yes, he does, but, well, I thought maybe—" Sue sounded breathless, as if she had been running, running or crying.

Crying? Asking if she had heard from Bobby? Fear, mindless and chilling, clutched at Meli's heart. "What's wrong, Sue?"

"He never came home from school."

Never came home from school. Meli's arm shook as she lifted it to check her watch. "But it's eight o'clock."

"Oh, God, I know it. I—" Sue broke off in a gasp and all Meli could hear was muted weeping.

"Meli?" David's voice, firm and in charge, replaced Sue's.

"David." Meli's fingers braided nervously through the coiled telephone wire. "What's going on there? Sue's not making any sense."

"I wish to God she wasn't. Unfortunately she is. Bobby's disappeared, and we have no idea where he's at." David's voice faded into an anguished sigh. "Look, Meli, I'll call you back as soon as we hear anything, but right now the police want us to keep the line clear."

"Police? Wait," Meli said. "Don't hang—" Too late. The connection had been severed. She stared at the telephone for one brief, indecisive moment, then crumpled the paper she was holding and stuffed it into her pocket. She couldn't just stay here and wait for David's call. If she did, she would probably bite her fingernails clear down to the knuckles. Besides, she thought, snatching her coat and scarf from the closet, Sue wasn't the calmest person in a crisis, and Meli was usually able to reassure her. Now, if only she could reassure herself.

Which is exactly what she tried to do as she drove toward Georgetown. Bobby had probably gone to a friend's house and had forgotten to tell them. By the time she got there he'd be home. Sue would be scolding him hysterically while smothering him with kisses, and David would be giving him a stern talking-to. But there were two police cars parked in front of the blazingly lighted house. An officer approached Meli's car as she pulled to the curb. Everything is okay, she told herself. So why were her hands shaking? And why was she silently praying that Bobby hadn't been hurt?

No news is better than bad news, she decided after she had identified herself to the policeman and he had informed her that they still hadn't heard from Bobby. But when she walked into the silent house it was obvious that Sue and David didn't believe that hogwash any more than she did.

They were huddled on the maroon leather sofa in David's den staring at the mute telephone. David had his arm around Sue, and her face was buried in his chest. Their features were taut and pallid, and they seemed to have aged twenty years since she had seen them at Bobby's birthday party.

"Meli, oh, Meli," Sue said, lifting her head for a moment before covering it with her hands. "Something terrible has happened. I know it. I just know it."

"Don't be ridiculous," Meli said, tossing her coat on the leather wing chair next to the unlighted fireplace. Chill and gloom, she thought. Everything was chill and gloom, but she couldn't let Sue and David know how frightened

she was. She had come to reassure them, not to add to
their fears. "I wouldn't be surprised if he's having dinner
at a friend's house and just forgot to tell you." She bent
down, rolled up some newspaper and started a fire. A
blazing hearth was cheerful, wasn't it? Well, they needed
all the cheer they could get.

"It's after nine," Sue said, shedding her crumpled
tissue into wispy little pieces. "I've called all his friends.
I just don't know what else we can do."

"Take it easy, honey," David said, wrapping his arm
around her shoulders. "The police are working on it."

"Hmm, the police," Sue snorted. "They keep telling
us that it's too soon to start worrying, that his teacher
reprimanded him in school, that he might have run away."

"That's preposterous," Meli said without thinking.
"Bobby wouldn't do that." She crammed her hands into
her pockets, fingering a handkerchief and a crumpled
piece of paper.

"Thank God someone agrees with me," Sue said.
"Now, if only we could convince them." She motioned to
the two policemen speaking in the entryway. "If only
there was someone who knew Bobby, who understood
that he would never run away."

"Meli, what about Jud?" David asked somberly.

"Yes," Meli agreed, wondering if that was why she
had unconsciously stuffed his phone number into her
pocket. "Jud would know what to do."

And he did. Less than ten minutes after her phone call
he walked through the front door and began questioning
the policemen.

"You know Bobby," Meli whispered. "Tell them that
he wouldn't run away."

"They don't think he has," Jud said, putting his arm
around her shoulder and guiding her into the kitchen

where David and Sue were making a halfhearted attempt to drink some coffee. "But there's always the poss—" He stopped mid-sentence as the telephone rang.

For a moment everyone stared at the jangling instrument. They had been waiting for so long, and now that it was finally happening, they were frozen in their seats.

Sue was the first to move. "It's him," she shrieked, reaching for the receiver.

"Wait." Jud's hand clamped over hers. "Let me get on the extension." He trotted into the hallway, grasped the extension, then signaled to Sue.

David stood beside her, his arm around her shoulders. "Bobby?" Sue asked, her voice quavering. David bent his ear to the outer edge of the receiver.

"I've got him," a gruff voice said. "If you want to see him again, get rid of the police."

"No," Sue cried. "Wait a min—"

The line went dead. Sue lowered the receiver for a moment, stared at it in silent disbelief, then brought it back to her ear. "Hello . . . Hello." No response.

David grabbed the receiver. "Hello? Are you there?"

"David, what's wrong?" Meli asked.

He stared at her blankly. "He's been kidnapped," David whispered. "Bobby's been kidnapped. But why? Who would want to hurt Bobby?"

As Meli watched David's face crumple she could feel the blood draining from her own. The fear that had been building since Sue had phoned her apartment nearly two hours ago had become an ugly reality.

"Hang up," Jud told David. "He's gone."

"But you don't understand," David said. "He's got Bobby."

"And we're going to get him back," Jud said, calmly accepting the portable telephone a policeman handed him.

"Oh, no," Sue said. "You're getting out of here, all of you."

"The police are leaving," Jud said as the front door opened and closed and some car motors started up. "I'm staying. I drove here in my own car. I'm a friend of Meli's. No other explanations are necessary."

"Maybe Sue is right," David said. "Maybe we shouldn't take any chances. Maybe we should do as he says."

"You know better than that, David. The Bureau is set up to handle this sort of thing. You can't go it alone." Without waiting for David's answer Jud crossed to the telephone. "I'm phoning my chief," he said. "He knows the best men in the field. He'll put a team together." The phone rang as he reached for it.

Sue lunged for it, but Jud held her back. "Take your sister upstairs," he told Meli.

"Come on," Meli said, gripping Sue's shoulder. She felt as if two separate people were living within her body. One of them wanted to scream like Sue while the other was holding her back, forcing her to think rationally, to make sensible decisions. She knew that Jud was right, that he was better equipped to handle this type of situation than they were. "We have to listen to Jud."

"Get the phone," Jud told David as his own hand closed over the portable extension and he attached a tape recorder to the receiver.

"They're gone. Good," the gruff voice said.

"Who is this?" David asked.

"How does it feel to be on the other side, Judge Linton?"

"Where's Bobby? Is he all right?"

"Mack Joplin," the voice said softly. "Remember me, Judge Linton? You sentenced me to life. My wife took my kid and disappeared, but you're going to help me find them, and then you're going to help me get away.''

"You don't know what you're saying. Bring Bobby back and I'll see what I can do to help you.''

"Uh-uh. You'll do what I tell you to, otherwise I'll mail your kid back to you piece by piece.''

"No. Don't. I'll do anything you tell me, anything at all.''

"Good. That's good. I like to hear you beg. Just stay by the phone. I'll call you back, and remember, no police.'' The telephone went dead.

"Well, at least we know who he is,'' Jud said as he unhooked the recorder, then dialed the F.B.I. and explained the facts to the person on the other end of the line. The rugged planes of his face were set in the same tense determination that Meli remembered from their first meeting. Strength and confidence tempered by gentleness and caution. "Run a check on Mack Joplin and put a tap on this phone,'' he said, leaning his hip against the desk. "No, I'll handle things here. You'd better keep everyone else away. I think he's watching the house. He could be anywhere—across the street, up the block. It doesn't matter. As long as he has the kid, he's got us by the throat. Okay, I'll wait to hear from you.'' He hung up the phone, reached for a pad and turned to David. "Tell me all you know about Mack Joplin.''

"The Burger Shoppe murders,'' David said, pressing his fingers into his temples as if doing so would activate his memory. "He robbed the place, then shot the manager and counterman. But it can't be him. He's in for life, no possibility of—'' He broke off as the phone rang and Jud signaled for him to answer it. "It's for you.'' He handed the phone to Jud.

Jud's conversation was brief, and when he hung up, he

explained that there had been a fire at the prison. They were still checking through the rubble for missing prisoners. "I told them to forget about Joplin," Jud said. "Unfortunately we don't know exactly where he is, but he's definitely not in prison."

The room grew silent, and the only sound to be heard was Sue's hysterical sobbing from the upstairs bedroom.

Jud listened for a moment, then handed David the phone and told him to call Sue's doctor. "She's on the verge of a crack-up." But not Meli, he thought. He knew how much she loved her nephew, the anguish she had to be feeling. Yet she was keeping her emotions under control, acting calmly, doing what had to be done.

He walked to the window, pulled the curtain aside and stared into the street. Joplin could see the front of the house, so he had to be close by, but where? Where the devil was he? Jud drew back as a white van turned into the street. The words PIZZA PALS—WE DELIVER were emblazoned across the sides in bold red letters, but the two delivery men were F.B.I. agents.

"We thought this was the best way to get by Joplin," one of the agents explained, handing Jud a pizza box. "Hal's parked around the corner and the tapping equipment's in here. You can start setting things up while we go out to the van. It's not going to start, so Todd will open the hood and be fiddling around while I come back inside and install the tap and set up radio communications with headquarters."

Jud and the two other agents executed the plan with calm precision and had just completed the radio hookup when the line buzzed. "A black Cadillac is turning into the block," Hal said, following it with the license plate number. "A man's driving. I don't see anyone else, but the kid could be in the trunk or tied up in back."

"Bobby," David said, racing to the door and flinging it open before Jud could stop him. His shoulders slumped as he stared at the man getting out of the car. "It's only Dr. Carrow," he said tonelessly. "I'll take him upstairs."

When David brought in Dr. Carrow, Meli left and walked down the hall to Bobby's room. Everything looked the same as it always had, yet something was different. An ominous silence shrouded the atmosphere, dusting the furniture, the toys, the books—all the things that Bobby had touched. Would he ever touch them again?

Resting her hands on the maple dresser top, she leaned forward and closed her eyes. "Please let him be all right," she prayed. "Please don't let Joplin hurt him."

A quiet knock interrupted her supplications, and opening her eyes, she turned toward the door. "Are you all right?" Jud asked.

Meli nodded. "Is there any news?"

"The woman who drove Bobby home from school stopped to pick up her dry cleaning. The other two boys in the car said that Bobby decided to walk home. He wanted to test his metal detector."

"The metal detector?" She shuddered at the possibility that her birthday present had caused Bobby's problems.

"Hey," Jud said, stepping behind her and curving his fingers gently into her shoulders. "Don't start putting yourself on a guilt trip. Once Joplin made up his mind to get Bobby, he would have accomplished it one way or another. This just happened to be his first opportunity, but if it hadn't been now, he would have kept waiting. A man like that doesn't give up, so don't go blaming—"

"Yes." She turned slowly and stepped into his arms.

"You meant well." He was working now, and he needed a clear mind, but when he was close to Meli, the only thing he could concentrate on was her.

"And so did you." But you're still on a guilt trip, she wanted to say, still punishing yourself for something that was never your fault.

"And so did I." He knew she was asking him to forget the past and give their love a chance. He wanted to, but still . . .

"Jud?" Her arms clung to her sides, tight fists burrowing into her hips. "I know you have work to do and we should both be thinking of Bobby, and I am, but would you think me awful if I asked you to put your arms around me and hold me for just a moment?"

"I could never think of you with anything but love," he murmured, putting his arms around her and rubbing his cheek against her temple. "What you want now is comforting, someone to reassure you and tell you everything is going to be all right." He caught her face between his hands and tilted it toward his. "And I can't do that, Meli. All I can promise is to do my best."

"I love you, Jud. I love you so much." Her arms curved around his neck and she pulled his lips down to hers. There was a wild desperation in her kiss, as if his love could ward off the evil lurking just beyond these walls, yet she knew it couldn't, knew there were times when love was simply not enough.

They tensed and pulled apart as the phone rang. Jud raced into the master bedroom and signaled for David to answer the phone while he listened on the portable extension.

"I been following you in the papers. All the time I been following you and planning," Joplin said, dispensing with any form of greeting. "You got a plane and you're going to fly me out of here. My wife Mary and my kid are with her family in Roanoke. Name's Beltine. Find them and bring them to the airport. I'll meet you there at five A.M.

You fly us out of here and I give you back your son. Otherwise the kid's chopped liver."

"But I can't get—"

"You'd better do it, Judge Linton, or you get him back one piece at a time." The line clicked into silence.

"Beltine in Roanoke," David said, writing the information on a pad beside the phone. "I'll have to contact them, convince them to come with me." He reached for the receiver.

"No," Jud said, covering David's hand with his own.

"What do you mean, no? You heard Joplin."

"Even if we could convince his wife to go with you," Jud said, "which I very much doubt, there's no way we could allow her to place her child and herself in such danger."

"What about my child?" Sue moaned. "Doesn't he matter?" She lifted her head briefly, then slumped back on the pillow. "Damn you all, doesn't he matter?"

"The sedative's taking effect," Dr. Carrow said. "I suggest we continue this conversation somewhere else and let Sue get some rest." He shut the light and led them out of the room.

"Sue's going to be all right, isn't she?" Meli asked.

"If nothing else happens. Sue's always been high strung. You know that as well as I. When things are okay, she's fine, but under pressure . . . she's not like you, Meli. Speaking of which—" He scanned her face for a moment, then lifted her hands and checked her fingernails. "Sensible as you are, you haven't been taking care of yourself. You look pale and I think you've lost some weight. I think the anemia's getting worse. Have you been taking your medication?"

"Well, under the circumstances," Meli said.

"Call my office for an appointment." Carrow said,

loping down the stairway. "You're stronger than Sue, but you're not made of steel. I want to see you next week." The door slammed behind him as he left the house.

"Who would have thought it," David said, leaning against the bannister. "I never thought my job would endanger my family. How could this be happening?"

"It's not your fault," Meli said. "We all take chances, and there are no guarantees in life, not for anyone, no matter how safe a job seems."

"Meli," Jud said, touching her shoulder. He hadn't missed the concern in Dr. Carrow's voice, and he was suddenly terrified at the possibility that she might be sick. What if something were to happen to her? Yet what right did he have to be concerned? Hadn't he sent her away? Still, he had never really considered losing her forever.

Meli shook her head and shrugged him off. She had been speaking to David, not to Jud; Jud had known how she felt long before this. She was willing to take her chances with him regardless of his job.

"Look, David," Jud said. "You know as well as I that you can't make deals with criminals. I realize that this is a lot to ask, but you've got to let me handle this."

David shook his head. "You don't understand. He's my son. If anything happens to him . . . I can't, I just can't."

"I know what's involved here, David, and I'm going to do my best to save him." Jud's husky whisper was choked with emotion. "You have to trust me. It's the only chance we have."

"He's right," Meli said. "We'll only be hurting Bobby if we panic. We have to let Jud handle it."

"Do what you have to," David said. "I'd better get back in there with Sue."

"Thanks," Jud said as he and Meli walked downstairs. He wanted to ask her why Dr. Carrow had been concerned about her, but she was holding herself so rigidly apart from him that he knew she would never tell him. Besides, after the way he had hurt her, what right did he have to ask her anything?

"For what?"

"Your vote of confidence."

"I trust you," she said as they reached the landing. "I've trusted you from the first moment we met when I took you into my room." And into my heart, she added silently. "You're the one with a shortage of faith, Jud."

"Faith, Meli? In you? You know that's not it."

"Not now, Jud. We'll talk when this is over. If you still want to." She stared at him for a long moment, then went into the kitchen to make some fresh coffee. Somehow she was sure they would all be needing it before this night was over.

Jud watched her leave and thought about going after her, but she was right; they could talk later. Right now he had more important things to do.

His mind had begun formulating a plan the minute he had heard Mack Joplin's demands. He went into the living room, sat down on the sofa and radioed headquarters.

"The first thing we have to do," Jud told his supervisor, "is contact Joplin's wife in Roanoke. Then we find a female agent who can substitute for her. I can stand in for Judge Linton. We're about the same size," he said, remembering how he had borrowed David's clothes when he and Meli had spent the night in Georgetown.

Once the plan was set into action, there wasn't anything to do but wait. They had to be at the airport by five. Jud checked his watch. Twelve-thirty. Good. They needed the time to put things in motion. He leaned back against the cushions and closed his eyes. Nothing more for him to do until the chief called him back, and doing nothing at a time like this was one of the most difficult chores he had ever faced. Less than two weeks ago he had thought that

David's job was safe. Now Bobby had been kidnapped. Maybe Meli was right; maybe there were no guarantees in life. You do your best and take your chance. He jerked to attention when he heard footsteps pad lightly across the carpet, and his hand automatically fingered his shoulder holster.

"Don't shoot me," Meli said, offering him a steaming china mug. "My coffee can't possibly be that bad."

"That's the problem," Jud said, accepting the mug and patting the cushion beside him. "I like everything about you, even your bitter coffee. In fact, I'm beginning to think of it as an aphrodisiac."

Meli slumped on the sofa and made no effort to pull away when his arm curved over her shoulder and drew her to his side. "Is this night ever going to end?" *Is Bobby going to be all right?* was what she meant, but she was afraid to ask, afraid to voice her doubts.

"We're setting up the airport meeting." Jud's hand stroked lightly down her arm. When all this is over, he thought, they would go somewhere quiet and he would hold her in his arms and make love to her. Then he remembered what he had told Meli about his job never being over. He had no right to love her, but he couldn't stop.

"But I thought you said it was too dangerous."

"We're going to use agents. In the dark, and with the proper clothing, Joplin won't know the difference." He stretched, then rose to his feet. "Which reminds me, I'd better ask David if I can check out his wardrobe."

"You're going in his place? What if Joplin finds out?" She tried to hide her fear, but she knew she wasn't succeeding.

"It's my job to see that he doesn't. Don't worry, Meli, we have agents watching this entire area. We know he's around here somewhere, so maybe we can catch him before he gets to the airport.'' He knew she was concerned about him, but he couldn't let her fear get through to him. Fear froze, and a frightened agent was often a dead agent. He winked at her confidently, then trotted up the stairs.

Four hours later Jud and Paula Stamford, who had volunteered to stand in for Joplin's wife, drove into the airport. A station wagon transporting Meli, David, and several other agents followed at a safe distance. Now the lives of two people Meli loved were in danger: Jud's and Bobby's. Yet she felt a certain confidence in knowing that Jud was protecting Bobby. After all, didn't she trust him more than any man she had ever known?

Jud was poignantly aware of that trust as he wove his car through the planes looking for David's. ''Bobby's our main concern,'' he told Paula. ''Nothing happens until we know he's safe.'' His glance drifted to several ''mechanics'' who had spent the night working on planes not far from David's. Other agents, waiting to back him up, if and when he needed them.

''That must be them,'' Paula said, pointing to a man with a blue wool cap pulled low on his forehead and the small boy he held tightly against his chest.

''Okay,'' Jud said, stopping the car. ''You stay in the car and let me do the talking.'' He tilted David's hat over his eyes and stepped out of the car.

''Where's Mary?'' Joplin shouted. ''Where's my wife and kid?'' He took his hand out of his pocket and began waving a revolver.

''In the car,'' Jud said, pulling David's scarf over his mouth to muffle his voice. ''Let Bobby go, and then I'll bring them to you.''

''Yeah? How do I know you'll keep your word once I let the kid go?''

''Let Bobby go and Mary and I will start walking

toward the plane. Your son will join us as soon as Bobby reaches the car.'' He motioned to Paula, who opened her door and stepped out beside him.

"Is he telling me the truth, Mary?"

Paula nodded. "It's the truth." Her voice was a rough whisper. "Laryngitis," she said, pointing to her throat as Jud began guiding her toward the plane.

"Come on, Bobby," Jud said, hoping Bobby wouldn't give away his identity. "Come on, Bobby. You go to the car and tell the other little boy that his father is waiting for him."

Joplin watched them for a moment and loosened his grip on Bobby while still holding him by the shoulder. His eyes narrowed as they came nearer. "You're not Mary," he snarled.

"Run, Bobby, run," Jud shouted.

Joplin tried to hold Bobby, but he wrenched himself free and ran toward Jud.

Shots rang out from all sides as Jud dove to the ground, covering Bobby's body with his own.

He felt the bullet burning through his back and the last thing he remembered before he lost consciousness was Meli's face and thinking that he might never see her again. I don't want to die, he thought. Please, God. I don't want to die.

Chapter 13

MELI STARED AT THE CLOCK ON THE WALL OF THE
hospital waiting room. Didn't those hands ever move? It
was only five minutes later than the last time she had
looked, yet to her it seemed like an hour.

The backup agents had shot and killed Joplin, but not
until after Jud had taken the bullet Joplin had meant for
Bobby. The bullet had lodged a hairbreadth away from his
heart and he had been in the operating room for more than
two hours. If he died, it would be her fault because he
would never have become involved in this case if she
hadn't called him.

Jud had saved Bobby's life, just as she had known he
would, but had he done it at the cost of his own? Hadn't
Jud always said that danger was part of his job and that he
couldn't ask her to share that danger? Yet she had asked it
of him, and now he was lying on an operating table,
fighting for his life.

Guilt lashed at Meli until her mind was as exhausted as

her body. Drained, she closed her eyes and slumped deeper into the vinyl chair. Cold, she thought, the upholstery felt so cold, as cold as death. She crossed her arms over her chest and shivered.

"Meli?"

Meli opened her eyes and saw Paula Stamford standing beside her chair. Paula had accompanied Jud in the ambulance, and now she, along with three other agents, maintained a somber vigil in the waiting room.

"You look like I feel," Paula said. "How about a cup of coffee?"

Meli stared at the swinging doors leading to the operating room. She couldn't leave, not until she had some news about Jud.

"Steve will let us know if there's any news," Paula said, motioning to the sandy-haired agent who was leafing through a dog-eared magazine.

They took the elevator to the second floor cafeteria. After pouring some coffee from the urn by the cash register, Meli carried her cup to a small table in the corner of the room. Sterile, she decided as she pulled the green plastic chair closer to the chrome table. Everything in this hospital was cold and sterile, even when it didn't have to be. This dining room, for instance, couldn't they have carpeted the gray tile floor, or put some posters on the bare beige walls? She busied herself with improving the decor of the room because she knew there wasn't anything she could do to help Jud.

"You met Jud in Hawaii," Paula said, lighting up a cigarette and inhaling deeply. "You haven't known him that long."

"A few months, but it feels like forever." She tried to imagine a life without Jud, but couldn't. Whenever they had argued, she had somehow expected that, given time, they would work things out. Yet life presented some problems that couldn't be solved, and if Jud didn't recover . . .

"I've known him practically all my life," Paula said, "yet it seems as if we've just met. I don't know where the years have gone, but then again, I guess most people don't feel their age. I still feel like that little girl on the reservation who used to trail along behind Jud."

"Jud lived on a reservation?" Meli knitted her brow. Hadn't he told her that he had spent his childhood on Air Force bases?

"Well, at first it was only for brief vacations, and then, after his father died, he spent all his school holidays with his grandfather."

"And his grandfather lived on a reservation?" She remembered Jud saying that he had lived with his grandfather, but she hadn't envisioned that home being on an Indian reservation. Yet, why not? Hadn't he told her that he was one-quarter Navaho?

"Jud wasn't like the other boys, not as rough, I mean. The first time I met him, I must have been four or five years old." Paula flicked her cigarette into the ashtray, then toyed with the plastic rim. "The older boys were playing baseball and I was running onto the field, trying to get into the game. The other boys picked up pebbles and began tossing them at me, but Jud, who had been pitching, put down his glove, took my hand and led me off the field to his grandfather's house. His grandfather was the gentlest man; he didn't deserve to die the way he did."

"How did he die?" Meli cradled her cup between her hands. Paula's muted tone had indicated evil and violence.

"The reservation had always been governed by a counsel of elders. Jud's grandfather was their leader. Long hairs, they were called. They would meet and talk things over until they reached an agreement. Then a group of younger men became impatient and decided to take over. They believed in guns and violence, anything to get what they wanted. Jud's grandfather threatened to go to the authorities.''

"So they killed him?" Meli's mind rejected the idea. People in a democracy didn't get killed for voicing their beliefs.

"Not right away. He kept talking to them, trying to change their minds. They called him a turncoat. Said they couldn't trust him because he had been living on the outside for so many years and didn't care about them anymore. When he was younger he had worked as a mechanic on an Air Force base in New Mexico. That's where he met Jud's grandmother. When she died, he retired and moved back to the reservation. Jud's father stayed on at the base and became a pilot.''

"When did all this happen?" Meli asked, remembering what Jud had told her about living with his grandfather. His father had died in a plane crash, then he had been deserted by his mother. How had he been affected by this threat to his grandfather?

"About fifteen years ago when Jud was twenty-two and just finishing college. Jud asked his grandfather why he couldn't keep to himself and mind his own business. His grandfather told him that we can't turn our back on evil. We have to fight against it or it will envelop the world. Two days later he was found outside his house, shot in the very back which he had refused to turn.''

And Jud shared his grandfather's beliefs, Meli thought, recalling his remark about the good guys having to vanquish the bad guys. Would he share his fate as well? Would the bullet that had plunged through Jud's back kill him also? Why had she ever called him? Why hadn't she let someone else investigate Bobby's kidnapping? Because she had wanted Bobby safe, and there wasn't anyone else she trusted as much as Jud. Still, what if . . . She suppressed the thought, but she knew she would never forgive herself if Jud didn't recover.

The paper napkin she had been tearing was a pile of white confetti when she looked up and saw Steve standing in the doorway surveying the tables. Jud, she thought. He had some news about Jud. Despite the coffee, her mouth felt dry and stale. All this time she had been waiting for news about Jud and now she was afraid to hear it.

"They got the bullet," Steve said. "Jud's in the recovery room, then they'll probably take him to intensive care. His head hit the ground when he dived over Bobby and they're concerned about a concussion. The chief is posting a guard outside his room, but he's told us to go home. Come on," he told Meli. "I'll drop you off at Judge Linton's house. They're waiting for you."

Meli knew that she wouldn't be able to see Jud until evening, so she followed Steve to his car. The early morning sunlight glinted off the car tops as a new shift of hospital workers drove into the parking lot. Life's everyday responsibilities never stopped, Meli mused, even if, for the moment, she had forgotten about her own.

She was not going to be able to go into work today, she thought as Steve drove toward Georgetown. In fact, she had better call Ned and ask him for an indefinite leave. As long as Jud was in the hospital, she wanted to be at his bedside. She would explain what had happened and hope that Ned would understand.

Bobby and his parents were sitting at the kitchen table when a grim-faced Ingrid showed Meli into the house. Meli caught Bobby in her arms and hugged him tightly.

"That man was bad, Aunt Meli," Bobby said. "He said he was going to kill me. Why did he want to kill me?"

"I don't know," Meli said, remembering the story Paula had told her about Jud's grandfather. What was it that made people hurt so much that they could relieve their pain only by lashing out at someone else?

"How's Jud?" David asked, his joy in having Bobby safe subdued by Jud's condition.

Meli repeated everything Steve had told her, then excused herself and went upstairs. She closed the door to her usual room and called Ned Fodin to apprise him of the situation and ask for some time off. Then she undressed quickly and stepped into the shower. There, while the warm water streamed down her face, she finally allowed herself the indulgence of tears, letting them merge with the shower until no more would come.

As she toweled herself dry she was engulfed by an overwhelming relief that admitted the exhaustion she had been eluding all through the night. Jud was going to be all right, she thought as she stretched out on the bed and drew up the covers. Now more than ever she knew that she and Jud belonged together. All that remained was for her to convince him. But how? How was she going to do that? Hadn't she used up all her arguments long before this?

Closing her eyes, she curled her knees against her stomach and tried not to think. She had been so worried about Bobby and then about Jud. Now they were both going to be all right. Everything was going to be all right. With that comforting thought in her mind she drifted into sleep. Two hours later she came instantly awake, as if some internal alarm had buzzed, warning her not to sleep too deeply or too long.

Sitting up quickly, she left the bed and dressed in the clean clothing Sue had laid out for her. The beige slacks felt loose around the waistline. Sue's figure had always been more rounded than her own, but these slacks were really big. Had Dr. Carrow been right about her losing weight? Even so, she couldn't be concerned about that, not when Jud's situation was so much more serious.

Frowning, she reached for the phone, dialed the hospital and asked for intensive care. At first the desk nurse refused to divulge any information about Jud's condition, then when Meli persisted, she asked her to wait and put her on hold. Her fingers drummed the top of the night table while she waited.

"Miss Fancher?" a deep male voice inquired. "This is Elliot Hodges. I met you at Judge Linton's house last night."

"Yes, I remember," Meli said, visualizing the spare, boyish-faced agent who had been masquerading as a pizza delivery man. "I wanted to know about Jud."

"Awake and complaining. He's out of danger if he just rests and takes it easy, but you know Jud."

"Yes, I know Jud. Is he allowed visitors?"

"On a limited basis. Investigative personnel and immediate family, but Jud's been asking for you. I'll check with the doctor and let you know."

Pain surrounded Jud, a burning knife that transcended the physical and drove torturous nightmares into his mind. Painkillers made the torment bearable, but left his perceptions hazy. Not the ideal moment for serious contemplation, but he had the time, and there were decisions that had to be made.

His limbs felt too heavy to lift and an IV was attached to his right arm, but he was alert enough to notice the scents and sounds of the hospital; an antiseptic odor combined with pinging bells, calls for physicians and a steady passage of people, whom he began to identify by their footsteps. Funny, how different one was from another, brisk, authoritative, slow, relaxed. He could recognize the visitors, doctors, nurses and orderlies.

For the next few hours he dozed on and off. Although still heavily sedated, he was fully aware of a nurse disconnecting the IV just before two orderlies moved him out of intensive care and into a private room. He dozed again, and when he woke, he felt more perceptive. The sedatives must be wearing off. He would have to tell them not to give him any more. He didn't like the way they dulled his senses.

He forced his eyes open and looked up at the ceiling. Not much to see there, just a dull white enamel. The overhead lamp was off, and the only light came through the window. He could hear birds chirping. His room probably overlooked a garden.

He closed his eyes and thought about Meli, recalling how he had seen her face just before the bullet hit, and how her image had swum before him when he was coming out of the anesthesia. Elliot had told him that she had waited at the hospital until he had come out of surgery and had then gone home to rest.

She's probably exhausted, he thought; we're all exhausted. It's a lousy world where little boys are kidnapped and old men get shot. A time of violence, sliding deeper and deeper into chaos, an outcome which he had devoted his life to preventing. Had he succeeded? he wondered. Yes, this time he had. Joplin was dead and Bobby was safe at home with his family. Chalk up a win for the good guys. He smiled as he closed his eyes and let himself float over the edges of sleep.

Time drifted aimlessly. He was aware of sponge baths, short trips off the bed, bland meals and visits from other agents. There wasn't much about the case that they didn't know, but he filled in the blank spots to the best of his ability. In between these mundane activities he dozed, and when he awoke he couldn't be sure which events had actually taken place and which were part of his dreams.

Was he dreaming now? he wondered as he became

suddenly conscious of the surrounding sounds—the door creaking slowly open, then clicking shut, tiptoeing footsteps crossing to the chair at the side of his bed. He didn't have to open his eyes to know who was there. Her clean sweet scent of soap and talc drifted above the hospital's medicinal odors. He inhaled deeply, relishing the memories they brought, then he opened his eyes because his body hungered for the sight of her.

"Hello, Meli," he said, lifting his hand in a welcoming gesture.

"Jud." She caught his hand between both of hers. "They said it was okay. I didn't mean to wake you." She had spent all of yesterday and most of today in the hospital waiting room, but they hadn't allowed her in to see Jud until now. "I'll leave if you want to rest." Her gaze flickered over him quickly, noting his pallid complexion and gaunt features. He had endangered himself because of her. If she hadn't called him, he wouldn't be lying in this bed. She gripped his hand tightly, a gesture of both gratitude and reassurance. "Oh, Jud, I was so worried about you."

"I'm all right." He lifted her hand to his mouth and kissed it. "And I don't want you worrying about me."

"You can't stop me."

"If I could, I would. Worrying doesn't agree with you. You're all pale, and Dr. Carrow was right. You have lost weight."

"It's the outfit," she said. "I borrowed it from Sue. Beige isn't my color, and she's more curvy than me."

"I hadn't noticed."

"Liar."

"Well." He cocked his eyebrow and grinned. "Maybe just a bit, but I've always preferred the lean, leggy type. If you're going to stay, why don't you sit down?"

"All right," Meli agreed, edging toward the chair.

"Here, next to me," Jud said, still holding her hand while he placed his on the mattress. "Whatever I've got, it's not contagious."

"Good thing too," Meli said, settling herself beside him and letting her feet dangle over the side of the bed. "If it were, I'd probably be chasing after half the men in the world."

"But you're not." He reached up and ran a knuckle over her cheek. Soft, he thought. So smooth and soft and very feminine. God, how he had missed her.

"No. You're the only man who has what I want." She tilted her head and caught his hand between her cheek and her shoulder. Lovingly she nuzzled him and kissed his wrist. "What I need."

"What you need, love, is some common sense."

"Um-um. I've never liked anything that was common. I've always been attracted to the unique, the one of a kind."

He reached behind her and twirled a tendril of hair around his finger. "Pink anemones and oyster-colored cats with sapphire eyes."

"A man who makes dramatic entrances from the sea and risks his life to save a little boy."

"Bad choice. You'd be better off with any of the others. Why look for problems?"

"Why create them?"

"Only a fool ignores the obvious."

"And you're not a fool."

"Not when I can help it."

"Then how can you ignore me?" As far as Meli was concerned, her need for him, their need for each other, was the most obvious thing in the world. She stared at the sheet and made tiny little accordion folds in the fabric.

"I can't," Jud admitted, looking up at her. "You really do look bad." Why did she have to look so weak and vulnerable? If only she looked stronger and he felt better, but at the moment he felt too tired to duel with his emotions. "Maybe you should be in this bed instead of me."

She shook her head.

"With me?" His palm curved around her neck and he urged her down beside him. "Come on. Lie down beside me."

"I can't, Jud. You're sick."

"I'm not planning on any acrobatics. I just want you near me."

"And if someone were to walk in?"

"We'll tell them you're my medicine." His hand stroked down her back, fingering her spine.

"And they'll tell you to stick to your pills," she said, dipping her head and lightly kissing his forehead.

Three short raps sounded on the door and she straightened away from him. By the time it creaked open, she was standing primly beside the bed.

"What this hospital needs is a Do Not Disturb sign," Jud told the gray-haired, bushy-browed man who had just walked into the room.

"If they suspected that you needed one, they would discharge you. Besides, I thought you'd be happy to see me. I brought you some flowers." He reached into his jacket sleeve and pulled out two red carnations, then three white ones came out of each pocket. "There you go," he said, handing the haphazard bouquet to Jud.

"Thanks, Roger, but I thought I'd be spared your repertoire of tricks while I was flat on my back."

"A helpless audience is the best kind." Roger winked.

"Why don't you pull some trick to get me out of here?"

Jud asked. "There's nothing I'd like better. Come on, let's see what you can do."

"Something in particular you're eager to get home to?" Roger asked, smiling at Meli. "Or should I say some-one?"

"What do you think?" Jud asked. "Miss Fancher is Judge Linton's wife's sister, and Meli, this prankster with an extremely bad sense of timing is Roger Gorman. He's in charge of our training program, but he spends most of his time thinking up practical jokes."

"Taught him everything he knows," Roger said, offering Meli his hand. "Well, almost everything." He chuckled and winked, then a hesitant silence fell between them. "Some things he managed all on his own."

"Pleased to meet you," Meli said, shaking Roger's hand. "Look, I'm sure you two have things you want to discuss." She picked up her purse and slung the strap over her shoulder. "I'll see you this evening, Jud."

Roger waited until Meli had gone, then he pulled the chair closer to Jud's bed and sat down. "She looks like a nice lady."

"She is," Jud agreed. "Very nice, the kind that goes with a mortgage and kids."

"Which is exactly what you need. Marrying Helen was the best decision I ever made. You're not getting any younger, Jud, and it's time you started putting your life together again."

"Why? So some trigger-happy thug can rip it apart? Do you know what would have happened if this bullet"—he pointed to the bandages plastered across his chest—"had been just an inch lower?"

"You would have been killed. Is that what you wanted, Jud? It was after Carrie died. That's why you kept volunteering for these dangerous assignments, wasn't it?"

"Maybe." Roger was right. When Carrie had been

killed he had been so laden with guilt that death seemed to be the easiest way out.

"Do you still feel that way?"

"No," Jud said emphatically, remembering how he had thought of Meli and prayed for a second chance.

"Good. Because that's what I want to talk to you about. You know this is my last year with the Bureau. Helen's arthritis has been bothering her. She's been bugging me to retire so we can move to Florida and be near the grandchildren. My oldest boy's down there with NASA. I know how you feel about working behind a desk, but I'm recommending you for my job anyway. You're getting too old to keep chasing around the world. It's time you left that stuff to the younger guys just starting out. Training's where you'll do the most good now, teaching them everything you learned over the years. It's an important position, Jud, one you're uniquely qualified to handle."

Jud stared at him for a moment and the adrenaline racing through his veins did more to dispel his pain than any medication. Chief of training. Entirely out of the field. He'd be in a risk-free position, stable hours, more money, home every night. A life he could ask Meli to share.

"Of course I can't promise you anything. There'll be other people applying as well. I know for a fact that Ray Johnson and Hal Walker are interested, but my recommendation should carry some weight."

"I appreciate what you've done," Jud said, his elation arcing into embarrassment when he realized he had mistakenly assumed that the job was automatically his. "You know, Roger, if I had had a shot at this job a few months ago, it wouldn't have meant very much to me. In fact, I might even have turned it down. But now I want it more than I've ever wanted any other assignment. It's more than just a promotion. It's—"

"A mortgage and children?" Roger said, smiling as Jud

nodded. "Don't worry about it. I'm going to push for you, and if I have anything to say about it, the job is yours."

Don't worry about it. Advice, Jud thought, after Roger had left, that was easy to give, but hard to take. And seeing Meli every day made not worrying that much more difficult. She came to the hospital bringing magazines, flowers and cookies. They played chess and talked about Hawaii, the kidnapping, their jobs, what Meli was going to do with Muffin's kittens. The only subject they didn't discuss was the one that was really on their minds. Them. Jud knew that Meli was waiting for him to broach the matter and tell her that his ideas about their relationship had changed, but he couldn't say anything, not until he had heard from Roger.

The situation was still unresolved when, ten days after Jud had been admitted to the hospital, the surgeon told him he was well enough to go home.

"But not back to work," the paunchy, pink-faced physician said. "I'll want to see you at my office next week, but you can plan on being home for at least a month. I don't think you'll need any painkillers, but I'll give you a prescription just in case." He reached into the pocket of his white jacket, pulled out a pad and began writing. "Lots of rest, no driving and no heavy lifting. Where will you be staying?"

"I have a house in Virginia," Jud said, picturing the small fieldstone cottage deep in the woods, secluded, the perfect place to rest.

"Someone will be with you, of course," the doctor said, tearing the top page off his prescription pad and handing it to Jud.

"No." Jud furrowed his brow as he let his legs dangle over the side of the bed. He hadn't thought about having someone stay with him. He had never needed anyone before. Damn, he hated being dependent, hated asking for favors.

The doctor shook his head. "Then forget about the discharge. You can't stay alone."

"I'll be all right. I'll manage just fine."

Watching Jud, Meli was reminded of their first meeting and of how difficult it had been for him to ask for her help. She'd have to choose her words carefully or he would refuse her now. Tentatively she reached out and touched his shoulder. "Jud, please let me stay with you."

Chapter 14

JUD'S HOME, A SLATE-ROOFED FIELDSTONE COTTAGE NES-
tled at the end of a curving dirt and gravel road, had been
built early in the nineteenth century. Originally the
carriage house of a vast Virginia plantation, the remod-
eled white-shuttered structure was now separated from the
main house by a neglected forest of overgrown hedges and
trees.

"A brook runs around the back," Jud explained. "The
lake it feeds into isn't on my property, but I have
permission to use it for boating and fishing."

"Nice," Meli murmured as she swerved to avoid
a drooping pine branch and pulled up next to a Jeep at
the side of the house. But she wasn't thinking of the
lake; her gaze was fastened on the mullioned windows.
Sunlight streamed across them, catching the edges
of each tiny prism and reflecting them with a diamond-
hard shimmer. "Something out of a fairy tale," she
said.

"More like a horror story," Jud said. "The place was falling apart when I bought it two years ago. Since then it's consumed money faster than a kid eating a chocolate bar."

"You don't seem to mind it too much," Meli said, noting that his complaint pulsed with hidden pride.

"It's the only home I've ever owned. I went house-hunting with an agent who was being transferred to Washington. I wasn't in the market myself, but when I saw this— Come on," he said. "I'll give you a tour." He swung himself out of the car, walked around to the back and waited for her by the trunk. "We might as well bring in the luggage."

"*I'll* bring it in," Meli said, unlocking the trunk and opening it. "You're not supposed to lift anything, remember? That's why I'm here."

"Is it really?" He crossed his arms over his chest and watched her lift out the luggage.

"Why else?" She placed her overnight case on the ground next to her two other pieces and closed the trunk.

"Oh, I can think of one or two other reasons."

"You're not allowed to do that either." She blinked in the sunlight and smiled, a smug grin that Jud found completely maddening. Then she picked up a suitcase and started toward the front door.

For a moment Jud leaned against the trunk watching her, then he lifted the overnight case with his good arm and began following her. "I wouldn't count on it," he said softly. "I wouldn't count on it at all."

When he opened the white front door Meli walked into a rectangular oak-floored foyer that led to a large living room with a fieldstone fireplace and french doors that overlooked the brook Jud had mentioned.

"The only furnished bedroom is downstairs," he said, leading her to a small room at the end of the hall. The

walls were sky blue, the furniture, curly maple, the
fireplace, red brick, and a patchwork quilt covered the
four-poster. "I haven't gotten around to doing much with
the upstairs. Another thing this place consumes is time."
He dropped the overnight case on the hooked rug beside
the bed.

Meli left her suitcase in the hall and stood in the
doorway staring at the bed. She had offered to come here
with Jud, had slept with him before, so why was she
hesitant about sharing this bed? When she caught Jud
watching her, she lowered her gaze. She hadn't meant to
be so obvious.

"Something bothering you?" Jud asked, covering the
distance between them in two swift steps and tilting her
chin with his thumb. He knew it was the sleeping
arrangements, but he didn't understand why. The one
thing that had never been a problem between them was the
physical attraction they felt for each other. So why the
sudden shyness?

Meli looked at Jud, studying the lean, chiseled planes of
his face, the high cheekbones and jutting jaw which had
become so much a part of both her dreams and her
reveries. She had offered to come here with him, had
pushed herself on him actually; he hadn't asked her to
come, perhaps he hadn't even wanted her with him. And
even more embarrassing, just a few minutes ago, out by
the car, hadn't he taken it for granted that she would be
sleeping with him? Suddenly she didn't want Jud to take
anything about her for granted; she wanted to be special,
wanted Jud to think of her as special. "Perhaps I ought to
sleep on the sofa."

"The sofa?" His eyebrow rose quizzically, and her
cheeks reddened beneath his bemused scrutiny.

She felt foolish, behaving like a reluctant virgin when
Jud knew that she was neither. "I thought it might be

better for you . . . with your injury, I mean . . . If I rolled over during the night I might hurt you.''

''I'm willing to take that risk.''

Sighing, Meli closed her eyes for a moment. If she looked at him, her resolve would vanish. Why was he making things so difficult? Did he want to make her crawl? Admit that she loved him enough to accept him on any terms and that she had come here because she felt a shriveling loneliness whenever they were apart? She couldn't say it, not without some declaration from him. ''Look,'' she said, opening her eyes and indicating the wound beneath his open-necked tan shirt. ''You wouldn't have gotten hurt if I hadn't called you. You saved Bobby's life and I'm—''

''Grateful?'' he finished for her, his jaw flexing tightly. ''Is that why you've come here with me, because you're grateful?''

''Of course I'm grateful for what you've done, but that's not why I'm here, Jud. You know me better than that.''

''Of course I do.'' Hadn't she once told him that when she wanted to be charitable, she wrote out a check, but that she had to really care to give of herself? He knew that she loved him, but he also knew that there were problems between them that they still hadn't resolved, and tonight he felt too exhausted for any long, drawn-out discussions. The morning would be soon enough to resolve the tension separating them. They had both been through so much recently that they needed time to rest and think and become used to being together again. Besides, even if they were to talk now, what concrete offer could he make to Meli when replacing Roger was still so tenuous? He released Meli, plunged his hands into his pockets and strode out of the room. ''You take the bed and I'll sleep on the couch.''

"No, Jud, please." She scurried after him, catching up just outside the kitchen. "You don't have to." Fantastic help she was turning out to be, tossing him out of his own bed. He would have been better off if she hadn't come with him. "I don't want you to. Please?"

"We'll work something out," Jud said, keeping his back to her as he adjusted the thermostat. "In the meantime, we'd better get the rest of the things out of the car before it gets dark." This time he didn't protest when Meli said she'd take care of the unloading.

The kitchen was a large square room with golden oak cabinets and stainless steel appliances along two adjoining walls, a multipaned bow window on the third, and a brick fireplace flanked by bookcases on the fourth. A bentwood rocker, a chintz-covered maple sofa and a matching chair sitting on a red and blue hooked rug formed an inviting group around the hearth.

In the few minutes it had taken Meli to bring in the remaining piece of luggage, Jud had started a fire, and now flames stretched around a bulky cedar log, flickering fingers of orange and yellow and red. Meli watched as Jud knelt to poke at the embers and fan the fire.

"I phone a woman in the village to stock the pantry and clear away the dust whenever I'm coming here. Her husband makes sure the Jeep is in good working order. Four-wheel drive is the only thing that gets me through some of these back roads," Jud said, rising to his feet and crossing to the refrigerator. He opened the door and peered inside. "I make a wicked spaghetti sauce, but it takes hours to cook. Tomorrow," he promised. "But for tonight you'll have to settle for something less exotic. This." He pulled some vegetables out of the refrigerator —eggplant, romaine lettuce, tomatoes. "You make the salad." He handed her the lettuce and tomatoes. "And I'll take care of the eggplant."

"You're supposed to be resting." Meli cradled the salad makings in the crook of her arm and reached for the eggplant. "I'm supposed to be doing the cooking." Her hand covered his as it circled the eggplant, their fingers meshing.

"Stop me if I'm wrong, but when I stayed at your apartment, you undercooked the instant coffee."

"I thought the water had boiled," she explained, remembering the unappetizing white haze that had pooled across the top of the coffee. "All right, so I'm not the world's greatest cook." She released the eggplant, crossed to the sink, dumped the lettuce and tomatoes on the tile counter and stared out the window into the darkness. *I never should have come,* she thought. *How can I take care of Jud? He needs someone domestic, someone like Sue.*

"It doesn't matter," Jud said, coming up behind her, putting the eggplant into the sink and letting his arm rest around her waist. "Look." His chin nuzzled her forehead as he indicated the scene beyond the window where a doe was picking her way between the tall pine trees, sniffing the air, then signaled for her fawn to follow her to the brook. "When I first bought the house I tried to put in a vegetable garden, but my friends from the forest devoured the shoots as soon as they began to show. So now I plant it just for them. I figure I can buy mine at the store."

Meli watched the deer as they wandered through the yard picking at the earth, then she refocused her eyes and studied Jud's reflection. What an enigma, to spend his own life on the edge of danger, yet be concerned about the hunger of a deer. She loved him more than ever.

"And I figure if my lady has two left thumbs in the kitchen, then there's no reason why I can't do the cooking."

"Definitely not two left thumbs," Meli said, holding her hands up in front of her. "And when you're better you'll get no arguments from me, but for now, you supervise and tell me what to do."

Dinner was prepared with delightful ease. "I had no idea cooking could be so much fun," Meli said, tucking her legs under her as she reached for a thin slice of breaded eggplant and dropped it into some butter sizzling in the electric skillet.

They were sitting on the rug in front of the fireplace. Meli had prepared the salad, then peeled, sliced and breaded the eggplant. Now they were sipping glasses of chilled Burgundy while sautéing, then eating thin rounds of eggplant which they dipped into a mixture of sour cream, onion juice and red caviar.

"Like anything else, it's all a matter of whom you do it with," Jud said, smiling. "This is a bachelor specialty. Fast, relaxing and filling."

"And absolutely delicious. Where did you learn to cook? Your scrambled eggs were impressive enough, but this is gourmet stuff." Jud was right. She enjoyed everything she did with him, absolutely everything.

"It's a Greek recipe. I was vacationing on one of the smaller islands—in a little white-washed cottage built into the side of the cliff—the caretaker's wife used to make this."

"I'm going to Rhodes during winter break," Meli said, "to check on a marine conservation project their government is financing." Now, while she was there, she would think of Jud. Wherever she was, she would think of Jud, and she couldn't bear the thought of losing him. She swallowed the last bite of the eggplant she'd been nibbling on and felt her appetite vanish. The fire cast a soft, flickering light, and she leaned back to study the dancing reflection in her wineglass. "I'm stuffed, couldn't eat another bite.'' She flipped the two remaining slices onto his plate and unplugged the skillet.

"What if you should change your mind?''

"I couldn't. Believe me.'' She rolled her eyes and motioned to the eggplant. "They're yours.''

"Not this,'' he said, shoving his plate aside and moving closer. "I meant about Greece.''

"Why should I change my mind?'' Her heart beat faster and she found herself hoping that he would say that he didn't want her to go, that he wanted her here with him.

"If something should come up?'' If my situation should change and I can offer you security, children, a home, he wanted to tell her, but how could he? The job was a toss of the coin and if he didn't get it, then what?

"Like what?'' Like you telling me that you want me to stay with you?

"Nothing. Forget I mentioned it.''

Silence fell between them, uncomfortable and oppressing, with neither of them able to voice their true thoughts or emotions.

"I'll put on some coffee,'' Meli said, picking up the dishes and carrying them to the sink. Why did she have to be such an optimistic fool, always hoping that Jud would change his mind?

"Okay,'' Jud said. "I have to make a few phone calls.'' He opened the cupboard and took out a brandy bottle and a snifter. "I'll be in the bedroom if you need me.'' He'd call Roger and see if there was any news.

Meli washed the dishes—surprisingly few for such a delicious meal. When the coffee was ready, she poured two cups and carried Jud's into the bedroom. The patchwork quilt had been folded down and he was stretched across the bed with his left arm cushioning his neck. When she walked into the room, he stirred, mumbled something and turned on his side.

For a brief moment Meli stood beside the bed and studied his face lovingly. Slumber had relaxed away the tension lines and he looked young and gentle, almost boyish, she thought. Moving silently, she set the coffee mug on the night table next to the brandy, then reached for the phone, which lay on the bed beside him. He must have fallen asleep right after he had made his calls. Carefully she slipped off his shoes and covered him with the quilt. The doctor had said that rest would now be Jud's most important medicine, so she decided that it would be wiser to let him sleep in his clothes rather than risk waking him.

Jud was settled nicely, but where was she going to spend the night? Beside him, or on the sofa? It would be so easy to just slip in beside him, to reach out and feel the warm strength of his body pressing against hers. Yet where was her pride? How could she keep pursuing him when he set up roadblocks at every turn? With quiet determination she picked up her luggage and carried it into the living room. She found linen in one of the hall closets and made up the sofa, then she changed into her flannel nightgown and turned out the light.

Meli awoke slowly as a bright autumn sun blazed through the windows, breaking the pattern of her sleep. Still drowsy, she blinked and let her gaze wander from the oak-beamed ceiling to the brightly colored Navaho wall hangings. Jud's house, she remembered, sitting up and tucking her feet under her. She leaned back against the cushions and stretched. Umm, she was tired. The sofa might be comfortable enough for sitting, but for sleeping it left much to be desired.

Birds chirped outside the window. She heard footsteps crunching across gravel and then a twig snapping. She drew the blanket over her shoulders, sat up on her knees and looked out the window. Jud held a sack of birdseed awkwardly with his injured arm and tossed handfuls to the sparrows swooping to pick them off the ground. His face looked as relaxed and youthful as it had when she had seen him asleep last night.

She remembered their first meeting, when she had yearned to stroke his forehead and erase the tense furrows. Now the signs of strain had vanished. He was as at home in these woods as she was in her marshes, and just as concerned with preserving life. Kindred spirits in all ways but one, the one that really mattered—commitment.

Sighing, she folded the blanket back on the sofa and padded to the bathroom. By the time she had showered and dressed she could smell the aroma of fresh-brewed coffee. Jud was a man of unlimited talents, Meli decided as she hurried to the kitchen.

He was standing by the sink looking out the window. When he heard her footsteps, he turned, smiled and poured some coffee into a mug. "I didn't forget," he said, holding it out to her. "Coffee first."

"Thanks." She carried it to the table and sat down. "Mmm," she said, inhaling the rich aroma. "I hate to admit it, but you're a much better cook than I am."

"Okay," he said, taking the seat beside hers. "So we'll keep you out of the kitchen, but what about the rest of the house? Is the living room the only place where you feel comfortable?"

"There's a lot to be said for the view. You were up early this morning."

"I was lonely, and it's amazing the friends you can make with a handful of birdseed for the sparrows and some peanuts for the squirrels. Too bad I can't please everyone as easily."

"How do you want your eggs?" Meli asked, carrying

her mug to the counter beside the refrigerator. Jud was right. She wanted more from him than sunflower seeds or peanuts. When two people loved each other, they wanted to share that love, to build a life together. That was what she wanted from Jud.

"Scrambled with some sautéed scallions and tomatoes. They add just enough spice to make the eggs interesting."

Jud was right. The eggs were as delicious as any she had tasted and Meli told him so later that morning when they were tramping through the woods. The warm mid-morning sun caught the dew still shimmering on the needles of the cedar and pine trees. A scattering of red and yellow leaved lingered on the gray-brown limbs of the oaks and maples, but most of them had fallen to earth.

Hushed silence covered everything, making the woodland sounds all the more obvious—birds chirping, squirrels scuttling, Meli's and Jud's feet crushing the brittle leaves. Meli looked at the sky—blue, cloudless, utter peace. At this moment, in this place, she felt as if they were the only people in the world, and she wished it could go on forever.

"What's that?" she asked, pointing to a series of slanted boards climbing up the barreled trunk of a gnarled oak.

"There used to be a treehouse up there," Jud said, leaning back against a mound of rocks and pointing to the oak's lower branches. The kids who lived in the main house used it for their hideaway before I bought the place. I had to tear the platform down. It was falling apart and I was afraid one of them would get hurt. I never did get around to taking down the steps."

"My father built me a treehouse when I was eight," Meli said, walking in a small circle and kicking the leaves into a pile. "It's the greatest place for a kid to go . . . to be alone and think . . . dream." She turned and looked from the woods to the stream, clear watery ribbons curving around rocks and twigs, then the house, a fairy tale cottage. She paused, remembering what Jud had once said about children not needing to travel all around the world, that all they needed was two loving parents, a stable home and some trees to climb. "Everything about this place is ideal for children."

"Meli. I know how you feel, but right now—"

"Right now I'm going to do something I haven't done for years." How had she ever let that slip out? The moment she mentioned children she realized she had made a mistake. Hadn't Jud told her that he wasn't interested? "Have you ever built a pile of leaves?" she asked, scooping up bunches in her arms and then tossing them on top of the ones she had kicked together. "First you make a gigantic pile, then you sit and roll in them," she said, plopping herself down and flinging the leaves in the air so they fell all around her. "It's the most fun in the world." She held her hand out and motioned for Jud to join her.

"Looks kind of silly to me."

"Your problem, Mr. Thompson, is that you've never learned to have fun. Now, are you going to come along willingly, or am I going to have to get up there and drag you down?"

"And you would, wouldn't you?" Jud asked, chuckling as he sat down beside her.

"Mmm, you know I would," Meli agreed, rising to her knees and letting her gaze run carefully over him as if she were measuring him for a suit. "Now, you're new to this, while I'm a pro, so I guess you're just going to have to let me show you how to do it."

"I'm all ears."

"Ah-ha, a pretty funny-looking guy, ears coming out

of your arms." She shifted closer and flexed her fingers over his arms. "And shoulders." Her hands curved around his shoulders. "Are they really all over your body?" She flattened her palms across his chest and patted his thick gray sweater.

"Are you going to find out?"

"Nah, why bother. You've seen one ear, you've seen 'em all. Now," she said, "the main thing to remember about leaves is that they aren't any good at all unless you get them all over you."

"Like ears."

"Stop being silly."

"Right. And the first step in that direction is to get out of these leaves." He put one hand down at his side as if he were getting ready to stand.

"Oh, no, you don't," Meli said, pouncing on him. "Stay exactly where you are. Now." She placed her hand lightly on his uninjured shoulder and pressed him back against the leaves. "Because you've been hurt I'm going to have to be very gentle with you."

"Oh, please," he said, grinning. "Be gentle with me."

"If you were in better shape, we'd be rolling in the leaves and tossing them at each other like snowballs, but since you're not, I'll just have to do all the work." She picked up handfuls of leaves, flung them into the air, then patted them down around Jud, burying him in them.

"Hey, watch what you're doing," Jud said, grabbing her wrist and pulling her down on top of him. "You may be the pro, but I can think of several different ways to make this game more enjoyable." His arms circled her back and his fingertips reached languidly toward the rounded swell of her hips.

Meli rested on her elbows and looked down at him. "You're supposed to be playing, not thinking."

"Exactly." Jud cupped her hips, and his fingers flexed sensuously, tasting the sweet firmness of her flesh. "And right now I'm thinking about playing . . . my kind of game." He circled her thighs and rubbed his hand over the nubby green wool of her slacks.

A game, Meli thought. That's all it was to Jud, some kind of a game. The only problem was that no matter how often they played, she came out the loser. She studied his face: dark, glowing eyes, features warmed and softened by desire. It would be so easy to settle into his arms, to kiss and make love with him, and then—then what? No, she wasn't going to. Not when she remembered the pain that lingered long after the ecstasy had passed. "You're right," she said, pulling away from him and standing. "We are too old for this sort of childish nonsense. Besides"—she brushed off her slacks and looked at the sky, where the sun had drifted behind a swirling gray cloud—"we'd better get back to the house. It looks as if it might rain."

It did rain. Light sprinkles started two hours later, and by evening, the droplets had become a steady stream rushing down the windows. Meli and Jud spent the day preparing his special spaghetti sauce.

"Time," Jud said. "The whole secret is in the time. First you have to brown the beef and sausage, then you mix them with the tomatoes and spices and simmer everything for at least three hours."

The result was all that Jud had promised—thick and flavorful with just a hint of garlic. "The recipe's from my Italian grandmother; well, she wasn't really my grandmother," Jud explained. "She was my landlady while I was on an assignment in Atlantic City and we sort of adopted each other. Wait until you meet her. You're going to love . . ."

His voice trailed off as Meli swallowed her last sip of wine, then stood and began clearing the table. He was becoming used to her, finding it less and less possible to think of a life, any life, without her. Yet if he didn't get Roger's job, what could he offer her? How could he even consider marriage? He would quit, he decided. If he didn't get the training position, he would leave the Bureau, because for the first time in his life he had found something—someone—that mattered more to him than his work. "Don't do that now," he said, rising to stand beside her. "We can do that later." He inched closer. Their bodies touched. "Stay with me tonight, Meli, stay with me tonight." He slipped his arm around her waist, nuzzled his cheek against her hair and led her slowly into the bedroom.

The room was dark except for a glimmer of moonlight gliding between the clouds and shining through the window. "Have you ever slept under a down quilt?" Jud asked as he released the top button of her cardigan and then moved to the next. "It's the warmest thing in the world, so warm that when someone is next to you"—he released the last button and slipped the sweater off her shoulders—"you really don't need to be wearing anything else at all." Her sweater slid to the floor while Jud continued undressing her, kissing and caressing each newly revealed area of her body. "Just a cozy feather quilt and warm, welcoming flesh."

"Jud, please, Jud." His hands were a blazing sun, banishing the darkness and warming her body.

"I know, sweetheart."

Lightning flashed across the sky and rain battered the windowpane. Meli heard the voice of reason murmuring through her passion. "I don't want this. I don't want to play your games."

"No games. Everything about us is for real."

"But, Jud—"

His lips crushed down on hers, silencing her last whimpering protest. Holding her tightly against him, he led her to the bed, then folded back the quilt and pressed her down on the mattress. She watched while he shed his own clothes, then she felt the mattress dip as he stretched out beside her and pulled the comforter over them.

"See? What did I tell you?" he asked, turning on his side and shifting closer until the warm strength of his body was pressing intimately against hers. "Isn't this nice?" He stroked slowly down her back. "And cozy?" Over the curve of her hip, down to her thigh. "Nothing like it. A rainy night, a feather blanket and you next to me." His lips touched hers lightly, a gentle persuasion that made her skin tingle as his tongue slid into her mouth and circled lovingly over hers.

Meli ran her hands along his bare shoulders, needing to touch him just as he was touching her. She could feel his muscles straining, taut and strong. Her hand curved over his arm, down toward his chest. She felt the adhesive bandage. "Your wound," she said, pulling away from him.

"No problem." Jud drew her back. "Do you remember when we were out in the woods, lying on those leaves?" Still holding her with his good arm, he flattened his back against the pillow and looked up at her. "You told me you were going to show me how to have fun. That you were a pro, and because I'd been hurt, you were going to be very gentle with me." He tilted his head and kissed the hand she had resting on his shoulder. "Feathers are much softer than leaves. Show me how, Meli. Let's be gentle to each other."

Meli lifted herself on one elbow, ran her hand lightly

over his chest and felt his muscles tremble at her touch. Keeping her gaze locked into his, she dipped her head until their lips met in an intense, lingering kiss. She rose to her knees and her nipples brushed against his cheek as she nibbled on his earlobe.

Her warm breath curled seductively in his ear, weaving delicate patterns of ecstasy that made his body tauten in response. He shifted his head slightly and his lips circled the rosy tip of her breast while his tongue teased it with short, fluttery licks. Meli moaned softly and threw her head back as heated tingles raced through her body.

"Now." His lips tasted the swelling undercurve of her breasts, then lingered in the sultry valley between them. Cupping her buttocks tenderly, he urged her on top of him. "Now, sweetheart," he said. "I need you now." He entered her with a measured deliberateness that let her set the pace.

Meli closed her eyes and moved in a leisurely, rhythmic motion. Nice, she thought, very nice. What had Jud once said about wanting one moment to last forever? "Mmm." She gave herself up to the moment, and as Jud reached up and gently cupped her breasts, her languid strokes became more demanding until her control melted and she soared to the pulsating pressure binding them together.

"I love you, Meli," Jud said, his voice hoarse and ragged, as cradling her tenderly he rolled to his side and buried his face in her breasts. "No matter what happens, remember that I'll always love you." He held her tightly as they drifted into sleep.

Meli shifted her head on the pillow, turning toward the sound that had awakened her. The bathroom door had clicked shut. She glanced at the empty pillow beside hers and at the indentation where Jud's head had been. Jud had said that he loved her, that he would always love her. She smiled at the memory. This cottage was a magical place after all.

Perhaps, much as she wanted them, she wasn't meant to have children. If she saw Dr. Carrow and arranged for the surgery, then there wouldn't be anything keeping Jud and her apart. Jud didn't want children and she wouldn't be able to have them. It was a possible solution, but not one she enjoyed thinking about. The shower was turned on just as the bedside phone rang. Meli reached to answer it and Roger's voice greeted her.

"Jud's in the shower," Meli explained. "I'll see if I can get him."

"Don't bother. Just have him call me back. It's bureau business . . . his new assignment."

Meli dropped the receiver back into the cradle, then lay quietly staring up at the ceiling. Jud was being assigned to another case. Somehow she had thought that he would have been given more time to recuperate. Nerves tightened in the pit of her stomach. She didn't want him going back to work, facing danger again. But her own feelings on the subject didn't matter. She had to give Jud Roger's message.

The bathroom door opened just as Meli sat up and swung her legs off the bed. "Good morning," Jud said, combing his fingers through his damp hair. A short blue towel was tucked around his waist, revealing his muscular waist and legs. Meli saw only the scars and bandages. "I didn't mean to wake you up."

"You didn't. I was up already." For a brief moment Meli contemplated not telling Jud about Roger's call. Was it so wrong to want to stay here, all alone, cut off from the problems and dangers of the outside world? She rejected the impulse. Any decisions concerning Jud's job had to be made by him. "You had a phone call. Roger. About your new assignment. I told him you'd call him back."

"My new assignment." Jud smiled. "That's what I've been waiting for." He walked quickly to the bedside table, picked up the telephone and began dialing.

Meli folded her jeans over her arm, then went into the living room and began rummaging through her suitcase for fresh underwear and a blouse. The happy anticipation on Jud's face when she had told him about Roger's call had drained her of all hope. Obviously he had been waiting for the call, merely passing time until it came.

She glanced out the window while she buttoned her blouse. A misty rain clouded the glass panes and her heart tightened as she realized that Jud thrived on the danger that she dreaded. The lifestyle he had chosen was one she could never be part of. A flight of sparrows swooped through the windblown mist and pecked at the muddy earth, but the birdseed Jud had scattered the day before was gone. Meli deliberated for a moment, then went to the kitchen pantry and took out the sack of birdseed.

A yellow vinyl poncho hung beside the kitchen door. She slipped it on, pulled the hood over her head and went outside. Suddenly the house had become too confining, and she wanted to get away from Jud, away from the phone call he was making.

The wind was colder than Meli had expected, and the rain felt icy when it splashed across her face. She shivered while she tossed out the seeds, then watched the sparrows cluster around them. She felt so at home here, so much a part of Jud's life, at least this aspect of it.

"Meli." Jud's voice brought her out of her reverie. He was standing on the kitchen porch. "What are you doing out there?"

"Feeding the birds."

"You can do that in the afternoon when it clears up. Now, get inside."

Meli tossed out another handful of seed. She didn't

want to go in, didn't want to hear about Jud's new assignment.

"Meli." Jud started down the steps.

"Okay." Meli tossed out some more seed, then walked back to the house. It was childish to think she could run away from her problems. Sooner or later she had to hear about Jud's new assignment.

She was shivering when she walked into the kitchen and Jud pulled off her poncho, then led her into the bedroom. "Take off your jeans," he said, kneeling by the fireplace and striking a match. "The bottoms are soaked." He disappeared into the bathroom and returned with a thick bath towel. When Meli stepped out of her jeans, he began drying her legs.

The slow stroking felt so soothing. She loved having him touch her. For one forgetful moment she knelt beside him, brought his wrists up to her face and rubbed her cheek against the back of his hand. "I love you, Jud Thompson, and I hate Roger for calling. I don't want you taking any new assignments. I don't want you getting hurt again. You were right about my not being able to stand the danger of your job. When you threw yourself over Bobby, and the bullet hit you . . . I thought . . . if anything had happened to you . . . I wanted to die."

"And I didn't." His hands framed her cheeks and lifted her face until their eyes met. "For the first time in years I didn't want to die. I thought of you, of never seeing you again, and I didn't want to die." His fingertips traced the curve of her ears and stroked behind the lobes. "When I came to in the hospital I thanked God for sparing my life and I vowed that I'd never be apart from you again, not ever."

"But the new assignment . . . your job."

"In Washington behind a desk. I'm taking over Roger's job. If I hadn't gotten it, I would have left the Bureau.

How could you ever think I didn't need you?" He kissed her forehead, then the tip of her nose. "Will you marry me, Meli? For better or worse? For always and forever?"

"Oh, Jud. I've been so miserable. I love you so much."

"How much? Want to show me?" He pressed her back against the mattress and loosened the blanket slowly and gently, as if she were a piece of delicate porcelain. "Want to try for those exotic babies you were talking about?" He rubbed his hand over her abdomen. "It would be a pity to let this place go to waste. I'll have to rebuild that treehouse, and the brook is ideal for fishing."

"Jud. About children." She covered his hand with hers. "There's something you have to know." She wanted to tell him what Dr. Carrow had said.

"You're not ready for a family yet? You want to wait? I understand. It's only that I've waited so long."

"No, Jud, I don't want to wait, in fact I can't wait." She continued speaking, telling Jud in detail about Dr. Carrow's diagnosis. "My condition isn't serious, but Dr. Carrow thinks that if I'm planning on children, I should have them right away."

"That's no problem, no problem at all. Just stop talking. You're wasting time." He shifted himself over her and dropped kisses on her neck, down her shoulder and along the curve of her breast. "We've got more important things to do."

Meli's arms circled his back and drew him closer. How could she argue with the truth?

Fall in love again for the first time every time you read a Silhouette Romance novel.

Take 4 books free—no strings attached.

Step into the world of Silhouette Romance, and experience love as thrilling as you always knew it could be. In each enchanting 192-page novel, you'll travel with lighthearted young heroines to lush, exotic lands where love and tender romance wait to carry you away.

Get 6 books each month before they are available anywhere else!
Act now and we'll send you four touching Silhouette Romance novels. They're our gift to introduce you to our convenient home subscription service. Every month, we'll send you six new Silhouette Romance books. Look them over for 15 days. If you keep them, pay just $11.70 for all six. Or return them at no charge.

We'll mail your books to you *two full months before they are available anywhere else.* Plus, with every shipment, you'll receive the Silhouette Books Newsletter absolutely free. *And Silhouette Romance is delivered free.*

Mail the coupon today to get your four free books—and more romance than you ever bargained for.

Silhouette Romance is a service mark and a registered trademark.

READERS' COMMENTS ON
SILHOUETTE INTIMATE MOMENTS:

"About a month ago a friend loaned me my first Silhouette. I was thoroughly surprised as well as totally addicted. Last week I read a Silhouette Intimate Moments and I was even more pleased. They are the best romance series novels I have ever read. They give much more depth to the plot, characters, and the story is fundamentally realistic. They incorporate tasteful sex scenes, which is a must, especially in the 1980's. I only hope you can publish them fast enough."

S.B.*, Lees Summit, MO

"After noticing the attractive covers on the new line of Silhouette Intimate Moments, I decided to read the inside and discovered that this new line was more in the line of books that I like to read. I do want to say I enjoyed the books because they are so realistic and a lot more truthful than so many romance books today."

J.C., Onekama, MI

"I would like to compliment you on your books. I will continue to purchase all of the Silhouette Intimate Moments. They are your best line of books that I have had the pleasure of reading."

. S.M., Billings, MT

*names available on request